TRUST HER

JESSICA VALLANCE

sphere

SPHERE

First published in Great Britain in 2018 by Sphere

1 3 5 7 9 10 8 6 4 2

Copyright © Little, Brown Book Group 2018

Written by Jessica Vallance

A CIP catalogue record for this book
is available from the British Library.

ISBN 978-0-7515-7263-6

Typeset in Caslon 540 by Palimpsest Book Production Limited,
Falkirk, Stirlingshire
Printed and bound in Great Britain by
Clays Ltd, Elcograf S.p.A.

Papers used by Sphere are from well-managed forests
and other responsible sources.

Sphere
An imprint of
Little, Brown Book Group
Carmelite House
50 Victoria Embankment
London
EC4Y 0DZ

An Hachette UK Company
www.hachette.co.uk

www.littlebrown.co.uk

TRUST HER

Charlotte

Prologue

I've always found it easy to make friends.

I know how that sounds but I say it without a trace of conceit, I promise. There's plenty (seriously – plenty) I'm hopeless at. I just think for all our obsession these days with education and training and upskilling, for all the blogs and articles and shelves of books in Waterstones promising to help us better ourselves, the skills that really shape our lives are those things that come naturally. Those innate instincts that we're stuck with, whether we like them or not. And I do believe that even the most advantageous of personal attributes has its drawbacks. Even our strengths can get us into trouble from time to time.

For instance, I'm a people pleaser. I want people to know they can count on me. If I feel that I've let someone down, that there was more I could have done, the guilt nags at me like an itch I can't get to. I don't know why I'm like that but I always have been, even as a little girl. It's a bit pathetic, I know, to need other people's validation like that. It's had its uses though, over the years. I've had some good friends. I think people have appreciated me. I suppose I can hold my head up and say I've always done my best, even when things haven't worked out exactly as I hoped.

But I've no doubt whatsoever that my natural sense of duty, my amenability, was the reason I found myself trying to convince a taxi driver that a woman with blue lips and a Punch and Judy puppet on her hand was 'honestly, hardly even tipsy' whilst the woman in question undermined my case somewhat by waving the puppet in the air and shouting, 'That's the way to do it!' in a high-pitched squawk.

It isn't too much of a stretch then, to conclude that that same sense of duty was also the reason I didn't walk away from Luke. Not on that first night and not on any of the nights that came after. I kept coming back. I let him – I let all of them – get under my skin. I wanted to do the right thing, not just the easy thing. And more than that, I wanted people to *tell* me that I'd done the right thing. I wanted people to say, 'Charlotte's a good one, isn't she? Thank God for Charlotte.'

It's like I say – even our good qualities have their drawbacks.

Chapter 1

The evening had begun four hours earlier as I made my way through the twisting streets of Brighton's Lanes, the glow from the fairy lights looped between the buildings making the wet stones shine. Emily and Meredith, many of the women from work in fact, turned their noses up at the Lanes. They were 'overpriced', 'twee' and 'for tourist morons', they said. It was probably true, but I loved them. As I'd been in Brighton less than five months – I'd never even visited before I moved – I suppose I was still a tourist myself, in all the ways that counted.

The bar I'd chosen for our drinks that evening was called Laking's Dispensary and was styled around the theme of an old-fashioned apothecary. When I'd stumbled across it a few weeks earlier, I'd stared, mesmerised, through the windows at the dark wood interior, the shelves of brightly coloured mixers in glass bottles of assorted shapes and sizes backlit on the shelves behind the counter, the bar staff in Victorian waistcoats and bow ties, lab coats slung over the top.

Laking's Dispensary was different from most bars in that it didn't sell alcohol at all. Rather, customers were instructed to 'bring along a good-sized bottle of their favourite tipple' and then, for a fixed fee, the trained cocktail waiters would use the alcoholic base provided to create a whole evening's worth of exotic cocktails from the mixers, spices and syrups on their well-stocked shelves.

'You have to bring your own drink *and* pay for the privilege. Wonderful. Where do I sign up,' Emily had said in her usual weary deadpan when I'd suggested that one night we ought to give Laking's Dispensary a go. I knew, though, that she wouldn't miss a night out, whatever the format, so I'd stood my ground and sent her a text earlier in the week instructing her to meet me at seven-thirty on Saturday, to bring a bottle of decent gin and to see if Meredith was around too.

I'd arrived a little early and, as it was raining, decided to head straight in. The bar was small – perhaps just six or seven tables, each lit with a single tea light in a jar. Only two of them were already occupied: one with three men whose clothes, beards and tattoos were so similar I wondered if they'd agreed the uniform as a condition of the friendship; the other by a couple. He had his back to me, but something about them – the way she was staring down into her drink, using her straw to poke moodily at the ice, the way he was leaning back in his chair, looking around the room, out of the window, anywhere but at the woman – made me think that their evening wasn't going particularly well.

As I took my seat the barman approached the table. He was tall, with vivid ginger hair and round tortoiseshell glasses.

'Hey! So!' He clapped his hands together then held them like that, in a clasp. 'First time? Been before? On your own? Waiting for someone?' He reeled the questions off quick-fire, jerking his head from side to side as he delivered each one.

I smiled. 'First time, yes. Waiting for someone. Maybe two people.'

'OK! Great!' He clapped his hands together again. 'So, I'm Toby. I'll be your mixologist for the evening.'

I reached into my bag and took out the bottle of Glenfiddich twelve-year-old malt that I'd bought on the way. He picked it up and held it in his palm, nodding appreciatively at the label.

'Nice. I'll get you something while you're waiting. Any specific likes? Dislikes? Requests? Something you've always wanted to try?'

I shook my head. 'Surprise me.'

He nodded and grinned, and headed off to the bar with the bottle.

The man at the couple's table turned around briefly and as I caught a glimpse of his face, I felt I recognised him from somewhere. It took a moment, but I realised where it was: one of the dating apps I'd signed up to when I'd first moved to town.

I'd lost interest in them by this point – too many idiots only there to waste time – but I'd been quite keen for a few weeks and would log on to check for messages as soon as I got home from work each day. The same photos seemed to crop up on all of the different sites, so you got to know the faces of your local single population quite well. Still, it looked like this particular one had managed to find himself a date at last. Although from the look of things, perhaps he was wishing he hadn't.

A few minutes later the barman was back, carrying a tumbler garnished with a slice of orange and a cherry. 'Thought we'd get things off to a traditional start,' he said, setting it down in front of me. 'An Old Fashioned – just sugar, bitters and whisky.'

I thanked him and sipped at the drink, looking around the room. They had done an amazing job with the place, I had to admit. It was even better once you were actually inside.

Obviously I had very little idea about the historical accuracy of the decor. I had my suspicions that neither a mangle nor a set of Punch and Judy puppets would have had any particular purpose in your typical Victorian apothecary, but they gave the place the quirky, surreal impression I'm sure the owners were aiming for. With the rain now coming down hard against the window and the quiet, slightly off-key, saloon-style piano music tinkling gently in the background, I sat back in my chair and allowed myself a smile.

There had been many moments like this since I'd arrived in Brighton five months earlier. Moments where I'd looked around and thought, Yes. This is *exactly* what I had in mind.

Chapter 2

When I'd been working behind the admissions desk of Fourcross Medical Centre in Holten, a small market town in Devon, I'd daydreamed about scenes like this. I was twenty-seven, single. I didn't own a house. I had no children. I'd met people from up and down the country but had no particular ties to any one place. How then, I wondered, had I ended up in a town like Holten, where people went to settle down, to retire even?

I was no stranger to setting up life in new places, but up until that point there'd always been a trigger for my moving on that was beyond my control. The usual life developments – new jobs, the rental market, changes of circumstances. Things that made me feel that fate was leading me around by the nose, with little interest in what I really wanted. This time, though, the decision was all mine.

Once I was sure I wanted to move, it didn't take long for me to set my heart on Brighton and I began to scour the internet for jobs in the area. One of the first roles I'd applied for had been 'Digital Content Producer' at Good Stuff Ltd, a start-up that delivered boxes of organic produce to customers' doors once a week. It had been a long shot – I couldn't honestly have said what the job title even meant – but I'd figured I had nothing to lose by trying. A little friendliness went a long way, I'd always found, and, as it transpired, this was no exception.

Marcus was the name of the man who'd interviewed me and I made him laugh several times during the hour we spent together. Then, as we were finishing up, he closed his notebook, rested his hand on top and looked at me.

'I'll be honest with you, Charlotte. We've spoken to candidates with far more experience than you.'

I nodded, and smiled brightly. 'Of course. I totally understand,' I said, but I was furious with myself. If he'd wanted experience I could've given him experience, but I hadn't wanted to over-egg it. I'd thought the blank canvas, eager-to-learn shtick would make him feel flattered, important. But now I'd blown it.

'But,' he went on. I looked up hopefully. 'When we set up this business, it was about creating an ethos as much as turning a profit. We want people with the right attitude, the right mindset. God, we're all stuck in here forty hours a week, we want people who are fun!' He laughed, so I joined in supportively. 'The other stuff you can learn. I'm sure you'll pick it up. So as far as I'm concerned, the job's yours if you want it.'

Marcus was right, about the people being fun. Friends came quickly. I worked hard to get on with people, but the way things worked there made it easy. People were inclusive, welcoming. I liked everyone well enough, but it was Emily, Meredith and Alison who became my real friends. After a few weeks in Brighton, they were the people I saw not just for a shared sandwich in the park outside the office, or for a quick drink after work, but for dinner or an afternoon's shopping in town. They were the people I could ring if I was lonely on a

Sunday evening and wanted someone to watch television with. If I was passing any of their flats, I knew I could call in for a cup of a tea, and they wouldn't be worried that they were still in their pyjamas, dirty plates piled in the sink.

They were all great but Meredith had a little boy, so was often limited to social activities that were possible with a toddler in tow. Alison was a little older than the rest of us, and from what I could gather had spent the five years since her divorce working her way through a series of casual but insanely rich boyfriends, which meant that, come the weekend, she was often whisked away for a short break in Venice or to relax in a luxury spa retreat in a castle in the Highlands. Emily though, like me, was single, childless, completely free of responsibility and obligation. Emily was always up for fun.

It was strange then, I noticed, as I finished my Old Fashioned, that it was nearly eight and there was still no sign of her. I checked my phone for texts, fully expecting to see one of her hastily typed apologies – 'Fuck sorry, lost my fucking shoe. Found it now. On way' – her style of communication always giving the impression that she was flailing through life in a fog of swearing and chaos, which she was.

I scrolled through my contacts and hit call. She would probably be on her way, I figured, running through the rain, slipping all over the place in her heels, battling the wind to keep her umbrella under control. It would be easier to speak than for her to try to text.

She answered after three rings. 'Hello?'

'Hey!' I said. 'Are you coming?'

There was a pause.

'Sorry? Who's that?'

I laughed. 'It's me, Charlotte. Are you coming or what? This place is wicked, actually.'

'Oh, shit. Charlotte. No, sorry. I can't.'

I frowned. 'Oh, OK. Is everything all righ—? '

She cut me off. 'Sorry, really can't talk now.'

And then she was gone.

I looked down at my phone for a few seconds. The light on the screen went out.

Weird, I thought. But not unheard of.

Emily always tried to do too much. She kept a social diary that even an organisational wizard would've struggled to pull off, and Emily certainly wasn't that. She'd try to fit in a haircut at five, an early dinner with a friend at six, drinks with a guy from Tinder at half-seven and still be at her sister's in time to watch a film and would invariably manage less than half of it. So, although I was disappointed to be stood up, I wasn't surprised. I would get the full story later, I was sure.

I looked around the bar. The twenty-pound personal cocktail waiter charge applied whether I left now or stayed all evening, and twenty pounds seemed more than a little steep for one drink, especially as I'd had to provide the whisky myself. Besides, I liked the place. I'd wanted to try it for ages. I was a twenty-seven-year-old independent woman, I told myself. I was more than capable of spending an evening in my own company.

As I looked around the room I noticed that the table with the miserable couple was now just a table with a miserable woman. My friend from the dating app had obviously decided that he'd had enough for one evening. The drink that the waiter had just placed in front of the woman told me that she intended to proceed without him.

She caught me looking at her and lifted her glass in a toast. I returned the gesture. Then she got up, and made her way unsteadily over to my table.

'Mind if I join you?' she said, with a lopsided smile.

I opened my mouth ready to decline, to make an excuse

about somewhere else I had to be or someone else I had to be with, but I couldn't think of anything. And then, I thought, why not? Although it was true that I was an independent woman, capable of spending an evening in my own company, it would be more fun, wouldn't it, to have someone to talk to? Anyway, I wanted to know what her story was. It looked like something had gone down with her and the man. I was curious about what it was.

I smiled back. 'Yes. No. Absolutely. Please do.'

Chapter 3

The woman was called Kelly, she had turned forty-two the previous Wednesday, she had a twenty-six-year-old son from an accidental teen pregnancy and she was allergic to tomatoes, cats and penicillin. She told me all this within four minutes of sitting down at my table whilst finishing her cocktail in five gulps. Whatever she'd been drinking had contained enough colouring to give her lips a faint blue tinge, reminding me of a risen corpse. It was clear as she ploughed on that she wasn't particularly interested in a two-way conversation – she didn't pause to ask me so much as my name – but I didn't mind. I was happy to sit back and be entertained.

With the basics covered, conversation turned to the man I'd seen her with earlier. It was as I'd suspected: the date hadn't been a success.

'What it is,' she said loudly, leaning back in her chair as a waiter put a new drink in front of her, 'is that if you put in your profile that you're forty-two, all you get is fat, bald sixty-year-olds who think they're God's gift just because they drive an Audi and buy their wine from Waitrose instead of Asda. I swear they think just because you're over forty, you're grateful for their attention. So my mate Tina said, "Kel, you're fishing in the wrong pond, you need to catch them younger." So now I put myself down as thirty-two and it's a whole new world, honestly. The sex!'

She didn't say the word sex out loud, rather she mouthed it – but with such exaggeration that anyone looking in our vague direction would be left in no doubt as to what we were talking about.

'But not tonight?' I enquired, then immediately regretted leading the conversation down that path.

She shook her head and took a sip of her drink. 'Nah. No. That's the only problem, with these young, fit blokes. Keeping it going long enough to get to that stage. They're boring, you see, nine times out of ten. God, they're all into sports! Him tonight, for instance – mountain biking! A grown man, spending every weekend on a bike, chasing his little friends through mud for fun. What am I supposed to say about that? Conversation's dead after ten minutes. I knew he wasn't interested when he started talking about having to meet someone later. Never a good sign when they start setting up their escape route when you're still on the first drink. In the end, I said to him, "Just go if you want."' She sighed and looked out of the window. 'So he did.'

I remembered then his photos from the app. Lots of them had featured him on a bike, so I suppose you could say Kelly should have been expecting that. Luke – that was his name, I remembered now.

I nodded sympathetically. 'Oh well, I suppose sometimes these things . . .'

I wasn't sure exactly which words of comfort I'd been planning to offer but it didn't matter, because she started up again, this time telling me a story about another man she'd met, or it could have been two different men, it was hard to tell. Her stories were jumping around without any apparent chronology and she was slurring slightly now too. I frowned, trying my best to keep up, beginning to regret ever having agreed to let her join my table.

Then, after a fifteen-minute monologue about a man from Norwich who'd dumped her unceremoniously when she'd refused to say she was driving his car to help him dodge a speeding fine, she said, 'Shall I call him? The mountain biker? There are worse things in this life, I suppose, than mountain biking. Maybe I should've made more of an effort to sound interested.'

Without waiting for my opinion on this idea, she took her phone from her bag and lifted it to her ear. She held it there for a while, her other hand supporting her head, which was drooping further and further towards the table. Eventually she took the phone away and pushed it forcefully into her bag.

'Not picking up,' she said with a sniff. 'Probably shagging someone else by now.'

She stood up abruptly, jolting the table as she did so and sending her glass smashing to the floor. Toby the waiter looked towards us, then collected a broom from the corner of the bar. 'Do you think she's . . . had enough?' he said in my ear as he begun to sweep.

I nodded once. 'We're leaving.'

As we made our way across the bar to the exit, Kelly seized one of the Punch and Judy puppets from the table near the door and pulled it onto her hand. She crinkled her nose mischievously and I couldn't be bothered to risk an argument by suggesting she left it where it was.

I had planned to make my excuses and head off in whichever direction was opposite to Kelly's as soon as we got out the door, but once we were in the street, I saw she was even unsteadier on her feet than I'd realised. She was amusing herself by performing a puppet show to herself in the reflection of the window, waving Judy's club about with abandon.

I hesitated for a moment. The last thing I wanted was to see her face on *South East Today* in a few days' time: 'Brighton woman missing after night out'; 'Brighton woman drowns after drunken fall from pier'. The taxi rank was just around the corner. I could see her that far, I thought. It's what I'd hope someone would do for me.

Three taxi drivers in a row simply wound up their windows and drove on as soon as they caught sight of Kelly's dishevelled hair and stumbling gait, but one – an older man whom I assumed was acting on some kind of paternal instinct – gave in to my gentle persuasion, rolled his eyes and let her fall into the back seat. 'What's that she's got though?' he said, nodding towards the Judy puppet.

'Oh. Nothing.' I ignored her protests and slipped it off her hand. Then, between us, we tried to establish where she lived.

'By the Bingo. Rig bed block of flats. I mean, rig bed—'

'Big red?' The driver sighed and smiled wearily. 'I know the block.' He gave me a quick wave and drove off into the night.

Finally free of Kelly, I headed back into the Lanes. Initially I'd just wanted to disappear into the shadows in case the taxi driver changed his mind and called me back to take her off his hands, but once I was sure I was clear, I decided to take the long route home and call in at Emily's flat on my way. She still hadn't messaged or called about her sudden change of plan that evening and I wanted to check everything was OK.

The alley I took ran between the sea and the Lanes, behind a street of restaurants. It was the place they all left their rubbish at the end of an evening's service and the black sacks were always getting pulled apart – seagulls, foxes – leaving potato peelings and chicken bones strewn across the street.

I nearly turned back when I saw the legs poking out from behind the green bottle bin. There were often people sleeping rough in that alley at night, tucked into the doorways, their sleeping bags pulled up to their chins, and I felt there was perhaps some unspoken rule that this was their territory after dark, that it wasn't the done thing to use it as a thoroughfare after a certain time. I decided I was being silly though. It was much quicker than turning back and going up the main road, and anyway, I was only going to walk past quietly. It wasn't as if I was part of a shrieking hen do, clattering about the place with an open bottle of prosecco, dragging a pink helium balloon and an inflatable vicar behind me.

I'd meant to keep my head up, my gaze fixed forwards as I passed the man. I didn't want to seem rude by looking down at him, and neither did I want to inadvertently invite any kind of conversation, if it turned out that he was, in fact, awake. But something about his position caught my attention. The way he was lying diagonally on the pavement, his feet in the gutter and his head in the middle of the path, when surely the more natural choice would be to tuck yourself up against the building, out of the wind, out of the way of clumsy drunken feet.

It was then that I noticed his coat. It was a smart suit jacket, a blazer. He was turned away from me so I could only see the back but I could tell that, although it was wet and splattered with dirt, it seemed new. The jeans too were dark blue, crisp. I realised then that it was unlikely he was a rough sleeper, that he had chosen the quiet alley as a spot to bed down for the night.

I paused a few feet away from him and looked around, wondering if there was someone whose advice I could ask, but we were completely alone.

'You OK?' I said. My voice sounded louder than I'd intended in the quiet of the night. There was a clatter of a metal can behind me and I spun round, but it was just a fox knocking a bag of rubbish as it darted between the buildings.

I turned back to the man and tried again. 'Hello? Are you all right?'

He didn't move. The only sounds were the cars crashing through the puddles on the main road and the bass line of the music from a bar at the end of the alley.

I stepped out into the road and rounded the green bin. The alley was dim, the only light coming from the windows of the flats above the restaurants. The man's face was partially covered by his right arm but as soon as I was on the other side of him, I recognised who he was.

It was Kelly's date. It was Luke. His eyes were closed and there was a pool of blood by his head.

Chapter 4

I looked around me again. 'Hello?' I called out. 'Can somebody help us?'

But I was talking to an empty road. I approached the man and crouched down next to him.

'Hello, are you OK?' I said.

I'd instinctively lowered my voice, I noticed, as if he was asleep and I was afraid of waking him too abruptly. When he didn't respond I reached out for him, but then withdrew my hand at the last minute, afraid of causing any more harm.

I put my bag on the floor next to me and scrabbled around for my phone. I dialled 999 but hesitated before I pressed call. I'd never phoned the emergency services before – to do so seemed melodramatic somehow, as if I was being hysterical or had watched too many medical dramas on television. I looked back to the man. His mouth was hanging very slightly open and the blood was beginning to congeal on the pavement. I hit call.

'Which service do you require?'

'Ambulance please. Quickly, I think.'

'Putting you through.'

'Ambulance service. Can you tell me what's happening?'

'I . . . I don't really know. There's a man here, he's on the floor. He's bleeding. I think he needs an ambulance. I mean, he definitely needs an ambulance. I'm in the alley behind the main coast road, behind The Grand.'

Although I knew rationally that the operator's whole job was to receive calls like mine, part of me was surprised – put out, even – when she didn't change her tone at the news of the severity of the situation in front of me.

'Is the patient breathing?'

'I don't know.' There was a wobble in my voice that I hadn't expected. I wondered if it made it more shocking somehow, that I had just a couple of hours earlier seen this man up and about, talking and drinking and looking bored. If that made it harder to comprehend than if I'd just seen his face for the first time, passed out here in the alley.

'You need to find out if he's breathing for me, love. Can you get close to him and see? Put your ear near his mouth and see if you can feel breath, and watch his chest to see if it moves up and down.'

I did as I was told. 'I don't think so. He's not doing anything at all.'

'OK, in that case I need you to begin CPR straightaway.'

'CPR . . .' I said vaguely.

'Yes. Put the heel of one hand directly over the breast bone.' She went on, giving me instructions about keeping my arms straight and not being afraid to push too hard. 'Do you know the Bee Gees' song, *Staying Alive*?' She sang the line from the chorus, and I blinked, surprised by this sudden change of subject.

'What? Yeah I—'

'That's the rhythm you need to aim for.'

I nodded even though there was no one there to see it. 'Right. OK.'

She was speaking to me in the tone you'd use if you were trying to cajole a toddler into tidying up their paints, but I didn't mind. It was reassuring, really. I suppose that was the point.

'There's an ambulance on its way to you now. Keep doing that, don't stop. Put the phone on speaker.'

I did as she said, but I was surprised how much energy it took and how quickly my arms began to tire. Still, it was good to have something to do to pass the time. It was probably only six or seven minutes until I heard the sound of the siren, but it felt much longer. I looked up. Through the buildings I could see the flashing blue lights speeding along the main road.

'Ambulance'll be with you in a few moments, love. I can hear it in the background there. I'll hand over to them now, OK?'

'I . . . OK.'

I was worried the sirens would turn out just to be a passing police car but, as my call with the operator ended, I saw the ambulance round the corner. The alley was narrow, and the end of the road was lined with metal bollards, so the driver had to slow considerably to manoeuvre the vehicle closer to us. I lifted my hand to signal that they'd found the right place.

The ambulance door opened and a man climbed out. 'Hello, hi there,' he called, making his way over.

I stood up, and took a step away from Luke. As the para-medics came over to join me, I hastily squashed the Punch and Judy puppet into my bag. It had been lying on the floor beside me, dangerously close to the pool of blood, and I felt that its presence on the scene was somehow inappropriate.

I noticed then that Luke's wallet – brown leather with a sewn-on patch saying 'Easy now' – had slipped from his pocket. I picked it up and flipped it open. Behind a clear plastic window was his driving licence. *Luke James Burley* read the name. I saw from his address that he lived in Hanover, just a fifteen-minute walk from my own flat. He was thirty years old.

'I'm Ian,' the male paramedic said. He was around fifty, I guessed. Balding and rosy-cheeked. He nodded towards his colleague, a woman, much younger, her blonde hair in a messy bun on top of her head. 'And this is Helen.'

'Who have we got here?' Helen said.

'I don't . . .' I snapped the wallet shut and pushed it into my coat pocket. 'He's called Luke.' I kept my voice steady and calm. 'He's thirty. He's bleeding – from his head – but I don't know what happened. I don't think he's breathing so the woman on the phone told me how to do the heart thing . . . the . . .' I suddenly couldn't think of my words.

'Chest compressions?' Ian said, kneeling down beside Luke. 'That's great. You did exactly the right thing. Do you know what happened? Did he fall?'

'I don't know,' I said weakly. 'I really don't. He was just here . . .'

At this point, they both turned their attention away from me and began working on Luke. It was impressive, their demeanour. They spoke and moved quickly and urgently, but with a kind of methodical calm. I stepped back, not sure how I could help and not wanting to be in the way. They passed each other equipment from their large rucksacks and spoke to each other in low voices.

At one point, Ian held two panels on Luke's chest and shouted 'Clear!' and Luke's whole body jolted upwards. Ian looked at Helen but she just shook her head and I felt a wave of nausea hit me.

'He's not going to die?' I said quietly, but they either didn't hear or chose not to answer. Then Ian repeated the shock, and this time Helen gave a relieved smile and a nod, and although I didn't fully understand what was going on, I found myself doing the same.

As they manoeuvred Luke onto an orange stretcher and Helen placed a mask attached to a plastic bag over his mouth and nose, Ian said to me, 'You don't know how long he's been like this?'

I shook my head and Ian turned back to Luke. But then I had a thought: 'Although, he only left the bar a couple of hours ago so it can't have been any longer than that.'

'And you were in the bar too?' Helen said.

I nodded. 'He left before me though.'

As they both bent down to lift either end of the stretcher, Helen nodded towards the ambulance and said, 'If you just take a seat there, we'll follow you in.'

I looked over towards the plastic flip-down chair she was pointing to and obediently stepped into the back of the ambulance. I was so overcome with the shock of the situation, so desperate for everything to be taken care of by someone who knew what they were doing, it didn't occur to me that I was preparing to join them and Luke on his journey to hospital. I was just glad to be able to see the chair and follow this simple instruction. It wasn't until the ambulance doors were shut and Ian was in the driver's seat and starting the engine that I realised that, not only were we heading to the hospital, but that perhaps it wasn't appropriate for me to be there.

I heard Ian speaking into a radio as he drove. 'All teams on hand for this one please, serious head trauma.'

I'm not sure if it was the grave tone of Ian's voice, the reality of what was happening catching up with me or just because I'd had one drink too many, but I found that I'd started to cry. I didn't cry often but it often happened like that – I wouldn't even know it was happening until I saw it in the reactions of others.

Helen put her arm around my shoulder and squeezed my upper arm. 'What's your name, love?'

'Charlotte.' I sniffed.

'It's all a horrible shock, I know,' she said. She had an accent, I'd noticed. Midlands. I liked it. It made her seem warm.

I nodded but couldn't say anything.

'You're wishing he hadn't left the bar, I bet?'

I blinked. Then I nodded, because it seemed the right thing to do. I suppose she was right. If he was still sitting at the table with Kelly, yawning and looking bored, then he wouldn't be here.

'We all have rows from time to time,' she said, giving me a sad smile and putting her hand on my knee.

I nodded again, but I really had no idea what she was talking about. It was only a minute or two later, as we took a sharp left towards the hospital, that I realised she was under the impression that Luke and I had been together in the bar, perhaps on a date ourselves, and that he'd left before me. And, going by what she'd just said, she thought we'd had some kind of falling out.

I felt my cheeks flush. I felt self-conscious suddenly, and silly. I should have pointed out that I was just a member of the public when Helen had suggested I get into the ambulance, rather than merrily climbing in like a dolt. My role should have been to pass on what little information I had, then to make my exit with dignity, and not to intrude any further on a situation that was absolutely nothing to do with me. But here I was, not only coming along for the ride but crying about it, like one of those bizarre people who attend the funerals of strangers out of morbid fascination.

My mother always said I was an expert at being where I shouldn't.

Chapter 5

It wasn't the time to come clean there and then, hurtling up the hill with the blue lights flashing. It hardly seemed to matter, anyway, in the greater scheme of things. They were far more concerned with Luke and whatever specialist care he needed at the hospital to be interested in the exact nature of our relationship and whether we had or hadn't had a row. When the ambulance reached the hospital and Luke was moved inside, I would take the opportunity to slip away.

A few seconds after we'd pulled into the ambulance bay, Ian was out of the driver's seat and hauling open the back doors of the ambulance. As directed by Helen, I hopped down and stood out of the way as a whole gang of men and women in various uniforms and plastic aprons emerged from the hospital doors. Working together, they transferred Luke to a trolley to be wheeled inside. As you'd expect, I was far from the focus of anyone's attention, so although Helen took a moment to turn to me and say, 'Get yourself a cuppa and take a seat, darling,' she didn't hang around to see that I followed her instruction.

As the crowd of people flanking Luke's trolley disappeared through the double doors into the hospital, I hung back. The car park was quieter now, although still busy with people on crutches or in wheelchairs, or clasping injured hands to their chests, shuffling in and out of the hospital doors and into cars.

The drizzle wasn't heavy, but I'd been outside for a while and my clothes were damp. I shivered. I just wanted to be at home, in bed. I turned and crossed the car park, hoping to find a taxi dropping someone off that I could jump in.

I pulled the zip of my jacket up to my chin and pushed my hands into my pockets, but as I did so, I felt something inside. I took it out. It was Luke's wallet. I'd forgotten I was holding onto it.

I paused, and looked back towards the hospital. I felt sure that Luke wouldn't be looking to spend any money in the next twelve hours, so I could easily return it in the morning, couldn't I – when everything had calmed down?

I began on my way again, but then I had a thought: no one had any idea who he was. I'd told the paramedics he was 'Luke' but that was all. They would probably search his pockets for any clues as to his identity but with all his bank cards with me, they'd be unlikely to find anything. And then what? How would they know who to contact?

I had an image of Luke's mother – a dumpy middle-aged woman in a floral apron, is what sprung to mind – preparing a Sunday lunch. Then, when Luke didn't turn up as arranged, calling his friends to see if they knew where he was, getting increasingly anxious about what had happened. And what if – oh god – what if he didn't make it? What if I denied his family the chance to see him one last time because I'd walked off with his wallet? Because I was a bit damp and didn't want to delay my nice warm bath?

I spun around and headed back across the car park. I didn't use the doors the ambulance had pulled up in front of, but instead entered the building via the main public entrance.

The reception was bustling. A man about my age with red spots on his shirt and a bloodied tissue pressed to his mouth stumbled and bumped into me. His friend pulled him out of my way. 'Sorry,' he said with an apologetic smile. 'Drunk idiot.'

The rows of chairs were filled with glum-looking people clasping whichever part of their body they'd injured or staring at the wall with anxious furrowed brows, every so often looking at their watches and sighing. The reception desk was surrounded by a crowd three-deep, and the two women sitting behind it were patiently processing each new patient, delivering the same lines over and over again – 'Everyone's working as fast as they can'; 'We're very busy this evening, someone will be with you as soon as possible.'

I hovered behind the crowd, still holding Luke's wallet in my hand, as if I was afraid someone might pickpocket me and it would be gone for ever. I considered my options. Even if I waited in the queue and handed the wallet over at reception, I wasn't sure it would find its way to Luke. What if the receptionist put it in a drawer and it got lost, forgotten amidst the throngs of grizzling toddlers and limping pensioners? I wasn't sure how I'd explain where it needed to get to anyway. I could describe Luke's injuries – 'Please give this to the thirty-year-old man with the head injury who was just brought in' – but was that clear enough a brief? Or was that a description that could be applied to many?

I looked towards some double doors labelled RESUS ONLY that led to the area where ambulance admissions arrived. I wasn't really sure what 'resus only' meant, but there was nothing explicit to say people weren't supposed to go in there. I could go through, I decided, and find a person I recognised – one of the crowd of professionals who'd rushed out to meet the ambulance – and hand the wallet directly to someone I knew was caring for Luke.

Almost at once I spotted a woman I'd seen meet the ambulance, recognisable by the distinctive blue plaster covering a nose piercing. She was wearing pale blue scrubs, so I had no idea of her role or rank, but as she walked quickly past me, I stepped forward, causing her to stop abruptly and look up at me.

'Excuse me,' I began. 'I came in with Luke . . . a man . . . he was bleeding . . .'

She looked at me blankly at first, but then her face cleared and she nodded. 'Yes. Of course. Sorry, sweetheart, I really can't stop now but we're doing everything we can for him.'

Before I could reply, she continued on her way down the corridor and I was left holding lamely onto the wallet. Then, just as I was about to head back out to reception, she turned back.

'Although . . .' She walked back over to me. 'I should warn you, you might be asked to make some tough decisions, I just want to prepare you for that.'

'What decisions?'

'Someone will be out to chat to you soon.' She squeezed my arm, and then carried on walking.

'Please don't let him die,' I called after her, surprising not just me, but everyone around me.

I stood still for a moment, with busy doctors and nurses swerving around me, trying to take in what she'd meant. What decisions?

I realised I still had the wallet. Once again, I considered just going home, taking it with me and coming back in the morning, but again, I was struck by the potential impact of that decision if things took a turn for the worse in the night – and from what I'd just heard, that seemed more likely than I'd realised.

I decided just to wait for a while and see how things panned out. I turned around, trudged over to the rows of metal chairs and sat down. I'd give it an hour. By then, hopefully, the initial frantic burst of action needed for Luke's care would be over and things would have calmed down. Someone would come to speak to me, I could clear up my role in the situation, pass the wallet on and be on my way.

There was a small low table next to my row of chairs covered with colourful information leaflets. I picked them up and shuffled through them, looking for something to pass the time. Details of how to treat an acid burn, a list of clinics offering free flu jabs, contact information for a therapeutic bell-ringing group. One pamphlet been put together by an organisation called FAROP – Friends and Relatives of Patients – and was a sizeable publication featuring more than forty pages of glossy photographs accompanied by personal accounts of people's experiences of having a person close to them admitted to A&E. I took this one back to my seat and spent a few moments reading gentle stories about a dad's panic when his two-year-old son pushed a plastic Santa hat into his ear and the kind support an elderly lady had received from A&E nurses when her husband had put his foot in a bonfire. Then an article caught my eye.

Its headline was, 'I begged them not to let her die – but I wish they had.'

The photo was of a woman in her fifties, hair streaked with grey and bags under her eyes, clasping a photo in a frame of a young girl of about sixteen or seventeen in a football kit with a ball under her arm.

As I read, I discovered the woman's daughter, April, had been knocked down by a drunk driver a few weeks before her eighteenth birthday and had been rushed to hospital with serious head injuries. The mother recounted how, when she'd been told what had happened and had rushed to the hospital, she'd been greeted by a doctor who had explained to her that, with injuries that severe, it was unlikely that April would ever make a full recovery.

'I felt like what he was saying to me was basically, "She's probably never going to be running around, playing sport and being one hundred per cent fit any time soon, so should we just let her die?"', the article said. 'So of course, I was furious. And desperate and devastated and all these things. So I told them on no account should they let her go. They must not let her die.'

The mother went on, describing the agonising weeks and months April spent in Intensive Care, her move to a high-dependency rehabilitation unit – 'It was called a rehabilitation unit, but she never got any better. She was out of it, not a flicker, not a twitch, for nearly two years.'

Then came the part that really struck me, that made me tear up, as if I'd really got to know this woman and her daughter: 'In the end, we had to starve her to death. That was the only way. To remove her hydration and feeding tube and let her go that way. And there isn't a day that goes by that I don't wish I could go back to that conversation the night of her injury and let them stop then. To let her go peacefully.'

It was only a few moments later, when I replaced the leaflet in its cardboard holder and returned to my seat, that I realised the enormity of what I'd done.

Please don't let him die.

Had I just made a completely life-altering decision for someone I didn't even know?

Chapter 6

It had felt like an innocuous enough statement – obvious really, not something to be taken seriously. But even as I tried to rationalise with myself, I felt my chest constrict. What if I had set Luke on a path of invasive and ill-advised treatment that would lead to years of suffering? Would *his* family be forced to watch as he starved to death? My breathing was becoming fast and light, my heart beating frantically. As ever, the sensation made me want to stand up and call for help, but I'd experienced this enough times that I knew what to do.

I sat very still, I put my hands on my knees and began to list the capital cities of Europe, working from north to south.

Reykjavik, Helsinki, Oslo.

What were they doing to him right now? Was he on an operating table? Was one surgeon saying to another, 'I still think this is a bad idea, but here's goes nothing'?

Talinn, Stockholm, Moscow.

Was it fraud, that I'd ridden in the ambulance, that I'd misled them? Or worse, was it some kind of indirect violent crime? Assault by . . . unauthorised medical treatment?

My fingers ran over the leather of Luke's wallet as I tried

to decide what to do next. I was just thinking that it probably would be best after all if I just ditched the wallet at reception, went home and put this whole strange evening behind me, when a man in a blue shirt with rolled-up sleeves and a stethoscope around his neck emerged from the side corridor. He raised his hand when he saw me as if to catch my attention and made his way over.

'Are you Charlotte?' he said. 'I've been looking for you.'

I nodded. 'Have you been with Luke? What's happening?'

'Let's go somewhere quiet, shall we?'

As he led me back to the quiet side room, set away from the main reception, I knew he was going to tell me that Luke had died. I'd seen enough medical dramas to know how this goes. I was surprised though to discover that by the time we took our seats on the foam-cushioned chairs, that I'd started to cry again. Not hysterical sobbing, but silent sad tears. It was turning into quite the night for it.

The doctor, who introduced himself as a registrar called Pavel, passed me a tissue from the box on the table. 'I know this is a really horrible situation to find yourself in, but we're doing everything we can.'

I wiped my eyes then my nose. 'You mean, he's not . . . he's still . . . ?'

Pavel placed his hands on his knees. 'The current situation is that he's stable but very poorly. He has a very serious head injury. We've moved him up to our Intensive Care Unit where he has a machine to help with his breathing. We're going to monitor him for the next twenty-four hours, then decide what to do next.'

I nodded. 'Will he wake up?'

Pavel paused. 'It really is too early to say anything for sure. I think the best thing is if you go home and get some sleep and we reconvene in the morning.'

I nodded again. Sleep was exactly what I wanted.

'Is there anyone else we should call? His parents, other family? Of course, you're quite welcome to inform whoever needs to know, but sometimes people do ask for our help with this.'

'Can you do it?' I said, looking up at him. 'I don't . . . I'm not in touch with them.'

He nodded. 'Of course. He didn't have a mobile phone on him. Do you have it?'

I shook my head and Pavel nodded seriously. 'Stolen in the attack, perhaps. Don't worry. We can track down contact details.' He told me there was a poster listing local taxi numbers next to the reception desk and suggested that I should call one. 'Get some rest,' he said, standing up and putting his hand on my shoulder. 'Make sure you leave your details with Reception. The police will want a chat, too, to work out exactly what's happened. But get home for now. We'll talk soon, OK?'

'OK,' I agreed, even though as I left the room and the hospital, Luke's wallet still in my pocket, I felt sure I would never see him again.

Chapter 7

At home, exhaustion trumped adrenalin and I fell asleep quickly. When I woke up and saw it was nine a.m. on my bedside clock, it took a few moments to shuffle my memories of the previous night's events into order, to sort through which parts had really happened and which were scenes from my dreams.

I pulled my laptop from under my bed and flipped it open. Logging into Facebook, I typed *Luke Burley* into the search bar. There were several accounts listed under that name, but it was easy to spot the one I was looking for. His profile picture was the same as the one on his dating profile: him standing next to a bike on the top of a mountain, an impressive vista laid out behind him. I remembered Kelly's drunken vitriol about his mountain biking. Had that really only been last night? I clicked onto the page and opened the picture to get a better look.

He had a few days' stubble growth and his hair was covered by a helmet, but it was definitely him. He had a wide smile showing a row of neat white teeth. He looked far more attractive when he was smiling, I noted, than when he had been staring moodily out of the window in the bar. And when he'd been lying in a pool of his own blood.

I should have just logged off then – I'd done enough interfering as it was – but I felt compelled to find out more about this man who was now fighting for his life. It seemed he wasn't too concerned about privacy; I was free to scroll through his whole profile.

His work page told he'd recently started work as a 'Solutions Support Advisor' – whatever that meant – at a company that, from what I could gather from its website, helped other businesses arrange team-building events for their staff. It's funny, I thought, the ways people make their livings these days.

I turned my attention to the many photos he'd uploaded. About three-quarters of them showed him on, or next to, a bicycle, or were close-ups of his muddy, sweaty face, taken from what I assumed was one of those robust action cameras, probably attached to his handlebars. Clearly Kelly had been right when she'd said bikes were a big part of his life. He seemed to have a healthy social life too. There was photo after photo of him with a pint in hand, standing alongside other men with similar neat haircuts, similar bright smiles. In one, I noticed a large scar on his lower leg, and wondered if he'd come off the bike at some point. I suppose you could really lose some skin if you grated a leg along the pavement for any distance.

There was one photo of Luke with an old couple and a younger woman sitting at a round table in what seemed to be quite a smart restaurant. The physical resemblance between Luke and the older man was striking – the same colouring, the same wide smile, the same bright blue eyes. I could see from the photo's tags that the couple were Stephen and Jenny Burley, and the other woman was Rebecca Burley. It took only a few more clicks to access the 'family' tab of Jenny's Facebook page and discover that Stephen and Jenny were Luke's parents, and Rebecca was his sister.

I was just beginning to scroll through Jenny Burley's page, finding myself mesmerised by photos of some incredibly intricately decorated cakes she'd posted, when I realised I'd been immersed in the online world of the Burley family for well over an hour. It was time I got out of bed, forgot about Luke Burley and did something with my Sunday.

Chapter 8

I put my laptop on top of the chest of drawers and did a cursory tidy of my room, shoving the clothes I'd strewn about the place when I was getting dressed the evening before back into my wardrobe. Then I showered, dressed, ate a toasted cheese sandwich standing up in my kitchen and decided to head into town.

As I grabbed my phone from my bedside table I noticed I had three missed calls and a text, all from Yanis, my landlord. He'd seemed quite pleasant the first time I'd met him as he'd shown me around the flat. He'd said he was only renting the place out to cover the mortgage while he was working in Cork for a few years so I'd felt quite confident he wasn't going to be one of those unscrupulous greedy types, forever enforcing bizarre restrictions on the tenancy or cranking the rent up whenever he felt like it, and indeed, everything had been fine for the first few months. In the last few weeks though, he'd be calling more and more often, getting snippy and rude when I didn't answer the first time. I was just glad he was safely on the other side of the Irish Sea, else he'd probably be pestering me in person by now.

As I walked through the station and down the main road towards the sea, my thoughts drifted back to Luke. You don't get much to go on from a dating profile app. The photo of him on the mountain, together with his brief paragraph about wanting someone to get outdoors with, had given me the impression of someone lively, but perhaps a bit earnest – somewhere between an overgrown boy scout and a border collie. Lovable, but perhaps a bit exhausting.

Now though, having seen more details of his life, seeing him hungover on the sofa holding up his palm to shield his face from the camera, reading the comments bouncing back and forth between his friends, he seemed more rounded. More interesting, really.

As I waited at the pedestrian crossing, I took my phone out of my bag and tried to call Emily again. She hadn't texted me with any explanation since her no-show and subsequent strangeness on the phone the evening before but with everything that had happened, I hadn't had a chance to think about where she might have got to.

My call went straight through to voicemail.

'Hey, Em, it's me, Charlotte. Just checking everything's OK.' I paused. I didn't want to sound accusatory in case she had a good reason for standing me up. I was a bit irritated that she hadn't felt the need to contact me at all, but I decided I'd have to give her the benefit of the doubt for now. 'I had the craziest night, actually, in the end. I met this guy and . . . well, it was all weird. Call me and I'll tell you the whole story. OK. Hope you're OK. Bye.'

I did a few chores I needed to get done. I took a coat that I'd bought on eBay that still had the tags on back to Topshop in exchange for a credit voucher well in excess of the price I'd paid. No doubt my mother would have called that fraud but then she always did like to make her life harder than it had to be. I'd call it being savvy in a difficult financial climate.

I ambled around looking in windows, going into shops, picking up clothes and holding them against me, making for the checkouts but stopping before I got there and discarding the hanger on a random rail. I was supposed to be being careful about money.

As I headed into the shopping centre with a vague plan to head for the cookie counter, I heard a shout.

'Noah! Noah, come here now. I won't ask you again.'

I recognised the name before the voice. Although I've since been assured that every nursery in the UK has at least one these days, I'd never known a Noah before I met Meredith's three-year-old son. I stopped and turned in the direction of the shouting and saw that it was indeed Meredith, struggling with a pushchair weighed down with carrier bags, while Noah lay flat on his back in the middle of the main walkway of the shopping centre.

She was so distracted that she didn't see me until I was standing right next to her.

'Meredith,' I said. 'Hey!' I put my hand on her arm to get her attention and she jumped and spun round.

For a second her face was frozen in horror but then she realised who I was and relaxed.

'Oh hi!' she said brightly. 'Charlotte!'

'How are you?' I asked.

'Uh . . . fine. Oh, you know.' She nodded towards Noah. 'Nothing's ever easy, is it?' She laughed weakly. She went over to him, scooped him off the floor and wrestled his wriggling body into the pushchair.

'Do you know if Emily's OK?' I said. 'I was meant to meet her last night but—'

'As far as I know.'

'I tried to call her again just now but she's not picking up. I was just wondering if . . . I don't know. Maybe I'm reading too much in to it but I wondered if she was still annoyed with me about . . .'

Noah was kicking his legs in protest at being restrained by the pushchair straps. He caught the side of Meredith's face with his trainer and she winced. 'I really don't know,' Meredith said, a bit abruptly. As her son's wails grew louder, I decided to leave it. Now obviously wasn't the time.

'We should get together soon,' I said. 'I'm happy to come to you if it's easier.'

'Yeah, yeah. We should do that.'

'Maybe next week?'

Meredith picked a carrier bag off the floor and hung it on the side of the buggy. Then she reached into her shoulder bag and took out a cereal bar, unwrapped it and passed it to Noah. With the boy pacified for a moment she turned to me. 'Yes. I'll message you.'

I nodded. 'OK.'

She ran her fingers through her hair and looked towards the shopping centre doors. 'I've got to go but . . . take care. Bye.'

She began walking quickly out of the shopping centre, ignoring Noah's cries when he dropped his cereal bar and not stopping to collect it.

I watched her go then carried on through the shopping centre. It looked quite awful, sometimes, having a child. The thought of not being able to conduct a simple three-minute chat without a screaming sidekick flailing about next to you made me feel ill.

I thought about my question, about whether Emily was annoyed with me. Meredith hadn't given much away, but surely everyone was past it all now? It was weeks ago, the stupid misunderstanding. It was all to do with a mistake managing the website at work. Too boring and trivial to even explain to someone outside the company without them nodding off, but sometimes in the pressure cooker of a small office, little dramas can feel important. I suppose these things happen when you mix business with pleasure. I guess it's just one of the hazards of making friends with colleagues.

By mid-afternoon I was starting to flag. An evening of drinking followed by the late night I'd had after being in the hospital for hours was catching up with me and I headed home with plans for a bath, pyjamas and a juvenile comedy film.

I dragged my duvet out into the lounge and buried myself up to my neck. I paid only vague attention to the television while I scrolled through the internet, reading brain-rotting articles about celebrities I'd never heard of and weird call-outs the fire brigade had had to deal with. When I went to my Facebook page, I found it was still open on Luke Burley's profile. I looked at his photo again. There was something about his smile that was quite compelling. Maybe it was the teeth, I thought. I'd never been able to resist nice teeth. Or maybe it was the way his blue eyes looked right at you.

I wondered what was going on at the hospital. His parents – Jenny and Stephen – they were there by now, surely? And this sister too – this Rebecca – I expected she must be with them.

I scrolled down his page looking for clues as to what might be happening. I wanted to see if any of his friends had heard the news and had written the kind of heartfelt messages of support people like to leave at times like this, even though they know the recipient is in no position to see them. 'Hang in there, Luke!' 'Get well soon, mate, missing you on the tracks.' That sort of thing. I was very much hoping not to see, 'RIP pal,' or anything similar.

There was nothing though, which I suppose wasn't that surprising. It had only just happened really, and people always liked to make sure the nearest and dearest were abreast of the situation before inviting comments from the wider social group. I realised though, that there was a good chance I'd never know how things turned out for Luke. The best-case scenario was that he'd make a full recovery and be back posting pictures of himself riding around the countryside and having dinner with his family, in which case, I suppose I'd have my answer. But what happened if he didn't? If the page went without update for weeks or months? I'd never know whether he was still in hospital, or if something else had happened. Something worse.

I closed my laptop, slipped it onto the floor, and fell into a fitful daytime sleep, snippets of the film's dialogue invading my dreams. When I woke up, the sun was setting, an orange beam of light stretching across the room. The idea came to me before I was fully conscious, but I decided to act on it before I could change my mind. I threw the duvet off me, pulled on my jeans and jumper and picked up my bag from the kitchen worktop. I checked the bus times on my phone but it was Sunday, so I'd have to wait at least half an hour and even then there was no guarantee one would show. In the end, I scrolled through my contacts to 'Taxi – Brighton' and hit call.

'Taxi, when and where are you going please?'

'Royal Sussex County Hospital. As soon as you can.'

Chapter 9

The hospital reception was as busy as it had been the night before but there was a different flavour to the patients now. Fewer drunk young men, more fractious children. As I walked through the doorway, a girl of about six or seven met my eye and slowly turned over the hand she was cradling to show me a deep cut on her palm.

'That looks sore,' I said.

She nodded solemnly but said nothing.

Next to the reception desk there was a large grey sign listing the departments of the hospital with floors. Intensive Care Unit was listed in two locations – on floor 5 and on floor 7. I headed for the lift. I decided to get off at floor 5; if I had no luck there I could continue on to 7.

As I exited the lift, I found myself facing a set of blue double doors, the sign above them reading Intensive Care Unit, but there were no staff immediately available, no desk to report to, no one to ask if Luke was here, or how he was. There was a big green button with a sign above it: 'Buzz for entry,' it said, but the security system obviously wasn't rigorously followed because the door had been propped ajar with a roll of newspaper. I hesitated for a moment, but then, not seeing what other option I had, pushed the door open and immediately found myself in the ward itself.

It was quiet inside, the only sound electronic beeping and the rhythmic roar of the ventilators. It was long, but held only eight or so beds as each one was surrounded by so much equipment – screens, trolleys, tubes, tables on wheels – that it needed to be set well apart from the others. There were curtain rails lining the cubicles, and most were partially drawn, shielding the patients from the beds on either side, but open at the front onto the walkway that ran down the middle of the ward. The patients themselves looked tiny, tucked up to their chests in the blue and white covers. All of them were connected to the machines around them with plastic tubes and wires. It felt to me like perhaps their consciousnesses were connected to a virtual reality existence somewhere, and they were in this world in body alone.

It was Luke's jacket that caught my attention, folded up and placed on top of his shoes in the corner of one of the cubicles. I stopped and took a step closer to the bed. I had to look at him for a full thirty seconds or so before I was convinced it was him. I don't think I would have stopped at all if it hadn't been for the jacket. It's true what they say about people looking different in hospital beds. And, of course, I wasn't intimately familiar with his face anyway.

I was tracing the tubes and wires with my eyes, trying to work out what was connected to which monitor, and what each one was for when I heard the voice behind me.

'Are you all right there?'

I turned around and saw a woman of about fifty with grey hair tied into a ponytail. She was wearing blue scrubs, a pair of glasses hanging around her neck by a green cord.

'Is he OK?' I said turning towards Luke's bed. 'Luke?'

She peered at me for a moment, her head slightly on one side. Then she said, 'Are you Charlotte?'

I blinked, and then nodded.

She smiled and came closer to me. Together we stood side by side at the end of Luke's bed. I noticed she had a name badge: Maggie.

'He's currently critical but stable,' she said.

I nodded, but the words didn't mean much. It sounded like a contradiction in terms to me.

'It's still early days,' she said. 'Brain injuries are very complex things. Medicine is a lot more about wait and see than people would like. Even more so when it comes to the head.'

I realised it was coming up to twenty-four hours since I'd found him. The first twenty-four hours are crucial. Wasn't that what they said about head injuries? Or was that kidnapped children? I couldn't remember.

'When will he wake up?' I asked. Then I added, 'Roughly?', aware that my question had sounded childish.

She paused. 'Tell you what, I'll ask the consultant to talk to you as soon as she's free, but I think the short answer is we can't say anything for sure yet. The scans aren't giving any definitive answers. They often don't, unfortunately.'

I nodded and then I looked around me. I suddenly felt I shouldn't have come. At any rate, now I'd found out that at least Luke wasn't dead, I really should be going. I should have left it longer, before checking on him. Of course he wasn't going to be up and about and eating a yogurt in the chair next to his bed. They'd only been working on him for a day.

'Why don't you talk to him?' Maggie said, nodding towards a chair.

I looked from the chair to Maggie and then to Luke. 'Talk to him? But . . .'

'We always encourage families to talk to the patient as if they were awake. We're not promising miracles, but it can only help. And you might find it useful too. People say it's nice, to continue to chat to them as they would normally.'

I'd feel self-conscious talking to a comatose man at the best of times, let alone one who was a virtual stranger. But I didn't feel I had much choice. It would look strange, I knew, if I just shook my head and scurried away.

Dutifully, I took my seat at his bedside. I wouldn't have to stay long.

'You can touch him,' Maggie said encouragingly.

I looked at her uncertainly, but then reached out. I slipped my hand into his. It was warm and dry. I really hoped he was as out of it as he looked.

'I'll leave you to it,' Maggie said, giving my shoulder a squeeze and closing the curtain around the cubicle.

I looked at him, watched the lines on the monitor. He was completely still, apart from the up-and-down of his chest. It looked almost mechanical, the movement. Then I realised, that's because it was mechanical. It was being done by a machine.

For a moment, I couldn't think of a single thing to say to him. So I made myself consider: what would I say if he was awake, lying there with his eyes open, staring at the ceiling, thoroughly put out by his current situation?

'Hi, Luke,' I tried. I paused for a moment, waiting to see if he'd react in any way. When he didn't, I went on. 'Sorry about this. Can't be much fun, I know. I hope I did the right stuff, with the CPR. I haven't had any training in that sort of thing.'

I paused, as if giving him space to take in what I was saying.

'I guess you thought that date with Kelly was the worst your evening was going to get!' I laughed, then thought better of it. 'Sorry. I guess you're not really in a joking mood. But . . . I could see she wasn't your type. She was a bit much.' I paused. 'What else can I tell you? I went on your Facebook. Sorry. Is that weird? It's just, I was curious. I wanted to know who you were, who—'

I heard voices approach outside the curtain. I stopped talking and dropped Luke's hand guiltily.

'We were in Athens, when we heard,' a man's voice said. 'Obviously we were packing our bags and on our way back the second we got off the phone but it was twelve hours before we could find a flight with space and then there were delays . . . bad weather . . . and . . .'

A woman spoke now. 'But we came as soon as we could. And we're here now. Can we see him?'

'Yes, of course.' I recognised Maggie's voice. 'I'm not sure how familiar you are with hospitals, but it can be a lot to take in the first time you see someone in Intensive Care. There's a lot of equipment.'

'Yes,' the man said quietly. 'We're prepared for that.'

'He's actually got a visitor, just at the moment.'

'Oh? Really?' The man said. 'Who? His sister was going to . . .'

As I heard Maggie reach for the curtain, I stood up and smoothed down my jumper.

When she pulled it back, I recognised the two people standing at the end of the bed immediately from their Facebook photos.

Jenny Burley. Stephen Burley. Luke's parents.

Chapter 10

Under any other circumstances, I imagine that being unexpectedly faced with a woman you'd never met before would cause you to retain an air of formality, at least until the basic introductions had been covered, but it was clear that when the woman you didn't know was standing next to your son, who was unconscious and wired up to machines in a hospital bed, manners went out of the window. After only the briefest look at me, Jenny lurched forward, her hand over her mouth. 'My little boy . . .' She had an accent. Northern. I remembered her Facebook page listing her hometown as Halifax or Harrogate or something. Somewhere in Yorkshire, anyway.

She stood on the other side of the bed from me, one hand on Luke's arm, the other stroking the hair away from his forehead.

Stephen closed his eyes briefly and swallowed hard, the sight of his son obviously having just as much impact on him, but producing a more understated response. He too then stepped forward to the bed, resting his hand on the metal rail.

At that point, he looked at me. 'Hello,' he said. Then, 'Sorry, I don't think we've . . .' He gave Maggie a questioning look.

She blinked. 'Oh, sorry. I assumed you'd know each other.'
Stephen shook his head, his face blank.

Maggie came to stand beside me. 'This young lady very likely saved Luke's life. He's a lucky boy. Not every fella can say his girlfriend's done that.'

Jenny shot Stephen a look as if to say, 'Did you know about this?' and he shrugged. Then they both turned back to me.

'Sorry,' Stephen said. 'We don't know . . . we were away, you see. In Greece. We're just catching up now.'

'Well, as I understand it,' Maggie said, 'the way Charlotte was able to keep a cool head and follow the operator's instructions meant the paramedics were able to restart his heart at the side of the road.' Maggie gave me a pointed nod as if to say, 'Go on, you tell it', but I couldn't think of anything else to say.

'His heart stopped?' Stephen said.

Maggie nodded gravely.

'My God.' He put both hands over his nose and mouth and breathed out.

'Charlotte, was it?' Jenny said.

I nodded slowly. That was true enough, at least.

She shook her head. 'Sorry,' she said. 'We hadn't . . . I don't think Luke had mentioned you. Maybe he did, but . . .'

'Oh,' I jumped in, to save her from the awkwardness. 'It's kind of early . . . early on. We didn't want to do a big official announcement or anything. We were just . . .'

I let my words peter out but Stephen and Jenny nodded like they knew what I meant. Which was good, because I hadn't a clue.

Maggie smiled around at the confused, sad frowns. 'They have all sorts of words for it these days, the youngsters. All sorts of phrases. "Seeing each other" – that's the one my son always says, "She's not my *girlfriend*, Mum," he says, "I'm just seeing her." "What, like we see your grandma on a Sunday?" I always say – that winds him up!' She seemed to realise she was babbling then and stopped. 'Anyway. I'll leave you to it.' She gave us one last smile, and left through the curtains. I heard her whistling as she made her way down the ward, which seemed a bit inappropriately cheerful to me, but Jenny and Stephen didn't seem to notice.

'What happened?' Jenny said, looking up at me. 'You were there?'

'I'm Stephen, by the way,' Stephen said, extending his hand. 'And this is my wife, Luke's mum, Jenny. We're pleased to meet you, even if it is under these circumstances.'

I hesitated for a moment. 'Yes. Yes, lovely to meet you,' I said. 'Luke always talked about you so fondly.'

I said it without thinking – it seemed the right part of the script for the encounter – but I suppose it was a harmless enough statement.

'I just don't understand what happened?' Jenny said again. Her hand was resting on Luke's shoulder. 'How could anyone do this?'

I shook my head. 'I wasn't there at the time. I found him, just afterwards. I . . .' I wasn't sure what else to say. I didn't suppose they wanted a full description of the sight I encountered when I saw him lying on the floor, the way his leg was twisted, the smell of bins and urine. In the end I just said, 'He wasn't moving. The ambulance came really quickly. I just kept doing the chest compressions.' I clasped my hands together, one on top of the other as I had the evening before, to show them. 'One, two, three. One, two, three. Until the paramedics came.'

Stephen patted my upper arm. 'You did well, to do that. Thank you.'

He went over and joined his wife at Luke's bedside.

He sighed. 'Oh, Luke,' he said, shaking his head and smiling sadly.

None of us said anything for a moment. The ventilator carried on making its roaring sound, the rhythm never changing.

'I thought he'd come off his bike,' Jenny said, still looking down at Luke. 'That's what we thought, when they said there'd been an accident.'

I nodded. 'He does love his bike,' I said – one of the few things I actually knew about him.

'Have you spoken to her?' Jenny looked at me. 'That Morrissey or whatever her name is, the consultant?'

I shook my head.

'Moriarty,' Stephen corrected quietly. 'Anne Moriarty.'

'She was useless!' A sob enveloped Jenny, making her voice louder suddenly, and Stephen and I both looked at her, shocked.

Stephen opened his mouth. 'She . . . she . . . now, come on, love.' He went over to her and put his arm round her shoulder.

'"We just can't say"!' Jenny said. 'That's what she kept saying, over and over again. She couldn't say a bloody thing apparently.'

'It's early days. That's all she said. We don't want them to pretend to know things when they don't. It's like she said, there's no road map.'

My phone beeped and I saw it was a text from Yanis:
We need to sort this out. I'll come to the flat this afternoon.

Suddenly the complete bizarreness of the whole situation struck me. Why was I standing here, in the midst of this scene? This wasn't my drama. This wasn't my grief.

'I should get going,' I said, picking up my bag from the floor. 'I'll give you some space.'

Chapter 11

'No,' Jenny said quickly. 'Don't go. They say familiar people, familiar voices can help. Stay. Please.'

'I . . .' I looked from Jenny's face to Stephen, expecting him to give me permission to leave, to gently scold his wife for being demanding.

But he just nodded and said, 'Yes,' he said. 'Do stay. We're not normally like this, I promise. We're normally very friendly!'

He gave a weak laugh, but it sounded strange in the quiet ward and he stopped abruptly. He nodded towards the one chair at Luke's bedside and I found I had no choice but to take it, leaving his parents, his actual relatives, to stand on the other side of the bed.

I decided to concentrate on at least looking the part of the concerned girlfriend, whilst at the same time formulating a plan for extricating myself from the situation. Eventually the visit would be over, we would leave – probably making plans to meet again at the hospital, or to keep each other informed of any news – and I would go home, and never see any of them again. I would always wonder what happened to Luke, and remember this strange twenty-four hours in my life, but I would quite likely never know how it ended for this family.

I held Luke's hand again, mostly because that way I could stay in role without having to think of anything to say. I re-assured myself with the thought that it would be very hard to chat naturally to an unconscious person in front of strangers, even if I had known Luke intimately.

Stephen seemed to feel equally out of his depth and stood mutely, alternating between squeezing his wife's hand and voicing musings about the equipment.

'That's monitoring his heart, I suppose,' he'd say, nodding towards one machine, then 'What's that for, do you think?' standing in front of another, bending down and peering closely at the numbers.

'Don't touch anything,' Jenny said, slapping his hand away as he ran his fingers along a tube.

'I wasn't!' Stephen protested, lifting his hands in the air, palms outwards. He stepped away from the bed and sighed. 'I just feel . . . pointless,' he said quietly. 'Useless.'

There was a sound like a cuckoo calling and Jenny reached into her bag and took out her phone. She pressed the screen.

'Becky's here. Where are we? What floor are we on?' Jenny looked around for signs.

It took me a moment to make the connection of 'Becky' to Rebecca, the sister, the photos of whom I'd seen.

Stephen said: 'Why don't we go and get a cup of tea and a sandwich? We haven't had anything for hours.'

'God forbid you should be late for a meal,' Jenny muttered, not taking her eyes off Luke's face.

Stephen opened his mouth, and looked as if he was going to argue, but then shifted his demeanour, clearly making an effort to take a more calming approach.

He took both Jenny's hands in his, forcing her to look up

at him. 'It's like the doctor told us,' he said. 'We don't know how long this is going to last. We could be here for the long haul. We need to look after ourselves, look after each other, if we're going to be here for him.' He nodded his head towards Luke. 'Let's collect Becky and have something to eat. Nothing's going to suddenly change because we've gone downstairs for twenty minutes.'

Jenny took an anxious look at Luke but eventually nodded. I saw the opportunity to excuse myself.

'I really need to make a move,' I said.

Jenny and Stephen looked at me. Both seemed shocked. I wasn't sure if it was because they'd forgotten I was there, or at the suggestion I'd go home.

'You'll come for something to eat?' Jenny said. 'To meet Becky?'

'Or, you've met her before?' Stephen added.

I was glad then, for the time I'd spent reviewing Luke's Facebook profile. Having to say that I had no idea who Becky was, or even that Luke had a sister, would have been a very awkward moment indeed.

I shook my head. 'Not yet. Luke talked about her though.' Again, this seemed a safe lie and one that would likely be well received.

Stephen smiled. 'They were very close.' Stephen clocked Jenny's alarm at his use of the past tense. 'I mean, they were because . . . it was more when they were kids, wasn't it, that he would follow her around? I didn't mean . . .'

He trailed off. 'Luke's close to everyone,' Jenny said. 'He's just that kind of lad. Always thinking of others.' I nodded and gave her the warmest smile I could manage.

Although I'd never officially retracted my intention to head home, by some sort of mutual unspoken agreement we began to make our way down the stairs to the third floor. Jenny was talking to me – general observations about the hospital, the noises, which door to go through – in a way that meant that, whilst not requiring a reply, it was difficult for me to find a natural point to bid my goodbyes and break away from them.

On the third floor, Jenny ducked into the ladies' toilet and as soon as the door closed behind her, I noticed Stephen's shoulders visibly sag. He rubbed his hand the full length of his face and sighed. I could see then that he'd been putting on some kind of front for his wife.

'God,' he said, shaking his head.

I looked at him, unsure what to say. I gave him the tight, sad smile I'd already rolled out a few times that evening.

'Jen's only just lost her sister,' Stephen said. 'Six months ago. She's just getting over that and now . . .'

'That's . . . really bad luck.'

He nodded but didn't say anything. Then he seemed to make a deliberate effort to brighten his tone. 'Anyway, how long have you and Luke been . . . when did you meet?'

I smiled at his shyness, and also to cover my alarm at the question, as I tried to decide what to say. 'Well . . .'

'That'll be one silver lining, for Jen,' he went on. 'She does baby Luke a bit. She hates him down here "on his own" as she always says. She'll be delighted that you're here.'

It wasn't so much the thought of letting down Jenny's hopes of a dutiful daughter-in-law to dote on her son that stopped me – a desire for a thirty-year-old man to have someone to look after him sounded a bit silly to me – but more that it would have felt awkward, harsh even, to correct Stephen at that point.

Luckily, his run-on about Jenny's delight meant his question about the duration of our relationship had gone unanswered, and he hadn't seemed to notice.

'Where did the two of you meet? At work?'

I blinked, then shook my head. 'Online,' I said. 'On an app thing.'

Stephen nodded. 'Everything's online these days, isn't it?' he said. 'I suppose our generation missed the boat a bit, on that one. That said though, Jenny's very good at it. She's always "liking" photos and chatting to her mates and what have you. She's always been a bit quicker on the uptake than me.'

Jenny came out of the toilet then, hauling her bag up onto her shoulder.

'Ready?' she said. I noticed she'd applied lipstick. I wondered whose benefit it was for.

The three of us walked down the corridor and through the double doors labelled 'The Pier Café'.

It was quiet inside. There were plenty of people dotted around the tables, but many were alone, and those who were in small groups of two or three spoke quietly, their heads bent over their mugs.

'She said she was here.' Jenny said, scouring the room.

'There!' Stephen said, pointing to a table in the corner. 'There she is.'

'Oh,' Jenny said. 'Oh yes.' I thought I noted tension though, rather than relief.

The woman I recognised from Luke's Facebook photo was sitting at a small square table in the corner, her back against the wall and the table at her side. Her hair was neat, tidy and sleek. Her clothes too – smart, businesslike. A pencil skirt and a blouse – no, a shirt – with just the top two buttons undone. She looked ready for a meeting at the bank. She looked like she *was* the bank.

She was typing quickly on her phone. I assumed at first that she'd been so engrossed in what she was doing that she hadn't seen us approaching, but even when we'd arrived at the table, and Stephen had said, 'Hello, love,' she still didn't

57

look up immediately, instead taking a few moments to finish whatever she was doing before putting her phone on the table and saying, 'Yes. Hi,' in a tired, flat voice.

She stood up and gave each of her parents a peck on the cheek. 'Mum,' she said. 'Dad.'

It was strange, I thought. I'd imagined they'd fall into each other's arms, grief unleashed, sobbing and talking and sharing what little information they had. But this was tense. Formal.

'And this is Luke's girlfriend,' Stephen said, gesturing to me, 'Charlotte.'

Becky's face showed just a twitch of a frown. 'Oh,' she said. 'OK.'

I offered Luke's sister my hand. 'Becky?' Obviously I knew that's who she was but no one had used her name so far and it seemed polite to confirm.

'Rebecca,' she corrected, barely meeting my eye. She grasped my hand loosely for the briefest of moments before dropping it. There weren't enough chairs for four, so Stephen pulled one over from another table and positioned it at Becky's – Rebecca's – left elbow. She turned away from me and faced her parents.

'What's happening now?' she said, briskly. 'Any updates since I've been down here?'

Stephen shook his head. 'Nothing new to report since you were here earlier, I don't think. He's still sedated. The consultant was between patients, but she says she'll come and speak to us at nine, to fill us in properly.' Stephen looked at his watch. 'Twenty minutes.'

Rebecca nodded. Her clothes seemed out of place for a hospital. On a Sunday. She caught me looking at her and frowned. 'Sorry, what was your name again?' she said.

'Charlotte.'

Rebecca raised her eyebrows. 'Right. A new addition?'

I deliberately kept my tone bright. This has long been my tactic when faced with confrontation or aggression. Neutralise it by ignoring it. Pretend it hasn't registered. Kill it with kindness.

I nodded and smiled. 'It's early days.'

Stephen tried to put a positive spin on the information they'd been given so far by the doctor, drawing comparisons with, as far as I could see, a totally different case where his colleague had been concussed after a work incident. In a long-winded story, he concluded that the colleague had been fine, and therefore so would Luke. Neither Rebecca nor Jenny seemed convinced. Rebecca closed her eyes briefly as if she was trying to prevent herself from snapping at her father. Jenny twisted the tissue in her hand, her brow still furrowed. I felt sorry for Stephen so, for moral support, I chipped in with a – completely made-up – story of my own, with a similarly positive outcome, but after that our group fell silent.

Stephen looked at his watch. 'We should go back up.'

Jenny nodded and we all got to our feet. Rebecca's phone flashed and she opened a message, sighed and put it in her bag. As we reached the door of the café she turned to her parents and said, 'I assumed this meeting with the consultant would be family only?'

Stephen frowned and pushed his lips together disapprovingly. 'Becky, love, Charlotte's Luke's partner. That is family, in this day and age.'

Rebecca looked at me then, but continued to speak as if I wasn't there. 'She can't have known him more than two and a half minutes.'

'Rebecca!' Jenny said.

Such hostility was uncalled for in my opinion and, for a brief moment, I wondered if she knew that I was lying about my connection to Luke. But I realised that was paranoia on my part. There was no way she could know, not really. And anyway, if she did, she seemed the type to come right out and say so. I found her manner intriguing, in a way. Especially the coldness towards her parents. What was the woman's problem? Was this just how grief and anxiety manifested themselves in her, or was she one of those with some kind of personality disorder? I found myself staring at her curiously, wondering what her deal was.

Rebecca turned and walked quickly towards the lift, leaving the rest of us to follow. 'Don't take it to heart,' Stephen said. 'She always seems angry when she's upset. It's just her way of channelling these things.'

So that's it, I thought. I was disappointed. I'd have preferred a personality disorder.

Rebecca

Chapter 12

Obviously when my phone had started ringing at whatever ungodly hour it was the night before, I'd assumed it was Brendan.

He would often call late at night. 'Just checking in to see how you are, baby,' is how he'd usually start things off, with little regard for the fact I'd probably be considerably better if he didn't wake me up in the middle of the night when I had a breakfast meeting the next day. In any event, it was usually only a matter of minutes before we'd get on to more pressing matters – namely, him. 'I've just had such bad luck with women in the past. You're not like them though, are you? Promise me you'll never leave me?'

On and on it would go, this desperate seeking of reassurance. I honestly don't know why he thought I was a good option for him, given that his ego was in such frequent need of stroking, but that was what he had decided, and what he continued to decide every day. And the events in which we had become jointly embroiled over the past year meant that, while he was still insisting he wanted our relationship to continue, it would be dangerous for me to suggest otherwise.

So sure was I that it was Brendan that I nearly cancelled the call without looking at the screen. There'd be a fall-out in the morning I knew, but sometimes it was worth it for an unbroken night's sleep. Luckily though, as I tilted the phone towards me on the bedside table, I noticed the name on the screen. Jennifer Burley. My mother.

It was a source of fascination to Brendan, that I kept my parents' contact details listed under their full names in my address book.

'Why don't you just call them Mum and Dad?' he'd asked, seeming truly confounded by the issue.

'Why would I do that? I don't list anyone else by their relationship to me. I don't list Harriet Kirk as *Woman Who Does the Laundry*. I don't call Philip Matthewson *Brendan's Friend Who Wears a Smelly Jacket*.'

Brendan had smiled then. 'I suppose. I guess you don't have me in there as *Lovely Boyfriend*.'

He was quite prone to coming out with this sort of nonsense. But then what else would you expect from a man who had his own mother's number stored under 'Mama', followed by a pink heart icon?

Of course, I knew that something untoward must have happened as soon as I saw it was Mum. Aside from the hour, Mum never calls me. She may text, with brief, perfunctory messages or updates on family matters – 'There's a letter here for you'; 'Gillian's operation went well' – but she wasn't one to chat. At least not to me.

I knew they were away, touring the historical sites of Athens, and my first thought was that something had gone wrong that required my practical assistance. Perhaps they'd been pickpocketed, or there'd been a break-in at home, and they needed me to contact the insurance company. Whatever it was, I assumed the help they'd be looking for would be administrative in nature. They certainly wouldn't voluntarily come to me for emotional support.

'Becky, it's Luke,' Mum said as soon as I answered. 'There's been an accident.'

I sat up. 'What kind of accident?'

'We don't know, exactly. The hospital phoned. They said he might have been attacked! Mugged. Hit over the head!'

The spike in adrenalin caused by the unexpected phone call and Mum's opening line abated as I consciously wrestled it into check. Mum was prone to exaggerated displays of emotions at the best of times. Factor in that the situation involved Luke, her precious baby boy, and that she was out of the country, and unable to immediately put into place a number of frantic plans, and the effect was doubled. Tripled probably. I was sure it was nothing as serious as Mum was imagining.

'So, what's the current situation? Where is he and what exactly are his injuries?' I wanted to establish some facts, not just Mum's worst-case imagining of them.

'In hospital. We don't even know. They just said he's injured his head and that they'd know more as the situation unfolded. Your dad's packing now. We're going straight to the airport and we'll get on the first flight they have available.'

'You're coming home?'

'Of course! So listen, he's in the Royal Sussex County Hospital. I don't know where exactly but you can give his name at reception, explain you're his sister—'

'You want me to go there?'

'Of course!' she said again. 'We all need to go there now. I don't know what's happening, Becky, but we all need to be there.' There was a definite tone of reproach in this last sentence.

'Right. Things are little tricky my end right now.'

I knew this wouldn't be well received.

'What do you mean, "tricky"?' Her tone was frosty. Even frostier than normal.

'I'm away. For work.' There was no way for her to know I was in fact in my own bed, in my flat in Brighton, less than two miles from Luke.

'Away where?'

'Edinburgh.' I had no idea what possible reason I could give for needing to be in Edinburgh, but I took the gamble that she wouldn't ask.

'Well, how quickly can you get back down to Brighton? Can you fly? It's only a short flight, isn't it?'

I was tempted to argue that the flight time between Edinburgh and the south of England was beside the point, that I shouldn't be expected to abandon my life to travel the length of the country at great personal expense when I felt quite sure she wouldn't be making the same demands on Luke if the tables were turned. I knew, though, that that was pointless. Instead, I needed to make a few vague promises, extricate myself from the conversation and try to get some sleep before my alarm went off at 5.45 a.m.

'I'll get there as soon as I can.'

Mum sniffed. 'OK. Thank you.' Her voice was formal now, which was I suppose an improvement on hysterical. 'I've got to go. Text me, please, as soon as you're at the hospital and know what's going on. Please keep us updated.'

'Yes,' I lied. 'Of course.'

Chapter 13

When the call had ended, I lay in my bed, looking up at the ceiling. I felt sure the situation wasn't as dramatic as Mum was making out, as she no doubt believed herself, but the shock of her calling in the middle of night meant I was wide awake now. It was the first time we'd spoken in weeks. As my irritation ebbed, anxiety began to creep in. What kind of head injury was it exactly? I knew it was likely to turn out to be minor but even so, Luke would be scared when he came round. For all his bravado on that bike of his he could be really quite a baby when he'd hurt himself. I didn't like to think of him alone.

I turned the light on and propped myself up in bed. I took my notepad from my bedside table and put it on my lap. I needed to think this through rationally. I needed to assess my options.

The club where I worked – recently renamed The Watch – was owned by Brendan and me jointly, but I ran it virtually single-handedly. The place had been on the verge of insolvency when I'd met him, trading then as Candy's Lounge, the sticky carpets, cheap decor and cut-price spirits attracting only drunk salesmen working away from home who, from the name and the signage, usually assumed it was a strip bar.

When, just six weeks into our relationship, I offered Brendan a sizeable financial investment – raised through the re-mortgage of my flat – in return for a fifty per cent stake in the business, we both knew he had little choice but to sacrifice half if he was going to avoid the whole place being turned over to the administrators.

However, Brendan being as he is, a master of self-delusion, he chose to romanticise the whole arrangement. The day the papers were signed he insisted on taking me out for a champagne dinner and raising a toast to 'our business, our future, our love'. As bizarre as I found all this, I realised I could use it to my advantage and that by parroting back his declarations of affection and promising that I was committed to our union – both professional and personal – for the long haul, I was able to persuade him to let me take the reins when it came to the day-to-day running of the club, and relaunch the business as The Watch, an upmarket private members club, serving high-end liquor in plush surroundings to the type of people who felt their status required them to patronise establishments that afforded them a degree of exclusivity. It had been no easy task, the complete overhaul of interior design, branding and business model, but I'd felt sure – as I still did – that the business would take off and return my investment tenfold, just as long as I could keep Brendan at bay and stop his terrible taste tainting the endeavour.

And just as long as I could keep the members signing up.

That was the key to the success of the thing – a good lot of members, paying their ninety pounds a month subscription fee. That steady income would provide the backbone of the bank balance, upon which the cash from the actual visiting punters was a nice addition.

At first, sign-ups had flowed well, Brighton apparently housing a good number of affluent young professionals who rather fancied themselves as the kind of people to need an exclusive venue for their after-work drinks and business lunches. Things had started to slow though, and we were still a way from our target membership figure, so when Ewen Tanner, head of employee engagement at Activator, asked me for a meeting, I knew this could be the breakthrough I'd been looking for.

Activator was a fitness brand, selling gym gear and exercise equipment all over the world. The company was one of the biggest employers in the city, their head office, in a fifteen-storey glass-fronted building with a view of the pier, housing nearly four thousand workers. Ewen explained in his email to me that his team had been 'reviewing the employee benefits package' and wanted to speak to me with a view to offering membership of The Watch as a perk of employment, an alternative to the current options of subsidised train travel or gym membership. They were, he told me, hoping to attract some of the London workforce down to the coast by putting together a package that would rival 'that fancy London living', Tanner had said, in a Scottish accent suddenly so thick I wondered if he'd ever been south of Hartlepool before.

I was sure I could come to a deal with him. I'd already devised my negotiating strategy – my dream deal that I knew he wouldn't agree to but that I'd use as a starting point, the one I'd offer to make it look as if I was meeting him halfway, and the absolute bare minimum I would leave with – and I felt sure that by the time we shook hands at the end of the meeting, The Watch's bank balance would be very healthy indeed.

That was, of course, if I actually attended the meeting – the meeting that was due to start in less than seven hours – and if I wasn't forced to cancel it to go and pick up the pieces after my little brother's latest disaster.

If it had been any other situation, any other meeting, I would have postponed it but Ewen Tanner had cut short a conference in Houston especially to fly in early and had been very clear about the time slot he was able to offer me. He was well aware – as was I – of the power dynamic between our two businesses. I could talk a good talk, I could wear a good suit, but Activator was the shark, The Watch the minnow. I knew very well that the minnow should not keep the shark waiting while she ran a family errand, especially not when the minnow wanted the shark to give her a lot of money.

I realised that, when I thought about it rationally, my course of action was clear. Of the two places I could be – at the hospital, sitting next to Luke or at the club, sitting opposite Ewen Tanner – there was only one where my presence would make any real difference. As much as Mum wanted someone there, holding her favourite child's hand while the nurses put plasters on his grazes, texting her regular updates to ease her guilt about being several thousand miles away, I wasn't a doctor. There was nothing I could do for Luke. I was, however, a businesswoman and a negotiator, so there was plenty I could do in that meeting. If it went well it could mean financial security for years to come and get me a step closer to a life free from Brendan. I *had* to go to the meeting. I would head straight to the hospital, to Luke, as soon as it was over.

There was no need to make life harder by letting Mum know about my decision. My mother was a woman who frequently posted photos on Facebook of sunny meadows overlaid with swirling letters reading things like *When your purse is empty of coins but your heart is full of love, you know you are rich indeed*. I couldn't expect her to have any comprehension of the realities of business. Or, in fact, what that business meant for my life. It was all very well for her to say that family comes before money from her four-bedroom country house with two nearly new cars in the drive. She might feel differently if she was two months overdue on her mortgage payments and stood to be made homeless if she didn't get things in order very soon.

Chapter 14

To buy myself some breathing space, the next morning I sent Mum a vague, breezy text as I waited for Ewen to arrive into the upstairs meeting room of the club, that I'd set up with fresh coffee and pastries.

At the hospital. No news yet but will keep you updated.

She'd texted back at once, of course, demanding details – had I seen him? What did the doctor say? How did he look? – but at that point the buzzer to the club had let me know that Ewen was outside, so I'd turned my phone off.

The meeting had gone well. So well, in fact, that after a tour of the club, it had turned into a lively lunch with Ewen's two colleagues, and a game of poker, my winning of which seemed to impress him more than anything I'd said in the business discussion that morning.

Ewen had been a tough nut to crack, but I thought I'd managed it. Although he'd have to go away to 'check a few figures' I felt confident that there would be a deal. The over-running timings meant that when Dad had texted to let me know they were pulling into the hospital car park I wasn't in fact sitting at Luke's bedside as I'd led them to believe, but rather just leaving the club and trying to hail a cab to drive me up the hill to the hospital.

It was after a short exchange with the harried receptionist that I realised things were more serious than I'd assumed: Luke was in the Intensive Care ward, reserved for the most critically ill patients. It seemed like, for once, Mum's panic might have been justified.

I knew straight away then that I should have got there sooner, but it was too late for that now. I dreaded facing my parents; they would be furious once they discovered how long it had taken me to come. I was reprieved though, when confusing hospital signage sent them on a wild goose chase to the oncology department via x-ray and, by the time they worked out where they needed to be, I was able to announce that I'd headed to the café to take a break from my vigil at Luke's bedside. Any guilt I felt about this lie was assuaged by the knowledge that it was better for Mum if she thought someone had been with Luke the whole time.

When they arrived, I felt a pang of pity at the realisation they'd come directly from the airport – directly from a relaxing picnic at the Acropolis probably. Mum was still wearing the linen tunic I knew she'd bought for the trip (I knew this from Facebook – long gone were the days when she would have shared this kind of detail with me). But just under the surface of my sympathy were the more familiar feelings of vague distaste. Could they not have found somewhere to swap into a fresh change of clothes?

As I slipped into position at a table in the run-down third floor hospital café, I caught a glimpse of myself in the reflection in the window and wondered if my parents would wonder why I'd dressed so smartly for a hospital visit. But then I realised, of course they wouldn't. They had never seen my flat; they barely knew what I did for a living. They wouldn't be able to say what was or wasn't typical attire for me, and little would they care anyway, when their favoured offspring's health was in question.

As I was waiting for them, my phone buzzed with an email from Ewen, asking me to confirm the bands of subsidisation I could offer him in exchange for the various numbers of memberships he was promising to buy. I began to reply at once, wanting to keep the momentum going on the deal and get the figures over to him while they were still fresh in my head. I was just writing the closing paragraphs as Mum and Dad came in, and I heard Mum's haughty sniff that I had the audacity to continue my business correspondence in her presence. No doubt she'd have preferred me to have thrown my phone to the floor and fallen wailing into her arms.

It was only after the email was sent, Mum's disapproval and Dad's unease both noted, that I properly looked at the girl they'd walked in with. She was a little blonde thing, in a bubble-gum pink sweatshirt and those awful slouchy fur boots that are really barely passable as slippers, much less something to be appropriately worn in public.

When my expression queried her presence on the scene and Dad announced she was Luke's girlfriend, I almost laughed.

'Oh,' I said in the end. 'OK.'

The girl – Charlotte Wright, it transpired her name was – made her first faux pas with her overfamiliar introduction. 'Becky,' she'd gushed, her syrupy smile fixed, as if she'd known me all her life. I'd kicked that idea away at once. I'm Becky only to people who have known me over thirty years and, frankly, I'd rather even they dropped the habit.

It became apparent that Mum and Dad had only just met this Charlotte themselves, but whether they'd known of her existence before today wasn't clear. Whoever she was, she talked a lot.

Dad went off on tangent, a story about some former colleague, which as far as I could see had no bearing whatsoever on matters as they currently stood. Charlotte was clearly delighted at this opportunity to prattle, and chipped in with her own, equally irrelevant and rambling anecdote. Shut up, both of you, I wanted to say, but didn't. Mum, no doubt, was loving it.

Dad mentioned the meeting with the consultant at nine and I quickly pretended I was already aware of this, and had received my personal invite earlier in the day. I relaxed a little then. It looked like this would be the first formal debrief so I hadn't really missed anything by not turning up earlier.

I got a brief reply to my figures from Ewen, who said he'd get back to me 'in the week' and I heard my sigh of frustration out loud. Why must everyone deliberate for days over every little thing? When you know what you want, do something about it. That's the way I've always done things.

My irritation was further compounded when I noticed the bubble-gum princess seemed to think she could tag along to meet Luke's consultant with us. I couldn't be bothered to be polite about it – didn't she see how inappropriate this was? She couldn't have known Luke more than two and a half minutes. As I suppose I should have foreseen, my bluntness horrified Mum and embarrassed Dad and in the end I couldn't be bothered to argue about it. No doubt Luke would tire of the bimbo quickly, as he usually did, and her solicitous wifey routine would be rewarded with an unceremonious dumping via text one evening soon. Even as we made our way to Intensive Care I couldn't imagine a scenario where Luke wouldn't be his irritatingly bouncy self, sitting up in the hospital bed wondering what all the fuss was about. Everything would be back to normal within the week and I could get back to my life.

As we pushed open the double doors to the ICU, I followed Mum down the ward. I could see her counting the curtain cubicles to find Luke's. Suddenly she stopped abruptly in front of an empty cubicle, the curtains drawn back.

She looked at Dad. 'It was this one, wasn't it?'

He rubbed the back of his head. 'Yes . . . I was sure. So where is he?'

Chapter 15

Charlotte stepped into the cubicle and picked up a jacket from a small pile of clothes in the corner. 'His jacket's here?'

'Is that definitely his?' I asked. I'd certainly never seen the jacket before, and moreover I couldn't see Luke choosing one like it at all.

'He was wearing it when . . .' She paused. 'He had it on last night. It's definitely his.'

I didn't know why she was being so combative about it, but I couldn't very well stand there and argue that black was white if she was hell-bent on saying it was blue. Or whatever the expression was.

A nurse walked passed and Mum stopped her. 'Excuse me . . . my son, Luke Burley? He was here. Where *is* he? Do you know where he is?' I could hear the rising panic in her voice, and it prompted the first real tightening of anxiety in my chest. This was a familiar scene in films, wasn't it? Relatives arriving to find the patient missing, the empty room telling them everything they needed to know?

The nurse looked perplexed for a moment, then she shook

her head slightly as if remembering. 'Ah. Yes, that's right. We tried to find you but—'

'We were just downstairs!' Mum wailed. 'Just for a moment! They said come back at nine!'

'Why don't you come through here?' the nurse said, pointing us in the direction of a wooden door labelled *Relatives' Room*.

The world began to take on a slightly surreal feel at that point. It was no doubt a combination of tiredness and stark hospital lighting but I could hear my pulse in my ears and I felt like everyone was looking at us as we were led away. Led to the room where, I was sure, we'd be told that they were dreadfully sorry, and that they'd done everything they could, but I no longer had a brother.

'The consultant will come and speak to you as soon as she can,' the nurse said, sitting down heavily and making the foam chair squeak, 'but the monitors showed a dramatic increase in the pressure in Luke's skull. The bleeding, we think, had caused it.'

'So,' Dad said quietly. 'What does that . . . ?'

'The only way to release the pressure,' the nurse said carefully, 'is to do something called a craniotomy, where the surgeon will remove a tiny flap of bone to give the brain room to expand. Normally we let relatives know before we carry out this operation, but time was of the essence so—'

'But where *is* he?' Mum asked again, looking around at all of us, like we all knew the answer but were keeping it from her as a trick.

'Surgery's in progress at the moment,' said the nurse. 'If you stay nearby, he'll be back on the ward as soon as they've finished and the consultant will be able to let you know more then.'

'So he's not – ' Mum laughed suddenly, not with mirth but a kind of hysteria ' – he's not dead?'

'Oh no, goodness no,' the nurse said. 'They will bring him back to the unit as soon as possible.'

The news that he was still alive prompted a simultaneous sigh from the four of us. I saw Charlotte close her eyes briefly and breathe out slowly.

Around an hour later, a woman who introduced herself as Anne Moriarty, consultant neurosurgeon, asked us to join her once again in the relatives' room.

She cleaned her glasses with a tissue she took from the pocket of her scrubs. 'As we spoke about earlier, Luke's head injury is a real cause for concern. The bleed on his brain was causing a build-up of pressure that would have killed him – and killed him quickly – unless we released it.'

'So did the operation go well?' Dad asked.

Anne Moriarty put her head on one side. 'Yes, in that it released the pressure and tackled the immediate threat to life. That said, the CT scan does show damage. It's impossible to know how this damage will affect Luke's cognitive abilities while he's still unconscious. We have, up until this point, kept him sedated to ensure he didn't fight his breathing tube, but we will reduce this sedation and . . . take things from there.'

We all just looked at Anne Moriarty, waiting for her to go on. I understood what she'd said, but at the same time, I felt she hadn't said anything at all. What was happening? What was going to happen? This was what we wanted to know.

'So . . .' Mum blinked. She seemed shell-shocked. I could tell her questions were the same as mine, but she didn't know how or where to begin asking them.

I realised I needed to take charge.

'Sorry,' I said, 'I'm not quite clear. What exactly is the situation here? What's the prognosis?'

I knew my tone was forthright, perhaps too forthright given

that the woman was only trying to help us, but I wanted some unambiguous facts.

Anne Moriarty shook her head. 'We just don't know. As I say, it's impossible to tell from the scans how cognition will be affected. We really can only wait and see.'

'When you say "cognition",' Dad said slowly, 'do you mean his memory? Will he remember who we are? Or do you just mean, he might be a bit forgetful?'

'Cognition is more than just memory,' Charlotte piped up. 'It's thinking, learning . . . everything.'

I rather hoped Anne Moriarty might point out that she didn't really need the help of a bimbo in slippers to explain basic terminology when she herself was a qualified brain surgeon, but she just nodded and said, 'Yes, exactly.'

Mum looked at Dad. 'It will take a long time. Is that what you're saying?'

'It could be,' Anne Moriarty said. 'That's one scenario. But you also need to prepare yourself for the fact that "recovery" might not mean what you think it means – what you hope it means. Brain cells aren't like other cells in the body in that they don't regenerate. However, the brain is good at finding workarounds and often other areas learn to take on the activities of the damaged regions. So Luke may recover *some* functions, but maybe not others.' She was quiet for a moment, then her tone was brighter again. 'But, let's see how the next twenty-four hours pan out. We can meet again tomorrow and see how things have developed. I'm sorry that I can't tell you exactly what you want to hear but my job isn't to give you false hope.'

'Can we see him now?' Mum asked quietly.

'Of course. He's back on the ward.'

As Dad followed Mum back onto the ward, I noticed him hold out his arm to let Charlotte go ahead of him. I suppose the gesture wasn't intended as anything more significant than good manners, chivalry, but I wanted to tell him not to allow himself to be demoted like that. He was Luke's father. He should be going to him ahead of some flash-in-the-pan floozy.

When we reached Luke's bed, I had to swallow hard to prevent the gasp escaping from my mouth. As far as Mum and Dad were concerned, I'd already seen Luke in this state so I needed to control myself, but this was worse than anything I'd been imagining. The whole scene was almost too perverse to comprehend. Not just the machines, which seemed impossibly complex, engulfing the small figure in the bed, but Luke himself. Anne Moriarty had warned us there'd been swelling from the operation, but his face seemed twisted and grotesque. His hair had been partially shaved away and the tube pushed into his mouth, forcing his expression into one that didn't look like him at all. I didn't truly believe it was.

Mum began to cry. Not quiet weeping, but great gasping sobs. Dad put his hand on her arm, but he seemed absent, like he was acting on autopilot, like he wasn't fully in the room. It was Charlotte who stepped forward, who went to Mum and pulled her into a hug, who rubbed her back and said, 'It's going to be OK,' over and over again, when of course she had no grounds on which to base such a statement.

For the first time, I didn't resent the girl's presence. I wouldn't have known how to initiate such a gesture, even if I'd felt Mum would have wanted it, so I was glad, briefly, that she was there to soak up some of excess emotion of the scene.

'She has to talk about the worst-case scenario,' Charlotte said, pushing Mum away from her and holding her by the top of her arms as she looked into her face. 'She has to cover all eventualities.'

Mum nodded. Charlotte produced a tissue from somewhere – I suppose her type keep these things about their person –

and Mum wiped her nose on it. She seemed to recover herself a little. 'It was just a shock. He looks so . . .' She lifted her hand and pointed weakly at Luke's bed.

'I only spoke to him yesterday morning,' Dad said. 'He rang to tell me about a race . . . a bike race he's qualified for next month.' He turned to me. 'When did you last speak to him?'

'A few days ago, maybe,' I said. 'Not long.'

I wasn't sure why Dad wanted to know that, like it was in any way relevant to how he'd ended up here. And I didn't really want to revisit the last time I saw Luke.

I could remember the afternoon quite clearly. I very much hoped that it wasn't going to be the last one we spent together.

Chapter 16

The last time I'd seen Luke in person had been some weeks ago – 25 February. That had been a Sunday too, and he'd invited me over to his new flat.

Until that point, Luke had been living with his oldest school friend, Anthony Sullivan, with whom he'd (finally, at the age of twenty-eight) moved out of our parents' house and struck out on his own, 250 miles away. His big move was celebrated with much fanfare by our mother, despite the fact we all knew he'd chosen Brighton because that was where I lived, so I would be on hand to bail him out of the sort of scrapes he'd found himself in on a weekly basis – rejected bank cards, missed night buses – since he was a teenager.

He didn't deny that I was the reason for his choosing Brighton but, as usual, he managed to wear down my reservations about this with his charm. 'I thought it would be fun to hang out more, Becs. You can come over, I'll make you nachos and margaritas. We can go to the cinema and you can introduce me to your friends.' I highly doubted any of this would happen, but he was my brother, and the idea of spending time with him without my parents around was actually quite appealing.

At first, Luke's new adult life hadn't seemed very adult at all. The flat he and Anthony shared had mildew-covered walls, stacks of empty pizza boxes in the hallway and very little furniture, aside from the enormous television set atop a tangle of gaming console wires, a battered second-hand sofa positioned a few feet in front of it. Both boys – men? – had worked in bars at first, so they would get home late, drink and play computer games until the early hours, then sleep most of the day.

I'd been disappointed in a way. I suppose I had really believed that he and I might cultivate a more adult relationship once he had a place of his own. But it looked like instead, I was destined to be forever the dreary big sister, watching the spontaneous little brother's adventures from the sidelines. This was the only part I could play in the drawn-out student existence he had chosen.

But then came the new job – something in an office, one of the trendy digital businesses Brighton was awash with – and now the flat. A marked improvement on his last, I saw at once. As he showed me round I noted polished wooden floors, scatter cushions, cleaning materials in the bathroom. As he proudly opened his hallway storage cupboard for my perusal, I noticed he'd even bought an ironing board.

'It's very smart, Luke,' I'd said. 'Very grown up. I should think you'll be quite the envy of your friends, with this new job of yours too.' I was pleased. I thought, finally now he might start to grow up, he might start to see the world more as I did. That our lifestyles might align a little more.

He'd laughed, and given me a soft punch on the shoulder, which was often his response to things I said. He seemed to find me perennially amusing, which was a bit rich given some of the inadvisable decisions he'd made over the course of his life. But still, it was never unkind.

He'd shrugged shyly and run his hand along the picture

rail as if checking for dust. 'Just a little bachelor pad, I guess.'

I wondered, thinking back to it, if this was a clue that Charlotte hadn't been on the scene then. He'd certainly not mentioned her that day. Her, or any other girl.

We'd had a pleasant afternoon. Luke had made us soup from scratch using the new hand blender he'd acquired during a recent trip to Lakeland. Then he'd made tea – in a teapot, for heaven's sake! – and carried out with a wry smile, and we'd sat on his new sofa to watch a silly but diverting Sunday afternoon film about an enormous talking dog.

We would no doubt have parted on good terms and deemed the whole afternoon a success, had it not been for the film's final scene. The villain of the piece, an unscrupulous overweight dog catcher, had been safely incarcerated in an island prison, forced to work in the community's dog-grooming salon until the end of his days, whilst his wife was left living alone, shunned by the people of the small town her husband had terrorised.

I knew what was coming as soon as Luke had turned to me. 'Makes me think of Daniel Rubinstein,' he said, trying to keep his voice light, as if this was a casual observation.

We had once considered Daniel Rubinstein and his wife Sarah, a journalist, prime candidates for membership of The Watch, even sending them personalised marketing materials promising them a special rate. However, although Sarah had visited once, our discounted offer would forever go unclaimed, as she had died suddenly, just before Christmas the previous year.

I didn't say anything, didn't turn to look at him. I just kept my eyes fixed on the screen, as if he hadn't spoken at all.

'Because,' he went on, 'I mean, it is like that, isn't it? Like he's ultimately the one paying for what happened to his wife. I know Sarah's paying too – paid, I guess – but she's gone now. He's the one left to suffer.'

'Quite possibly,' I said vaguely, still staring at the screen, still silently willing him to stop talking. He didn't though, and really, I knew what was coming next.

'I think we should speak to him. Daniel. You and me should go to see him. Tell him exactly what happened. I think it would make him feel better to know the full story. That he was right, when he said Sarah wouldn't do something like that. And more than that, it's just right that he should know. He deserves to.'

'No,' I said simply.

'It was a baby, Becs,' he said quietly.

'I know! I *know*.'

Because I did know. And that's what I was finding most frustrating about these cyclical conversations we had been holding on the subject since that night. Each time, Luke would seem to be at pains to hammer home the sadness of the situation, to remind me of the consequences of what we've done, as if he thought I had somehow forgotten the details or that I just didn't care. But I *did* care. I cared very much. I dreamt about Sarah Rubinstein several nights a week. When I saw babies in prams I would find myself trying to calculate their age in relation to hers. She, Daniel, the whole course of events, was never truly off my mind. I just knew there was nothing we could do about it. I had only very briefly seriously considered Luke's suggestion of explaining the whole story to Daniel before coming to the conclusion that there was nothing whatsoever to be gained from doing so. The idea that a confession would ease our guilt was nonsensical. Why would it? Nothing would change. Sarah wouldn't be back. The past wouldn't be rewritten. There was no way to make any of it better. All Luke's idea would do would be to make everything much, much worse.

Luke opened his mouth to speak again, but this time I turned to look at him. I fixed him with the same unblinking, stony expression I'd used when he was eight and I was sixteen and he was threatening to slide his skateboard down the metal handrail of the stone steps in the sports centre car park. 'Absolutely not.'

He frowned and sighed. 'Well, I think you're being selfish,' he said quietly.

That's what really got to me, when I felt the frustration boil over. This blue-eyed man-child, who'd been mollycoddled and babied and rescued from every bad decision he'd ever made, who only now at the age of thirty was beginning his first real job, who spent his weekends bouncing around the woods on little bicycles, who still had the credit card in his wallet paid off each month by our father because he couldn't be expected to live within his means like every other adult in the world. He was telling *me* I was selfish.

'You have no idea,' I said, gripping onto the edge of the sofa with both hands, 'what it means to face consequences, do you? I don't think you can really imagine it. You think you can afford to say what you want, do what you want. You always have. Someone will always make sure everything goes smoothly for you. But this isn't like accidentally knocking the wing mirror off a neighbour's car. You can't get Mum or Dad to plead your case. You don't get to apologise and flash your best smile, and have everyone agree to say no more about it. We're talking about the police. And judges and *prison* guards, Luke.'

I had been on the verge of getting out my phone, bringing up the pages of research I'd been compiling. The statutes, the case law, the newspaper articles of what had happened to people who had done what we'd done, or close to it. I'd so far held off on sharing any of it with Luke, aware that doing so could backfire, and that emphasising our culpability might fuel his desire for absolution further. Now though, I realised it might be what was needed to give him a shot of reality.

But I didn't get the chance. There comes a point with Luke when he visibly shuts down, and this occurred somewhere towards the end of my short diatribe. At first, he had gaped at me, opening his mouth to argue back, but then, quite abruptly his mouth closed, his eyes became fixed and icy. When he spoke, his tone was bitter and clipped.

'It's probably about time you were going. I've got things to do.'

I knew from experience that the only way to deal with this shift in demeanour was to fight ice with ice. 'Yes. So have I.'

I'd emailed him the following day, once again setting out my reasoning – this time I hinted at, although didn't detail, the evidence that backed up my fears – and once again Luke's resolve proved impenetrable. I knew that any further conversation on the topic at that time would be likely to serve only to entrench his position, so hadn't tried to contact him again for a few days.

It was he who contacted me in the end, and there had been one further conversation after that, the last time we'd spoken before his admission to hospital. It was around ten days after our argument in his flat, when he'd called my mobile.

I'd been happy to see his name on the screen, hopeful that he was going to apologise for the way my visit had ended and admit that his talk of visiting Daniel Rubinstein had been at best fanciful, at worst dangerous. I thought back to that day in his flat, the easiness between us before we had argued. I didn't have that with a lot of people. With anyone else, actually. I just wanted things to go back to normal.

But there was no apology. In fact, he acted as though the disagreement hadn't occurred at all. This was no doubt a deliberate move on his part – least said, soonest mended was just the type of maxim a boy like Luke relied on. I knew there was something to be said for letting bygones be bygones so I'd responded in kind, but his failure to mention his Daniel Rubinstein plan – that is, his failure to explicitly tell me he'd revised the idea – made me nervous. I would never call myself an accomplished conversationalist, but the exchange was even more stilted than normal. We exchanged a few polite questions about work and he passed on some family news – a sporting success of a younger cousin – then we ended the call.

The fact his text had come through just five or six minutes after our conversation made me think its sentiment was probably the one he'd intended to deliver over the phone, but had backed out of at the last minute. It was a short message, just eight words long, but it was enough for me to know that everything I had acquired in my unremarkable life was at risk.

I just want to live honestly.

Charlotte

Chapter 17

The meeting with the consultant – Anne Moriarty – was intense. Surreal, almost. I felt like I was taking part in some kind of immersive theatre experience. It's not something I'd ever encountered before, being thrust into the middle of another family's lives like that, sitting there with them, shoulder to shoulder, while they received the kind of news that could quite possibly change their lives – ruin their lives – for ever.

It wasn't surprising, I guess, that the emotion had sucked me in. If I'd been watching the scene on the TV, if it had been part of one of the Sunday afternoon weepy movies I used to watch with Emily when we were hung over, I no doubt would've shed a tear or two, so of course I wasn't going to be able to sit there dry-eyed with it happening all around me, with Jenny and Stephen, and even that cold fish Rebecca, pale and wide-eyed on their plastic hospital chairs. I suppose it was only natural to cry.

I wasn't acting. I wasn't feigning distress because I knew that's what was expected. Nothing like that. They were the sort of family, I think, to inspire instant fondness. Not so much for Luke, whom I really had no way of knowing anything about, but for his parents. For Jenny, still in her crinkled summer dress, that she'd obviously bought when she had nothing more serious on her mind than what type of jacket she'd need in the evening in Athens in the springtime. The way she reapplied her lipstick every time she went to the toilet like it was an armour against everything that was happening. And Stephen too, clearly so desperate to do and say the right thing, to be the man of the family, to be a rock for his wife, but who just seemed bewildered and exhausted.

It was funny, I realised, how I had this strong sense that Jenny and Stephen were exactly as parents should be. Everything about them, from their clothes to their gentle Yorkshire accents seemed so right for the role, so comforting. It was exactly the sense I'd had about my Aunt Frieda, who'd been much more of a parent to me than my own mother.

I realised then that, in many ways, Jenny reminded me of her.

Chapter 18

It was in that meeting with the consultant that I realised that perhaps I wasn't just an imposter, and one who should make herself scarce as soon as practicable, but that there was a real role for me to play there – and one that, looking around at the family, it seemed they very much needed. I don't know that I believe in fate but I couldn't help feel that, perhaps, I'd been the one to find Luke, to be at his bedside when his parents arrived, for a reason.

Anne Moriarty was tall with a long nose and a square jaw. Her voice was calm and unhurried, and she spoke precisely, prioritising the delivery of facts over the provision of reassurance or comfort. I could understand that, I suppose. She was a scientist, a professional. Her area of expertise was the anatomy of the brain and it made sense that that's where she'd focus her attention. However, it seemed obvious to me that families like the Burleys really needed some kind of advocate with them during conversations like these – throughout the whole process really. Someone who was detached enough to be able to absorb and remember the information without becoming overwhelmed with emotion, someone to translate it, to repeat it back when they needed to be reminded. Nurses I knew had a reputation for providing the more human element of healthcare, but the fact was they were too busy to get to know families personally, to be there all the time.

I realised that the way the events of the last twenty-four hours had unfolded made me uniquely placed to be perfect for the job. I'd been with Luke right from the beginning, from the moment he was collected by the ambulance, so I was fully abreast of the situation and the care he'd received so far, but I was separate enough to retain a cool head. Obviously, Stephen and Jenny had no idea just how separate I was, but it meant that I was able to think more clearly than they could, that I could step in to provide what they needed – explanation, reassurance, a steadying hand.

There was no question then, when we came out of the meeting, and Luke was wheeled back onto the ward – now swollen and damaged and looking far more poorly than he had before – of what I had to do. What my responsibilities were. One look at Jenny's crumpled face told me there was no way I could leave them then. I was already in too deep.

The sister – Rebecca – seemed to radiate coldness. If I was going to be generous about it I suppose I could interpret this as shock, but that's not how it felt to me. I sensed tension between her and Jenny. It seemed strange to me that a cuddly Northern crumpet of a woman could have produced an ice queen like Rebecca. Maybe Jenny felt the same.

When Luke was back from his operation and Jenny began to cry, Rebecca actually took a step backwards, as if she found the scene distasteful in some way and wanted to distance herself from it. It fell to me then, to be the one to go to Jenny.

I gave her a little pep talk – I've always found that sort of thing comes quite naturally – and she was able to pull herself together, and I realised that it felt good to be useful again. To feel needed, and to feel I knew what to do. I knew it wasn't much to rave about as a skill, but this was my arena: caring for people, saying the right thing. Just trying to take the sharp edges off the reality of the situation. And it had been a difficult few months, with the move and the new job. I'd felt out of my depth for a while there, and that had given my self-esteem a knock. It was nice, I suppose, to feel I wasn't a social failure after all.

Chapter 19

As the family reminisced about when they last spoke to Luke, when they last saw him, Rebecca seemed anxious to make it clear that she was in regular contact with him. I wasn't sure whether this was for my benefit or her parents', but she seemed to want us to know that they were close. Strange though, as her doing so only made me feel the opposite was true. Insecurity, that's what it was. It was, perhaps, a dig at me – as in, 'we spoke all the time and never once did he mention you' – but I didn't rise to it. With Luke unconscious, she was just going to have to accept that, whether she liked it or not, Luke had chosen not to tell her about me and that his decision said much more about her relationship with him than mine. I knew that would annoy her though. I could tell she was a woman who didn't like to be relegated.

'It makes me so angry!' Jenny said suddenly, making everyone jump. 'Thinking of the bastard who did this. I bet wherever he is, he's just strolling around laughing with his mates and what have you. What kind of person can do that? How can anyone be so desperate for money, for drugs, for whatever it is they wanted, to do this to another human?'

Stephen squeezed his wife's hand. 'Like the police said, love, they were probably off their faces. They probably didn't even know what they were doing.'

Rebecca's head twitched. She turned from the monitor she'd been inspecting to look at her father 'The police?'

Stephen nodded. 'We spoke to the woman – DS whatnot – on the phone on the way down. She said there'd be an investigation, no stone unturned and all that, but she said that seeing as his phone was missing the most likely culprit was one of those druggies, looking for cash or something they can sell for their next fix.'

Rebecca nodded and looked back at the monitor. 'So nothing . . . nothing personal then.'

Jenny gave her a funny look. 'Of course nothing personal, but that doesn't make it any better, does it?'

Rebecca closed her eyes and opened them again slowly. She looked tired. 'Perhaps not.'

Rebecca looked lost in thought for a moment. She was standing awkwardly, shifting her bag from one shoulder to the other. 'I suppose it won't be easy though,' she said after a while, 'when they've got nothing to go on. Unless someone saw what happened, or saw someone running away, they won't know. Unless – until – Luke – '

'They have all sorts of technology these days, to track people down,' Jenny snapped. 'They'll get him.'

Rebecca nodded slowly but she didn't say anything else.

We stayed like that for another twenty minutes or so, saying very little, Jenny stroking Luke's hand, Stephen rubbing Jenny's back. Rebecca looking at the clock on the wall at the end of the ward.

'We should probably head home, love,' Stephen said gently. 'There's nothing else we can do, just for the moment. We should get some rest.'

99

'Will you go back to Yorkshire?' I said, wondering for a moment if I should offer them the floor of my flat before realising it would be far more appropriate for them to stay with their daughter.

'Oh, no. No, no,' Stephen said, shaking his head. 'My aunt, Arlette, has a house down here, on the seafront. She travels about, for half the year, so it's just sitting empty. She's said we're welcome to use it as a base until . . . until we know what's what.'

'What's your number, Charlotte, love?' Jenny said, taking out her own phone to capture it. 'We'll need to stay in touch. Twenty-four seven. I think that's a good idea, don't you? So we all know exactly what's what.'

'Yes,' I agreed, reeling off my digits. 'Definitely a good idea.'

Chapter 20

As I made my way home, I felt strangely energised by the whole situation. Although I felt desperately sorry for Jenny and Stephen, it seemed to me a positive thing that the series of coincidences and misunderstandings that had occurred meant I could be there for them. And it was good to feel positive about something because a few pieces of bad luck, at work, and with my flat, had got me starting to think Brighton wasn't the shining beacon of joy and carefree living that I'd built it up to be when I'd been living in Devon.

I'd only been living in Holten and working in the medical centre for a few months when I realised I'd be better off living in a city. I'd liked Holten well enough at first. The gentleness of the pace and the simplicity of my routine there was a relief after several years of bouncing around from one town to the next, doing casual jobs with irregular schedules – bar work, cleaning, running errands for a retired concert violinist. Whatever paid. My teenage years had been a bit chaotic, one way and another, so my education hadn't taken the priority it should have done and I knew there was a limit to how picky I could be when it came to work.

It had been nice, at first, to go to the same office every morning and return to the same home every night, but after a while I'd started to get bored. It wasn't that I thought myself better than the town, than the people. It wasn't that at all. Everyone there seemed happy and serene, and why wouldn't they be? It was a pretty little place on the edge of Dartmoor, with a few nice pubs, lots of shops. Everything you could need for a certain type of life. It just wasn't the type of life I wanted. Not yet, anyway. I felt out of place. As if I'd washed up there by mistake – which I had, in a way – and everyone else was as bewildered as me about what I was doing there.

I struggled to find friendship. I suppose because the only people I really had any contact with were my colleagues and it was hard to find a way to extend our relationship beyond the professional. Occasionally, as they headed out the door at five-thirty on a Friday afternoon for their usual half a cider in the Rose Bush, one of them would turn to me as I collected my coat from the back of my chair and issue a half-hearted invitation, an afterthought – 'You fancy one, Charlotte?'

I went along the first few times, but I could tell they didn't really want me there, that they'd only asked to be polite and hadn't expected me to take up the offer. They wanted to talk about whose kids had got places in which secondary schools, how the re-rendering of the brickwork at the back of the house was going, whether they were going to fix the mortgage for five years or take the gamble and go with the two-year option. Conversations that I had nothing whatsoever to contribute to. My life just didn't contain any of the things that mattered to them most. It wasn't long before they stopped asking me, or just pretended they weren't going out at all. They'd make a big show of talking about their busy evening plans – ferrying kids to karate lessons, stripping wallpaper in the dining room – and call loud, cheery goodbyes to each other across the office. They didn't know that my walk home took me directly past the window of the Rose Bush, and that I'd see them all there, quite clearly, laughing and talking around their usual table without me.

I felt the difference between that and my new life in Brighton almost instantly. My job, in essence, was to write articles about vegetables and paste them onto the company's website. There were three of us responsible for keeping the content up-to-date and relevant by researching and writing about anything we could think of that somehow related to organic farming, healthy eating, cooking . . . anything at all that could drive traffic to the Good Stuff Ltd site and, with any luck, persuade people to sign up for a weekly veg box.

Every Monday morning we'd have a meeting where we shared ideas, discussed who was going to take which article – who was going to go down to that new Asian grocers and interview the owner, who was going to write up the ten tastiest things you can do with a sweet potato. It was hilarious in a way, the three of us sitting around the table in that glass-walled meeting room, discussing our leads with serious faces as if we were at the cutting edge of hard-hitting journalism. As if we were about to blow the whistle on an international human-trafficking cover-up rather than reveal the secret ingredient for the perfect mushroom risotto. But I loved it really. It was exactly what I'd imagined. It was exactly where I'd wanted to be.

Marcus was right, about the people being fun. There was none of the whispered conversation and cliqueyness of the medical centre. On a Friday afternoon, usually a good twenty minutes before the official five-thirty knock-off time, someone would stand up and say, 'Pint?' to the office in general. There'd be murmurs of agreement, the fast clicking of computers being shut down, the odd call of 'I'll see you down there. Just got to get this email out.'

I suppose the truth was I'd got a little too carried away with the friendship side of things – mixed business and pleasure so much that pleasure had started to eclipse business without me really stopping to notice. That was why things had got a little awkward when I'd made my first mistake, three months into my new role.

Still, three months error-free wasn't a bad innings, and my mistake was silly really – Emily was the only one who was still dwelling on it weeks later. It had been sobering to have had to sit in a windowless meeting room being told off by someone you were more used to sitting in the pub with but I could see why it had to be that way. I had to reset the tone of things, establish some boundaries. Work was work, and I needed to remember to be professional while I was there.

Emily still hadn't replied to the voicemail I'd left her earlier, but I'd decided not to contact her again. Not for a while anyway. I'd left a message; the ball was in her court. I knew now I should just wait. It was hard though, to do nothing. It was in my nature to want to do *something* when I felt a problem was unresolved. I don't much like having to sit around and wait for things to happen to me. It was handy, in a way, the Luke situation as it was, because it gave me something else to focus on. Otherwise I might have been more tempted to go round to Emily's flat, to get the whole stupid thing put to bed for good.

Chapter 21

When I returned to my flat, I found a Facebook friend request from Jenny waiting for me, which I accepted at once, and spent an interesting hour and a half scrolling through her page, gleaning all sorts of information that would prove useful in my new role.

She was a prolific poster. As recently as twenty-four hours earlier there had been at least twice-daily updates on everything she was doing – photos of every stage of the holiday, of course, from the packed suitcases at the front door captioned 'And we're off!' to a smiling Stephen giving a thumbs-up in front of some crumbling European monument. Going back further I'd seen that Jenny had been on a spa weekend with her book club, that she volunteered in an NSPCC charity shop on her local high street every Tuesday afternoon and that she'd recently donated ten pounds towards the renovation of a local cat and dog shelter. I was on special lookout for mention of Luke, particularly any nuggets of information that I should already know. I saw a post from a few months earlier where she was congratulating him on his new job – the one in the team-building company I already knew about – and some photos of the three of them – Stephen, Luke and herself – having a roast lunch in a local pub. Rebecca was conspicuously absent from the page.

Later that evening, as I was getting ready for bed, I received a slightly rushed phone call from a DS Leech who told me she was investigating what had happened to Luke and that she'd been trying to get hold of me. I'd been surprised for a moment but then she explained that Luke's parents had passed on my number and I relaxed. That made sense. She said she needed to 'pin down a few specifics' around how and when I'd found Luke and if I'd seen anything that could help them 'identify the perpetrator'.

I'd found myself sounding quite proud as I recounted the way I'd leapt into action, my diligent CPR keeping Luke's blood flowing until the paramedics were able to restart his heart, but it quickly became clear DS Leech didn't particularly want to hear about all that. That had all gone on after the part she was interested in. She'd sounded weary when she realised how little I knew about what had happened to get him into that state in the first place. Disappointed, but not surprised. I got the feeling she spent a lot of time trying to get to the bottom of situations where she had no idea where even to start.

She asked me to come in to make a formal statement as soon as I could, but I knew that as that statement wouldn't stretch much beyond, 'I found him lying on the floor and have no idea how or when he got like that' it would be of limited value to her investigation.

Chapter 22

The next day, Monday, we had agreed to reconvene in the hospital café before going up to Intensive Care together. The atmosphere when I arrived felt brighter than it had the previous day. Jenny and Stephen looked tired, but Jenny in particular seemed hopeful, as if she'd spent the night loading herself up with optimism, and we headed up to Luke's bed with a spring in our step. When we arrived, though, he looked much the same as he had when we'd left him, and when the consultant, during a slightly harried meeting on her way through the ward, confirmed that nothing of significance had changed overnight and that they were no clearer about if and when it would, there was a discernible shift in the atmosphere. After a few moments' silence, Stephen put the deflation into words. 'It's hard to know what we should be doing.'

Rebecca seemed to take this as permission to retreat, and straight away said something about needing to go into work to meet a supplier.

Jenny pursed her lips and nodded. 'Yes. You get off.' It was obvious that Rebecca's prioritisation of work over her brother's health shunted her even further down in Jenny's estimations than she already was, but I don't think Rebecca cared.

She fastened a button on her jacket and left the cubicle, with a vague request to be kept up to date with any developments.

Then there were the three of us.

'Do you need to get off too?' Jenny asked, turning to me. 'For work?'

I shook my head. 'No, don't worry. I'm not going anywhere for a bit. My schedule is pretty flexible.'

Jenny nodded and gave me a tight smile. She seemed sad, but perhaps grateful too.

It really was very hard to know what to do for the best. It wasn't so much Luke that I was concerned about, as I knew the reality was that it made very little difference to him what the rest of us were doing. He just needed to lie there, in the warm, while his brain cells did their jobs and repaired the damage. The people who really needed me were Jenny and Stephen.

I knew from my own experience that having nothing to do, knowing you're utterly helpless and without a task, can be one of the most crushing realisations there is. I knew that giving Jenny a sense of purpose, a job to do – no matter how trivial – could be the difference between keeping her going, bravely ploughing on, or sinking into a pit of despair.

I began to try to formulate some ideas for an activity I could suggest. I often found cooking, cleaning and gardening worked well – lots to keep the hands busy, a real sense of progress being made – but that didn't seem appropriate here. The problem was, when Luke was unconscious and unable to notice anything, it was hard to think of anything that it would make sense to do for him.

Then I remembered something – something I'd heard about people in comas.

'They do say,' I began, assuming a tone of authority to give the idea weight, 'that music can provide real benefits to patients with brain injuries.'

I wasn't sure what the benefits were exactly – could the music help bring them out of it? Or was it just about providing comfort? It was something, anyway. Something like that. In all honesty, I couldn't remember the exact details of the insight, or whether I'd picked the idea up from a reputable scientific source or if I'd overheard it in a bar, but I didn't think it mattered either way. The point wasn't to help Luke – although obviously that would be a bonus – but to help Jenny. To give her something to do and keep her spirits up. I felt sure that if I could do that, then Stephen too would be buoyed, as his mood seemed so tied to his wife's.

Jenny eyed me suspiciously, but I'd pricked her interest I could tell. 'What kind of music?'

'Well, they did a range of experiments,' I said, getting into my stride, 'and what they found was that it wasn't the genre of music that was important, but the personal relationship the patient had with it.'

Jenny frowned. 'Personal relationship? You mean the person doing the singing?' She paused and looked over to Luke. 'Should I sing to him, do you think? He did like that, when he was a little lad.'

I put my head on one side as if considering this proposition, although I was well aware that Jenny bursting into a rendition of 'Wheels On the Bus' in the middle of the ICU might not help anyone right now, least of all the other patients.

'I think it's more about accessing memories,' I said. 'Tracking down the pieces of music that mean something to Luke, that represent significant events in his life. According to the research, the music taps into dormant memories which the brain then begins to relive, thus stirring the other areas of the mind into action.'

I was quite impressed with how plausible it all sounded. I wondered if anyone ever *had* tried researching the idea. It might be worth a go, at least.

Jenny was nodding, and looking off into the middle distance, obviously thinking hard. 'Significant events . . . What do you think, Stephen?'

Stephen began thinking too, his arms folded, his eyes fixed on a spot on the far wall. 'Significant . . .' he repeated. 'Well, I can't say I know what song was playing when he had his first kiss or anything like that. I'm not sure I'd want to, to be honest with you.'

I could see this activity would need some structured guidance if it was going to take off.

'I think what we should do first,' I said, 'is make a list of all the possible events that might be relevant – first day of school, day he learnt to ride a bike, all of that – then we can go through the list and we can assign music to each one, based on what was in the charts at the time. Between us, we should be able to create a playlist that might do the trick.'

I was worried I was overplaying my hand, speaking in such a chirpy and assured way about the theory, as if the right mix of songs would work like a magic elixir, instantly stirring Luke from his slumber in a cloud of pink smoke. Jenny and Stephen seemed taken with the idea though.

'OK,' Jenny said, nodding firmly. 'Yes. We can do that, can't we, Stephen? We can go into town and get him a Walkman from Argos. We'll need to get those little headphones that go right in his ears, won't we, because the over-the-head ones might ruck up his dressing. We can . . .' Her short burst of energy seemed to expire suddenly, and her voice became smaller. 'Where will we get the music from? CDs? Will they have it all on CD?'

'At my flat, I have an old iPod, with in-ear headphone like you said. I'll go back home now and get that, together with my laptop. Then, let's meet at – where was it you were staying? With a relative?'

Stephen nodded. 'My aunt's house, Arlette. On the seafront.'

'Does Arlette have the internet?'

'Oh yes,' Stephen said with a light chuckle. 'She enjoys the internet, does Arlette. She's big on online poker.'

'Great!' I said brightly. 'We can download all the music from there.'

'Oh, right,' Jenny said uncertainly. 'If you're sure they'll have what we need.'

'They will,' I assured her.

I took down the address of Arlette's house and we arranged to meet there in an hour.

As I turned into my own road, I was surprised to see my landlord, Yanis, standing outside my front door. At the sight of him, I instinctively turned and began walking in the opposite direction. He'd already seen me though, and he called out after me.

'Hey!'

I pretended I hadn't heard and continued walking, thinking that if I could get into a crowded area he wouldn't be able to accost me. He jogged to catch up with me though, calling my name over and over until he stopped in front of me.

'Oh, hi!' I said brightly, pretending that I hadn't seen him. I knew he knew that I had, but I felt that if I approached the conversation with a friendly attitude then he'd be less likely to be aggressive with me.

He didn't return my smile. Instead, he pushed a folded

piece of paper into my hand and said, 'Wanted to give you this in person so you can't pretend you didn't get it.'

I unfolded the paper. It was a single page of small, tightly packed letters. At the top, the title said: NOTICE TO QUIT.

I looked up at him. 'What . . . ?'

Yanis was looking at me coldly, his arms crossed. 'You've got twenty-four hours to clear out. On Wednesday, I'm changing the locks and anything left inside will be going down the tip.'

I blinked. 'But . . . it's my flat.'

He shook his head. 'It's *my* flat.'

And then he turned and left me standing in the road, staring blankly at the paper he'd given me.

Without knowing what else I could do, I carried on with my mission, returned to my flat – as it still was, for the time being – and searched my drawers for the old iPod I'd borrowed from a girl I'd lived with before I'd moved to Devon.

Then I went to my desk and flipped open my laptop. I opened my browser and took the precaution of deleting my internet history. I'd been doing a lot of snooping over the last few days and it would be embarrassing if any of my searches popped up with Stephen and Jenny looking over my shoulder.

Rebecca

Chapter 23

It was that Monday morning – when we found Luke much as he had been the day before, the consultant reporting no noteworthy developments – that it hit me the hardest. It was worse, even, than that first evening, when I realised how much I'd underestimated his injuries.

It was the sense of perpetuity, of limbo, that I found hard to stomach. The lack of control, or ability to have any influence at all, didn't sit well with me. I think Dad voiced what all of us were thinking when he said, 'It's hard to know what we should be doing.'

I knew it wouldn't go down well when I excused myself to return to work. I could feel Mum's glare without looking at her. But then she never understood that people were capable of feeling emotions without wearing them all over their face. Without writing them all over the internet.

Charlotte of course was pulling all the right expressions, making all the right sympathetic noises. Ricocheting between my parents, incessantly patting their arms and stroking their backs like they were angora rabbits in a petting zoo. It seemed she didn't have work, or indeed anything else, to do that Monday morning.

That week I stayed away from the hospital, although my parents didn't realise this. I pretended that I was stopping by twice or three times a day, that we kept missing each other. I did ring the consultant though, and established that, in essence, nothing had changed. A series of text message exchanges with Dad confirmed the same, despite his reporting of events occasionally including hopeful details like, 'Your mum thought she saw his eyelids flicker when she mentioned that Leeds had won at the weekend.'

When you imagine terrible things happening to you or your family, your imagination always jumps straight to the climactic moments – the moment you receive the news, the spectacle you're faced with when you first visit the hospital. Your imagination seems to have little regard for the life that goes on around the tragic event. The life that must continue to go on. The great long expanses of time that are covered if, as seemed to be the case with Luke, the terrible event is drawn out, over a number of days, with no neat conclusion one way or the other in sight.

There are meals to be eaten, laundry to be done, travelling to be arranged. There are bills to be paid and money to be earned to pay debts that don't care who is in hospital or why. They will continue to grow regardless.

Mum's Facebook habit meant there were few people associated with our family who didn't now know about Luke's accident. After a brief hiatus on the Sunday while she and Dad travelled back from Athens and established the situation we were facing, she had once again returned to broadcasting her daily news to her 104 followers, her journalistic style seemingly coming into its own now she had something more serious than her work in the shop and her morning sessions at aqua aerobics to report.

On the evening of Thursday of that first week, when I was scrolling through the messages of support that had been posted to her page, I noticed a message from Anthony Sullivan – Sully, as he was better known – the school friend of Luke's with whom he had made the big move to Brighton just under two years ago.

I had, in the weeks prior to Luke's accident, been toying with the idea of contacting Sully, with the thought that he may be well placed to talk some reason into Luke. Even as children they had been something of a yin and yang partnership, Anthony's shy, slightly anxious, quietness tempering Luke's puppy-like enthusiasm, and on more than one occasion we had Sully to thank for preventing Luke hurting himself or someone else with an idea he considered 'fun'.

I knew that, given recent developments, the need to hold Luke back from saying something he shouldn't was less pressing – he wouldn't be enacting any schemes, rash or otherwise, from his current position – but I still thought reconnecting with Sully could be useful. I could try to gauge from him first if he knew about the night of Sarah's death, and then, following on from this, whether Luke had spoken to him about his desire to bare his soul to the widower. This would be useful information to have so that by the time Luke did eventually recover – and he *would* recover, I felt sure of that – I would know more about how to handle him.

Sully was Luke's oldest friend. They'd played five-a-side football together when they were eight, then been in the same class since Year Seven at St Edward's, and been firm friends all the way up. Sully had always been short and chubby, with red curly hair, a turned-up nose. To look at, he seemed ripe for teasing, but he never was teased, at least not with any serious intent, because he was too likeable. Too warm.

I began a new message:

Hi Sully,

I paused. As adept as I was at drafting a persuasive business email, I felt far less sure of myself when venturing into more social, personal communications. Especially given the circumstances, and especially given my desire to keep to myself the true motivations for my contact. I decided to fall back on a trick I often used when unsure of the correct social etiquette – channel someone else. Put myself in the role of my mother – of anyone who was more emotionally . . . untamed . . . than I was.

Hi Sully,
    I'm sure you've heard about what's happened to Luke by now. We're all struggling here. The not knowing is the hardest.
    I wonder if you'd be free to meet up? It would be lovely to chat about Luke.
    love,
    Becky x

As I read it back, I realised what I'd done. The voice I'd used to compose it had been Charlotte's, her chirpy phraseology seeming exactly fitting for my purposes. It really was like another person had written it.

Which, all things considered, was probably for the best.

Chapter 24

Sully replied to my message quickly and kindly, expressing his concern for Luke and the whole family, and confirming that he would love to meet.

On my request, we arranged to meet in a pub – the King George. I didn't like to drink and, despite my occupation, didn't feel particularly at ease in venues where it was expected, but I knew it was better suited to my needs. People didn't keep such a close eye on you in a pub as they might in a café or restaurant, they were less keen there for you to finish up and be on your way. I wasn't sure exactly what I was hoping to achieve from my meeting with Sully, but I knew it would require careful handling on my part, and that could take some time.

I saw him at once, sitting in a corner, a pint of something dark on the table in front of him. He looked up as the door closed behind me, and his face broke into the wide smile that had barely changed in twenty years. There was an awkward moment where I wasn't sure what the appropriate greeting was, so stood quite still and waited for Sully to make the decision for me. In the end, he patted my upper arm and went to get me a drink from the bar.

'I couldn't believe it when I saw Jenny's message on Facebook,' he said when we were settled. 'I know it's a cliché, but you just don't think it's going to happen to someone you know, someone like Luke. A mugging, I mean . . . you see these things on the news, but you don't think people really go around, smashing people up for no reason.'

Sully asked detailed questions about Luke's progress in hospital so far. Although I couldn't tell him much more than Mum had already shared, I recounted every detail I could remember from the consultant's debriefs. Then we were silent for a few moments and I was aware of the awkwardness. I knew I was the one who'd initiated the meeting – who'd said I wanted to 'chat about Luke' – but I didn't know where to begin. I lacked the subtly to disguise the questions I wanted to ask as random reminiscences.

In the end, Sully spoke first. 'He'd been quiet, for a little while now,' he said. 'Preoccupied, it felt like.'

'Preoccupied in what way? With what?'

Sully shrugged, but then he said, 'I know you guys hadn't seen each other for a while.'

I pondered how best to respond to this. It was, it seemed to me, designed to elicit an explanation of our strained relations from me, but I didn't want to give one – even a false one – because what I wanted was to see if Sully *knew* why it was. To see if Luke had told him about our row, about his plans. And to see if Luke had got any further with carrying out those plans.

'Did Luke mention why that was?' I said eventually. I aimed to make this sound as if I was mystified about why he had suddenly retreated from me.

'Pretty easy to guess,' Sully said, taking a sip of his pint.

I felt my eyebrow twitch. 'Oh?' I said, as nonchalantly as I could manage.

'Yeah,' Sully nodded. 'Brendan, isn't it. No offence or anything but you must know Luke can't stand him. So I guess it makes sense that Luke would give you guys some space.'

'I know Luke and Brendan are very different people. I would never expect them to be friends but . . .'

I had been going to say, did Sully think that was the only reason Luke was avoiding me, to give him one clear chance to speak up if he knew anything about Sarah Rubinstein, but he cut me off with a sudden laugh.

'I think it was a bit more than that, Becs. Brendan threatened him.'

Chapter 25

I felt my cheeks redden in that infuriating way they do when panic sets in.

'What?' I said.

Sully laughed. 'I don't mean he *threatened* threatened. I'm not saying he held a knife to his throat or anything. But still, he was pretty nasty. Pretty *rude*, really. I think that's what wound Luke up.'

'When?' I demanded. 'When did this happen?'

'At the club,' Sully said. 'Think it was his last week. Last day even, maybe.'

It was actually Luke who had worked at Candy's Lounge, as it was called back then, first, and it was he who had introduced me to Brendan. Candy's Lounge was one of the run of casual bar jobs Luke had had before his recent foray into the world of corporate events and, on occasion, I would go to meet him there at the end of his shift and sit at the bar with a chilled tonic water while he wiped surfaces and completed the handover to the next member of staff.

It was during those visits that I'd noticed the bar was run abysmally. In a prime location with sea views from the upper windows but decorated like a run-down amusement arcade, staffed by layabouts – Luke included, I'm sorry to say – and managed by a balding, pointy-nosed shrew of a man who seemed to treat his customers like tiresome inconveniences in his life.

At first, relations between Brendan and me had been frosty. When he'd attempted to 'make a pass' at me (this was the phrase Luke used – he'd been there at the time – when he'd explained the encounter to me), I'd responded with something between disdain and confusion. I hadn't realised what had been happening, but I realised that if Luke was right, then perhaps here was an opportunity.

The club had potential. I saw that quickly. I knew that with the right management – with *my* management – it could turn a substantial profit. It took only the briefest scan through the business's public accounts to see it was on the verge of collapse and badly needed a cash injection, but I knew there was no guarantee that Brendan would accept it from me, and certainly not for the stake I was looking for, unless I could throw something else into the mix. The something else, I decided, would be my attention.

Getting into the relationship had been easy. Once I began to play along with Brendan's flirtations, I realised how susceptible he was to any kind of flattery. I also realised how important it was for him to have a woman on his arm, how he liked to parade me in front of his friends as though I was an impressive cheesecake he had made. He was dull but generally biddable back then, and attending candlelit dinners in his flat and feigning delight at the cheap jewellery he bought me seemed a small price to pay if it persuaded him to sell me half of his business.

In the end, it took just a few weeks for Brendan to begin referring to me as his girlfriend and just a few weeks more than that to accept my investment, change the assignation of shares on the paperwork and declare us partners – 'in all senses of the word', as he liked to say.

I had planned to extricate myself from the relationship eventually but I knew I had to play it carefully. If I ended things too abruptly he might get angry and begin throwing his weight around, demanding more of a hand in the day-to-day management and undoing all my good work. But I hoped that if I stopped showering him with compliments he'd simply get bored and move on to someone else. Our business partnership would then continue – the contracts were rock solid – but I told myself I could cope with that. He showed very little interest in work anyway so I reasoned that if seeing me no longer held any appeal for him, he might begin to stay away from the club altogether and become a sleeping partner.

Of course, when I had formulated the whole idea I had no idea what would transpire over the coming months and how I would come to realise I may never be truly free of Brendan.

I felt it important to the credibility of the charade that I kept up the pretence of a genuine fondness for Brendan to everyone, even Luke. So although I knew Luke thought Brendan was a fool – as I did myself – I had to let Luke believe I was beguiled by him. It pained me to let Luke think I could be so severely lacking in judgement, but it's as I often say: life is not without its inconveniences.

Fortunately, Luke decided to move on from his time at Candy Lounge shortly after I had begun my role as 'Brendan's girlfriend' so I wasn't forced to deceive him to his face too often. His last week had been at the very end of December, the end of the year before.

'What happened?' I asked Sully. 'What did Brendan say exactly?'

Sully frowned. 'I don't know exactly. Luke was cagey about it for some reason, but it was something to do with you.'

'Me?' Once again I feigned nonchalance, concealing the dark fear that we were creeping towards exactly what I didn't want to hear.

Sully shrugged. 'The gist of the threat seemed to be Brendan telling Luke that if he ever did anything to harm you, he'd kill him.'

'If Luke harmed me?'

Sully pulled a face. 'I know, weird isn't it? Isn't it meant to be the brother warning off the boyfriend, not the other way around?' He paused, then added. 'It was a kind of a dickhead move, by Brendan.'

I nodded. 'It certainly was,' I muttered.

'I mean,' Sully went on, clearly not finished on the subject. 'I know Luke was a bit of a freeloader when it came to lifts and money and somewhere to crash, but what did Brendan think Luke was really going to do to you?'

I just shook my head. 'I have no idea.'

But actually, I had a very good idea. All Luke would have to do was open his stupid, honest, well-meaning mouth.

Sully had said enough to convince me that he knew nothing of what had happened to Sarah Rubinstein prior to her death, and nothing of Luke's plans to reveal it. But any relief I felt was clouded by the seed of a thought that had been growing over the last few days: just how far was Brendan prepared to go to keep Luke quiet?

Chapter 26

'Is he allowed visitors?' Sully asked suddenly.

'Luke?' I said, surprised. 'At the hospital?'

Sully smiled. 'That's where he is, isn't he?'

'Yes. My parents and I go there every day.'

'Could I come?'

I wondered if I should warn him off, or at least make sure he realised what he was volunteering himself for. My brother was the most important person in the world to me but spending time with someone completely unresponsive could be deeply unsettling.

'I should think so,' I said. 'There's not much to see though.'

Sully gave me a funny look.

'He's unconscious,' I explained. 'You can't speak to him. Not properly. He won't know you're there.'

Sully nodded slowly. 'I'd still like to come.'

We made the twenty-minute walk to the hospital together. Conversation was difficult as we kept getting separated by people and roads that were too narrow to walk along side by side, so we gave up trying. The silence was awkward though and I wished that Luke had been there. I felt a pang of nostalgia for the old days, when Luke and Sully used to build camp fires in the overgrown area at the end of our parents' garden and lie next to it, eating penny sweets from paper bags. Whenever I'd gone down there – ostensibly to complain about the smoke drifting into my bedroom window – Luke had persuaded me to join them, handed me a Sherbet Dip Dab and insisted I listen to his exaggerated tales of schoolboy mischief. 'Seriously!' he'd say, grinning when Sully or I expressed any scepticism about his stories. 'I couldn't make it up if I wanted to!'

Luke never seemed to have any trouble making casual conversation, riffing off what people said, asking surprising questions, putting people at their ease. How does one learn to do that? I often wondered. What are the tricks of that trade?

At the hospital, I led Sully up to ICU. He seemed to hesitate at the double doors, as if nervous about what he might find on the other side of them.

'It's OK,' I said. 'It's largely just machines, and static bodies. It's not gruesome or dramatic in any way.'

We made our way to Luke's cubicle and I felt my teeth clench with irritation when I saw Charlotte was there, in her favourite position in his bedside chair. Unaware she had an audience, she didn't even seem to be paying him proper attention. She was looking at her phone.

She turned around, her surprise quickly replaced with one of her plastered-on smiles, and then she stood up to greet us.

'This is Charlotte.' I introduced her to Sully without enthusiasm. 'Luke's girlfriend.'

I wondered if she had picked up the sneer in my tone at the word. I hadn't been able to prevent it. She pretended not to notice if she had.

'And this—' I began, gesturing towards Sully.

'Sully!' Charlotte cut me off, raising her arms aloft as if in celebration of him, then wrenching him forward and enveloping him in a hug.

'I thought you two didn't know each other?' I said, frowning. Sully had confirmed he'd heard no mention of Charlotte from Luke on our walk to the hospital, and suggested this could be one reason for Luke's preoccupation. I'd agreed, feeling that was the safest conclusion for Sully to land on.

'Oh, we don't!' Charlotte laughed, for no good reason. 'But I've seen so many photos! And Luke talked about you, of course.'

Sully grinned shyly. 'Cool.' If he was as irritated by her as I was, he was hiding it better than I ever managed to.

Sully approached Luke's bed. He reached out tentatively and rubbed his shoulder. 'All right, buddy?' he said. 'You been in the wars then?'

It was clear that Sully, like the rest of us, wasn't quite sure what to do when faced with the spectacle that was Luke, in his current state.

Charlotte, as ever, was on hand to help Sully relax. She gave him a guided tour of the equipment, explained Luke's injuries in irritatingly juvenile and euphemistic terms – Luke had apparently had a 'bit of a bump', his craniotomy was a simple case of his brain 'letting off a bit of steam' and he wasn't just stable, he was as 'comfy as could be expected'.

After this, they began chatting about this and that as if they were at a coffee morning in a church hall rather than standing at the foot of the bed of a gravely ill man. They had just got onto the subject of Charlotte's recent winter jaunt to Goa – which frankly I'd heard more than enough about – when I decided to interject.

'Where are my parents?' The question came out more abruptly than I'd intended.

They both turned to look at me as if they'd forgotten I was there.

'They're in the canteen,' Charlotte said. 'They thought I might want some time alone with him.' She said it in that breezy way she had when she knew she was delivering something pointed, something that would irritate me. Then she added, 'Perhaps you should join them.'

And then she went back to fussing over Sully, jabbering away about that inane playlist she and my mother seemed to believe was communicating directly with Luke's soul, touching Sully's arm and back in a way that was hardly appropriate given the fact she'd only met the man five minutes before.

Charlotte

Chapter 27

When I'd suggested that making the playlist would help Luke's recovery, I hadn't anticipated quite how enthusiastically Jenny would embrace the idea, but I suppose my theory that she needed a project had been proved accurate.

I arrived with my laptop and the iPod at the grand seafront apartment belonging to Stephen's aunt. The plaque next to the front door told me it was called the White House, which seemed strange as the paintwork was blue. When I queried the name, Stephen laughed and said it had been so called by Arlette's friends and neighbours as she was known for her forthright presidential manner when dealing with neighbourhood matters.

Stephen welcomed me into the airy entrance hall with parquet flooring and tall plants in each corner, and showed me through to a formal dining room with long mahogany table in the centre, where Jenny was sitting hunched over a pad of paper, writing carefully.

She didn't say hello when she saw me, instead picking up our conversation about the music directly where we'd left off in the hospital.

'I've been trying to do it like your idea,' she said. 'Making a list of all the possible main events, the things that will be most important in his memories, so we can try to link songs with them based on the dates. I thought we could search,' she gestured to my laptop, 'online for the charts and playlists and things – for the relevant dates?'

I nodded seriously. I knew that, to keep Jenny going, it was essential that I embraced the project as earnestly and whole-heartedly as she was and that we worked on the basis that it was nothing less than a sure-fire route to Luke's recovery. I sat down at the table opposite her and got my own notebook out of my bag. 'So, talk me through what you've got so far.'

Jenny and I worked steadily and companionably on our project all morning, Jenny taking care of the dates from Luke's childhood – the summer he spent at an outdoor pursuits camp in Sweden, his first day of secondary school, the day he passed his driving test – but looking to me for more inspiration for more recent events. It was actually quite easy to manufacture what was most likely to have loomed large in Luke's psyche based on what I'd been able to glean from his online presence, and the time I'd spent with his parents. There were the obvious candidates – the day he moved to Brighton, his first day in his new job – but I added a few creative flourishes too – a song he used to sing in the shower before we'd go out for the evening, the time we'd made our own cider at an apple festival.

Over the course of that first week, I focused almost all of my attention on the family, all my energy on performing the role I'd assigned myself to the best of my ability, and, although I was a little embarrassed to admit it, I knew I was using it to some degree as a distraction from my own problems. So much so, in fact, that I left it until the last possible hour to pull all of my clothes out of my wardrobe and squash them into the two suitcases I kept under the bed, shove all my other worldly possessions into a holdall, sling it across my body and heave the whole lot out of my flat – or the flat that was no longer mine – while Yanis stood impatiently in the hall, saying, 'I can have a locksmith here in ten minutes, you know.'

It was only then, on the bus with my bags piled up on the floor and the chair beside me, a pot plant tottering precariously on my lap, that I began to feel nervous. I was used to new beginnings, to striking out on my own, but never before had I had no plans in place at all for the next step. Never before had I had no idea at all which direction to travel in, where to even begin.

I suppose if I'd found myself homeless at any other time I would have turned to one of my friends from work, someone I'd known for a few months at least, in search of a short-term place to stay, but as I had spent nearly all of my waking hours over the past few days either at the hospital or at the White House with Stephen and Jenny it seemed only natural that I should head there in the first instance. I had already arranged to call in later that day anyway and I reasoned I could use it as a base to trawl the internet for rooms or flats available at short notice. If the worst came to the worst, I thought, I could check into a B&B for a few days while I got myself sorted.

I hadn't intended to tell them about my housing issues at all. It felt inappropriate in a way, to whine on about my administrative hiccups given what they were dealing with. I was worried, too, that they might think I'd done something wrong to find myself, a grown adult, with nowhere to live.

My plan was to buy a ticket for the swimming pool next to the library and store my bags in a locker there until I managed to get the keys to a new place, so when I arrived at the White House they'd have no idea that just that morning

I had hauled everything I owned across town. What I didn't plan for though, was stepping almost directly into Stephen when I got off the bus at the stop near the pier.

'Charlotte!' he said. 'Look at you, loaded up like a carthorse. What on earth are you doing?'

If I'd been expecting the encounter, I could have perhaps thought of an explanation for my luggage, but I hadn't had time to prepare anything.

'Moving!' I said in the end. 'Just moving flats. Just moving a few bits across.'

His forehead crinkled with concern. 'Moving? Why didn't you say?'

I sighed, shook my head and did a tired laugh. 'It's not really planned. I had some problems with a landlord. People warned me but . . . ' I shrugged.

Stephen shook his head. 'Luke had exactly the same problem with his last place. They're thieving gits, all of them. No limits on their greed. Where's the new place?'

I hadn't planned to tell him the truth, but given that we were already midway through the conversation and I couldn't think of a reasonable response to his question, I decided it was probably easier to just come clean.

'I don't know. Nothing's confirmed yet. I've got a few agents calling me back.'

Stephen looked at me anxiously, his head on one side. 'So where are you going now?'

'Well, I thought I'd call in on you and Jenny, and then the hospital and . . .' I trailed off. 'I mean, with everything that's happened I haven't really been on top of sorting things out and . . .'

He nodded, finally getting the measure of the situation. 'Right, well, we can't have that.' He leant forward and took a suitcase from my hand. I flexed my fingers, relieved to get the blood flow back. 'You can stay with us tonight, at the house. And for as long as it takes you to get sorted. It's a huge place, rooms sitting empty, beds all made up and everything. And Jenny will be pleased to have you around. We both will.'

I felt I should protest, to insist they had quite enough going on without me imposing myself on them, but the truth was I was so grateful for the offer – the sense of relief was almost physical – that all I could do was blink back my tears and nod.

'Thank you. That would be amazing.'

Stephen had seemed serious about his offer, but I was nervous of what Jenny would say. Despite the time we had spent together, she probably still considered me a virtual stranger, so I worried she might reject the idea out of hand. However, to my relief, when we arrived at the house and Stephen hauled my bags through the front door to the hallway, she seemed delighted.

'It makes perfect sense really,' she said, taking my jacket from me and hanging it on the banister. 'We're up and down to the hospital all the time anyway. And, I don't know . . . everyone from back home is being lovely and trying to be supportive but it's only really us – the three of us – who really know what it's like. All the waiting. All the not knowing.'

'And Becky,' Stephen said.

'Yes, of course. And Becky.'

Over the next few days we established a routine. We'd visit Luke early on, straight after breakfast, come home for lunch and a rest – sometimes Jenny and Stephen would nap or go for a short walk along the seafront – then we'd go back to the hospital mid-afternoon, returning in the evening for a late dinner. After that, Jenny would turn her attention to her iPad, posting long, badly punctuated updates to Facebook detailing

Luke's progress and any other happenings at the hospital. She also sought her followers' input on our playlist, and was diligently writing down their suggestions in her notebook.

In bed each evening, I would open my laptop and keep up with the family's online lives. By monitoring the exchanges – who commented, what they said – and visiting the profiles of the people Jenny interacted with, I was able to continue to build my knowledge and understanding of their lives, of Luke's life, before I met them.

It was fascinating, in a way, every time something from that 2D, digital world came to life. If Stephen and Jenny told me an anecdote about someone from back home, I was able to match the characters up with the names I'd seen on Jenny's profile, and the messages of support they'd left. When Luke's best friend Sully came to the hospital, I was able to greet him like I knew him because I genuinely felt I did.

It was a wonderful thing, in that way, the internet. And it was wonderful to feel part of something again.

Chapter 28

Friday 4 May marked six days since Luke's admission to hospital, and although his condition remained the same, it felt as if it had been much longer.

Being thrust into the heart of the family at a time of such emotional turmoil had fast-tracked my relationship with them in a way that suited me. I'd never been good at the tentative early steps of getting to know someone, whoever they were. Formality didn't come easily to me. I struggled with the rules, what was appropriate to say and when. I was far more comfortable once I got to the stage that I had with Jenny and Stephen where they would make me tea without it being officially offered, where they could ask me to run to the shop for them without making a big show of manners – 'if it's not too much trouble', 'if you wouldn't mind', all of that.

Sometimes, often when I'd done something quite mundane like swept the kitchen floor after dinner, Jenny would say, 'What would we do without you?' But the truth was, I needed them just as much. They had come into my life exactly at the time I needed people like them around me.

That Friday morning, I found Jenny in the kitchen with

four leather-bound photo albums spread over the kitchen table.

'I got my cousin to send these down,' she said. 'I just wanted to make the place feel like home. And I wanted to have Luke – real Luke's – face to look at. You know? It's not the same, how he looks in there. I don't want that to be what I see when I close my eyes. I want to see my handsome boy.'

She smiled and Blu-tacked a photo of him as a gawky teenager holding an electric guitar and grinning at someone to the left of the camera. I hadn't seen any other photos of him playing the guitar. I wondered if he'd kept up the hobby. I made a mental note to check in case it came up.

'Do you have any, love?' She looked at me. 'Photos of you and him together?'

I frowned as if searching my memory. 'You know, I don't think I do actually.' I chewed my lip and looked out the window, as if the realisation troubled me.

Jenny smiled kindly. 'Everything's digital really these days, isn't it? I'm the same. All on my phone. But if you want to find any nice ones and email them over to me, I'm going to send a bunch off to get them printed. It's right that they should be up, around the place for us to look at every day, not locked away in a cloud, or wherever it is.'

I said I'd see what I could find, and hoped she wouldn't mention it again.

Chapter 29

We'd arranged to meet Rebecca in a café in town that afternoon, and when we were home from the morning hospital
visit, Jenny asked me if I wanted to walk in with her a bit
earlier.

'I start to go mad sitting inside all day,' she said. 'And I
barely know Brighton, despite both the kids living here. You
can give me a little tour, show me all the places you and Luke
spend time together.'

I agreed, knowing it would be quite easy to point out a few
lunch spots, pubs and cafés and claim them as our own special
places.

As we approached the steps that led to the shopping centre,
a woman wearing a bright pink T-shirt over her sweatshirt
stepped into our paths. She thrust a leaflet into my hand that
said: MUMS GO FREE!

'Ladies!' she said with a manic smile. 'How do you feel about
tea and cake? Good, am I right? And how do you feel
about *free* tea and cake?'

'Oh, I don't know . . .' I began.

The manic woman laughed. 'I can see you're suspicious

but there's no catch, I promise! It's not a trick! It's just to celebrate the opening of our new tearoom. If you go along, take your mum with you – ' she smiled at Jenny – 'then you pay, but Mum gets a cup of tea or coffee and a cake for free.'

'Oh,' Jenny smiled shyly. 'We're not . . . I'm not—'

'OK!' I jumped in before Jenny could say any more. 'We're up for that!' Then I added, 'Aren't we, Mum?'

Jenny still seemed nervous about our white lie, perhaps expecting a visit from the baked goods police, but once we'd ordered and were safely hidden away on a corner table, she began to relax a little.

'You never mention your own mum. Are you close to her?' she asked. 'She knows what's going on, does she? Had she met Luke?'

I shook my head quickly, firmly. And the shaking, I was aware, went on perhaps a touch too long. But it was just such an unlikely scenario, so undesirable, to imagine my mother – her shapeless sack of a dress, her wild eyes, her unkempt hair – anywhere near Jenny or Luke. Or, for that matter, anywhere near me.

'I don't see my parents any more,' I said. 'They weren't very well. They weren't very good parents.'

'Oh,' Jenny said, her face anguished. 'Are they still . . . ?'

'Oh yeah, they're alive,' I said. 'As far as I know, anyway. But . . . just some people aren't cut out to . . . to bring up children.'

I took a sip of my tea and didn't meet Jenny's eye for a moment, uncomfortable at the way she was looking at me, with a mixture of pity and wariness.

'But it was OK,' I said, to lighten the mood. 'I moved in with my aunt Frieda and she was great and . . . well, I'm OK now.' I gave her a brave smile. 'All's well that ends well, as they say.'

Jenny nodded and smiled, but her brow was still furrowed. 'And you're still close to her now, your aunt?'

I shook my head. 'She died, sadly, a while ago now but . . .' I shrugged, as if to say, that's the way it goes.

Because, sometimes, that is the way it goes.

Chapter 30

After our tea, Jenny went to buy some more Blu-tack for her photo wall so I headed towards the café where we were due to be meeting Rebecca in ten minutes' time. I'd already planned to wait on the corner until Jenny caught me up, not wanting to go directly there in case Rebecca too was early and she and I were forced to sit at a table alone together.

It was clear that Rebecca was, as far as possible, avoiding spending time with her parents, choosing to carry out her visits on her own, at times when she knew she would be alone with Luke. I still hadn't got to the bottom of the tension between her and her family. I suspected that perhaps the simple truth was that she just wasn't that nice, and if it wasn't for their biological connection, she and her parents would never choose to associate with each other. She remained a source of fascination to me. A curiosity, like one of those creatures you catch a glimpse of near the bins at dusk who seem to be neither fox nor cat.

As I turned into the road, I saw that Rebecca was indeed already there, sitting at a metal table on the pavement. As ever, she was typing furiously on her phone. And as ever, she was frowning. Although I was starting to realise that the groove between her eyebrows was permanent. Probably through over use.

I saw a man approach her then. He was short and skinny with severely receding strawberry blonde hair and a prominent nose and chin. Rebecca was too engrossed in her typing to see him approach and she didn't look up until he was standing directly at her shoulder. When she saw him, she flinched but quickly set her face into a fixed smile, and looked up at him. He leant forward to kiss her, but she – instinctively, it seemed – shrank away from him. He stood back up, clearly displeased by this reaction, and pushed his hands into his pockets. He scowled for a moment, but Rebecca said something to him, the fixed smile now stretching her face almost into a grimace, and he seemed placated. He nodded once, hung around as if not sure what to do for a moment, then walked quickly away in my direction. I tucked myself into a doorway, in case Rebecca should look up and see me spying on her.

As he walked past me, his phone rang. He looked at the screen and answered it. 'Brendan Scott?'

Later that night, when I was in the privacy of my own bedroom in the White House, I typed *Brendan Scott* into Google. There were too many results for me to even begin to narrow things down so I tried Facebook instead. This time I found a profile, with a photo clearly showing the small man I'd seen greet Rebecca.

When I clicked through the few of his photos viewable by the public, I found one of him and Rebecca together, his arm resting on the small of her back in a proud, proprietary kind of way. In the photo, as in the café earlier, Rebecca seemed deeply uncomfortable about Brendan's proximity.

Weird, I thought to myself. She didn't seem the type of person to be with someone she didn't want to be with.

Chapter 31

On Saturday morning, I woke up early so I went to the bakery at the end of the road and brought home a paper bag full of pastries. I laid them out on plates on the balcony with a pot of fresh coffee and, as I looked out at the sea twinkling in the late spring sun, it occurred to me how luxurious our accommodation was. Overworked London types would probably pay hundreds to experience these surroundings, just for a few days. I knew I'd feel differently if I'd really known Luke, but despite my growing affection for Stephen and Jenny, it was hard for me to view him as much more than a dark shadow, stealing the sunshine from moments that would otherwise have been happy.

'It is lovely, to be by the sea,' Jenny said, gazing out at the waves once she had joined me on the balcony. 'I've always wanted to live on the coast.'

'Maybe you should,' I said. 'Luke's down here. And Rebecca, of course. Were you never tempted to follow them?'

Jenny slowly turned her gaze away from the sea to look at me. 'Do you know what? I did imagine it, a few times, but I told myself we couldn't – I have the shop and Stephen has his squash club. But now – God, that all seems ridiculous! I can work in any bloody charity shop. We were just set in our ways. Took it for granted that we could visit the kids any time we wanted. Stupid.'

Stephen came out to join us, squinting in the bright sunlight and pulling on his cardigan. 'Stephen,' Jenny said, 'when Luke's back on his feet, I think we should put the house on the market and look for a place down here. Luke will need us as he gets better. I thought he'd come home with us but maybe it'd be better for us to come to him. It'd be good for us to have a change.'

'Well, we'd need to think about . . .' He looked at his wife's face and stopped. 'Of course, love. Of course, we can do that.'

I imagined what kind of house they'd get. Something with a sunny kitchen and big glass doors overlooking a well-kept garden, I thought. I imagined myself going over to visit them, finding Jenny sorting out cupboards, putting all the spices in alphabetical order, her smile when she realised I'd dropped in unannounced. Then Stephen coming in from the garden to meet me, his face lighting up in delight too. For a moment the daydream seemed so real I felt my face physically sag as I realised it was just a fantasy. Contentment turned to anger as I thought of my parents – something I hadn't done for a while – and how they'd robbed me of that reality. It wasn't a big ask, was it, to want to visit your parents, to find them happy and pleased to see you? Why had it been too much for them? For them to be normal?

When I'd left them, when I hadn't been able to stand any more, I hadn't simply moved out, never to return. I'd started off just staying at Frieda's for a few nights at a time, but gradually, as I got more comfortable there, as I moved more of my own things across, these stays got longer, until I was living there almost full time. But I had tried, several times, to go back home. To give my parents a second chance.

One of those attempts had been on my birthday – my fifteenth. They hadn't remembered it was my birthday, but I hadn't expected them to, so I think I'd chosen that date as a personal milestone rather than in hope of any recognition. Fifteen, I remember thinking, sounded an awful lot older than fourteen, so I thought perhaps I would be able to tackle my family, that house, with a new maturity.

My father had been working. I use the term loosely because there was never any clear economic value to what my parents spent their time doing. He was sorting a large bag of screws and nails into small bags of screws and nails, then placing each small bag into a Tupperware box and stacking the boxes on the floor. This was the type of thing he was always doing. I have no idea why. He'd nodded in acknowledgement when I'd entered the room, but that was the end of our interaction for that visit.

Not sure what else to do, I'd gone up to my bedroom on the second floor. Despite their many flaws, something my parents had always managed well, up until that point, was to stay out of my space. The house was large, so despite the hoarding and the clutter and squalor, I had been able to preserve a twelve-foot by twelve-foot sanctuary of space of my own. And that was, in fact, one thing I didn't have at Aunt Frieda's. I didn't really mind – I enjoyed the little ones running in to show me their drawings, I looked forward to the older ones smuggling me wine inside a hot water bottle, sitting on the end of my bed and telling me about their boyfriends – but sometimes the constant activity could be tiring.

But when I went up the stairs and crossed the landing to my room, I noticed a problem as soon as I'd pushed the door open. I had to shove hard to get it to open at all, and there was the sound of something heavy sliding across the carpet. And when I'd got it open wide enough to step into the room, I saw there were boxes everywhere. Cardboard boxes lined with plastic bags. I could see there was something on my bed and I went over to get a closer look. When I did, when I saw, I screamed – three times, I think. Three separate shouts.

On the bed were the carcasses of animals. Birds, badgers, foxes, maybe a cat. It was hard to make out any discernible shapes in amongst the mangled limbs, the fur caked with congealed blood.

My screaming had alerted my mother and she came into the room, her white smock smeared with dark red blood, her skin sallow and gaunt.

'What are you doing in here?' she snapped. 'It's not hygienic! Have you touched any of them? I'll have to wash them all over again if you have!'

I just stared at her. 'Where did you get them from?'

'The road.' She went over to the bed, seized one of the bodies and tossed it into a nearby box. 'People just leave them there to rot. Such a waste.'

'Why have you brought them here?'

'To do them up! We've got to make a living. Not that you'd know anything about that.'

I'd been going to ask why, how, what possible plan she could have for them, but I knew there was no comprehensible answer. Nothing my parents did made sense. They weren't capable of reason. Other people thought they were eccentric, that they lived an unorthodox lifestyle, but only those of us inside the house knew how unhinged they were becoming. How they were spiralling into madness.

But suddenly I realised I didn't care. I was done. I was finished with them, with that house. There was nothing I could do for them. And there was nothing I wanted from them, not any more.

As I turned to leave the room, I looked down into a box and saw that the fabric she'd used to swaddle one of the dead creatures was one of my school shirts.

Chapter 32

As Stephen tidied away our breakfast things, Jenny said, 'Stephen and I were saying, we should check in on Luke's flat. Check his post – see if there's anything urgent that needs attending to, turn the heating off and things. He won't be best pleased to get home to a huge energy bill. But we'll need to get hold of his landlord, I think, to get a set of keys. We couldn't find any in his things. I suppose we should think about getting the locks changed because—'

'Oh, I've got his keys,' I said. I'd completely forgotten that when I'd looked through Luke's wallet I'd found a set in the back pocket.

Jenny blinked, surprised for a moment, but then she smiled. 'Oh! OK. Great. Maybe you go over first then, love. Make sure the place is decent. He wouldn't want his mum and dad poking through his things, I'm sure.'

I knew Luke's address, having seen it on his driving licence, and couldn't believe I hadn't thought of calling round before. I felt excited as I made my way back from the sea and climbed the steep hill into Hanover, curious to see another part of the Burley world come to life.

The flat was on the ground floor of one of the brightly coloured terraced houses that lined the hill. There were a few keys on the chain and it took me a couple of attempts to find the right one, but eventually the door creaked open.

I'd expected to find a mountain of mail piled on the mat to sort through but I suppose it had only been a week and in these days of emails and online banking, how much paper mail did one person really get? I was a little disappointed to find there weren't any official-looking letters that I, the dutiful girlfriend, would need to open and carefully process. There were just a few pizza menus, a flyer for a carpet-cleaning company and a letter offering a discount on a broadband package.

His flat was kept very nicely indeed, I realised, as I made my way through. His lounge was simply furnished – one sofa, a large television and coffee table between them. His kitchen was spotless too, the only suggestion that someone had been there recently a coffee mug with a ring around the top in the sink. I felt a pang of sadness at the thought of him putting it there, ready to wash up later, not realising that later wouldn't come.

I busied myself cleaning out his fridge, throwing away half a tin of pineapple that had been left open, and pouring away a carton of sour milk. It made me feel better, being able to do that – like my visit was a genuine help and not just snooping.

I sat on the sofa and imagined Luke there beside me, his arm around me. It must be nice, I'd always thought, to have someone to come home to, to talk to about what to have for dinner. Someone to turn to and say, 'Oh, I saw a funny thing today.'

On the arm of the sofa there was a square envelope, sealed with little red sticker. I could feel something hard inside, so

I eased open the flap and tipped it out. It was a braided leather bracelet, with a round silver button threaded onto it. The button was engraved with the letters SFB. I slipped it on and tightened the cord.

It was then I noticed the laptop on the floor in the corner of the room. I went and picked it up, brought it back to the sofa and flipped it open. I hit the standby button and waited for it to start up. The computer had only been asleep I realised, not properly shut down, and on the desktop view, I saw there was a browser window minimised. When I opened it, three tabs automatically loaded.

The first one was the webpage of a dating app. It wasn't the one I'd first seen his face on, I noticed. He'd obviously tired of the options there. A little blue bubble in the corner told me he had five new matches and three new messages. He was obviously a popular guy, I thought, feeling something between pride and jealousy. I smiled to myself at the absurdity of either.

I looked at the messages, just out of curiosity. Once I'd read the new ones – variations on 'hi, how are you' – I scrolled through his older messages. I was able to read the whole exchange between him and Kelly that had led to the date I'd seen them on and was amused to notice at once that it was clear they weren't going to get on.

Luke had been friendly but reserved, clearly waiting until the face-to-face meeting before getting too involved. Kelly on the other hand had been forward, suggestive, making liberal use of winking-face and lipstick-kiss emojis. On the evening of their meeting, she'd sent him a full-length photo of herself, pouting at the camera along with the message: *hope ur looking forward to more of this!!!*

He hadn't replied. Perhaps he hadn't seen it. Perhaps if he had, he would never have gone to meet her.

On the next tab was his email account. There were about fifteen new ones, mostly from mailing lists. As I scrolled through I saw there was a message from Rebecca, from about eight weeks earlier. As it had already been opened, I saw no harm in taking a look.

I'm sorry my visit ended on uncomfortable terms. I just need you to think carefully about the consequences of your actions. I know you think speaking to that man is the honourable course of action, but I don't believe there is any moral high ground to be held by making matters more difficult for all concerned. I include Daniel himself in that number. I am of the firm belief your proposed intervention will make him feel more negatively about the situation.

As I read the message, I couldn't help but smirk. Why did the woman always have to talk like she had a pole up her bum?

Luke's reply was much briefer:

I'm not saying it's the easy thing to do, but it is the right thing.

Rebecca's respond ended the exchange:

You're making a mistake, and I hope to find some way to convince you of that.

My amusement at the tone of the exchange aside, I was intrigued. Who did Luke want to speak to, and why was Rebecca so adamant that he mustn't?

It was at this moment I realised: it wasn't just that I didn't like Rebecca. I didn't trust her.

Chapter 33

I heard a noise outside the flat and jumped. Instinctively, I slammed the laptop lid shut and I was already on my feet when the doorbell rang.

I hesitated, feeling inexplicably guilty and contemplating hiding behind the curtain until the caller left, but then I pulled myself together. It would, I knew, most likely be the postman or someone to read the meter. No one who would be the least bit interested in my specific relationship to Luke and how long it had – or hadn't – been going on for.

I opened the door and although he had his back to me and was looking out into the street, I recognised the red hair and slouchy green cords at once.

'Oh, hey, Sully,' I said.

He turned and grinned at me shyly. 'Hey,' he said. 'Jenny said you'd be here.'

'I was just . . . sorting out some things.'

He nodded. 'Yeah. She said. I was just going to say, there are a few of us going out for a drink later. For Luke . . .'

I frowned. 'For Luke?'

Sully seemed embarrassed. 'Yeah. I don't know. It's weird.

There were just a few of us – his friends, I don't know who you know and who you don't – we were just saying that we felt helpless, but we just felt like it was right to be together. So it's sort of like a drink to . . . his health? I don't know.' He shook his head.

I smiled warmly and nodded, and Sully instantly relaxed. 'That sounds great,' I said. 'I actually haven't really met anyone properly yet so it will be nice to. And to talk about Luke.'

'Great!' Sully beamed. He seemed relieved that his idea hadn't fallen flat. There was something really very sweet about him. 'Jugglers – you know it? Halfway down Lewes Road. We thought about seven, half seven.'

I was interested to notice that I didn't feel nervous as I approached Jugglers. Normally I would have, at the prospect of meeting lots of new people in one go, and actually I thought I probably would have had I been with Luke. If I'd been heading out with him, ready to meet all his friends for the first time, then I would have felt as if I was about to be presented, wheeled out for judgement. As it was, though, as I made my way down Lewes Road I felt a certain pride. I felt, I suppose, a bit like the guest of honour. The drink was all about Luke, about moral support in the face of what had happened, and who could have been more central to that get-together than me, his girlfriend, the one who kept his heart beating when she found him in that alley? Once again I noted how nice it was to feel part of something. How it was like being allowed into a warm front room after waiting on a cold doorstep for several hours.

Sully saw me come into the pub and stood up to wave me over. He took me under his wing at once, introducing me to people from Luke's work, a couple of boys from the bike club, a girl called Daisy, who, according to Sully's introduction, was just 'in the gang – can't even remember how Luke knows her originally'.

To their credit, they made me very welcome, and to my relief, none of them questioned how long exactly I had known Luke and how it had come to be that he had a girlfriend whom none of them had heard of, much less met. In fact, a number of comments made by different people at different points in the evening led me to realise that they all seemed to blame themselves for the fact they hadn't been fully up to speed with Luke's love life.

'I realised this morning we hadn't caught up properly since November,' Pete, a man from the bike club, confessed. 'It sounds ages when you put it like that but just . . . one month turns into the next and . . .'

'Yeah. Time really does fly,' I said blandly.

'The thing was,' Daisy said, 'that Luke and I always met late doors, so by the time he turned up, I'd be wasted and could never remember the details of what we said. Anyway, we never talked about anything serious. We just . . . dicked about, you know. Played pool. I wish I'd asked him though.' She seemed sad. Wistful.

'Oh, it's OK,' I said with a reassuring smile. 'We hadn't really told people yet. It was early days.'

'Man,' Sully said suddenly, running his fingers through his hair, 'I just want him to wake up, you know? I like, lie in bed, trying to send him telepathic signals. Wake *up*.'

Daisy put her hand on Sully's. 'He will,' she said quietly.

After an hour or so, Sully suddenly said, 'Hey, we should get Jenny and Stephen down – Luke's parents – they'd like to meet you all, meet his mates. They're lovely, seriously. I've known them since I was four. They're like second parents to me.'

Enthusiastic noises were made about the idea, and Sully ducked outside to make the phone call.

Jenny and Stephen looked tired when they arrived, but I

could tell Jenny had made an effort to look nice. I could imagine the exchange that had taken place between her and Stephen at home.

Him: 'Oh I'm sure they don't want us hanging around, they don't even know us.'

Her: 'We should go, when they've gone to the trouble of inviting us. I want to meet them anyway.'

I knew that, for Jenny, the occasion would be bittersweet – exciting to have an insight into Luke's new, independent life, the one she secretly felt excluded from, but sad that it was only happening because he was unable to be there.

Sully ushered them into seats in the middle of the long table and everyone immediately swapped into their best well-mannered, parents-present behaviour, saying how sorry they were that Luke was sick and how they knew he'd pull through because he was so determined. It was funny, I thought, how everyone in any kind of medical strife was always deemed 'a fighter'. I wondered what people would be saying about me, if I was the one in hospital.

Sully gently managed to coax Jenny out of herself by leading the conversation down a sentimental but upbeat path, the two of them sharing reminisces about the scrapes Sully and Luke had got into when they were small. Stephen was quieter, and I thought he was biding his time until they could make their excuses and leave. After a while though, I heard him turn to Jenny and say quietly: 'I've texted Becky. Asked her to join us. It's not right that she's left out.'

'Oh,' Jenny said, only a brief frown betraying her real feelings. 'She can come, can she?'

Stephen nodded.

I didn't want her there, making everyone feel on edge, making me feel like I didn't belong, that I shouldn't be there, when so far that evening I'd been feeling the exact opposite.

I couldn't picture her in a pub anyway. What would she drink? I couldn't imagine her chatting. She seemed capable of only the most transactional of conversations. Maybe she won't come, I hoped.

She did come though, and what's more, she didn't come alone. She brought along with her the small man I'd seen approach her outside the café. Brendan Scott.

I noticed Stephen and Jenny share a surprised look as they crossed the room but there wasn't time to comment before the pair arrived at the table.

'Hello, sweetheart,' Stephen said, standing up and kissing Rebecca on the cheek. 'Brendan.' The two men shook hands. 'Nice to see you again.'

Chairs were shuffled around to make way for the newcomers and Pete was despatched to the bar to get drinks. Only then did Rebecca nod her head in my direction, and say to Brendan, without making eye contact with me: 'Charlotte. Luke's new girlfriend.'

At least this time the audible quotations marks around the word girlfriend were absent. She just sounded tired and flat. I wondered then, for the first time, what impression I would have had of Rebecca if I'd met her before all this had happened. I couldn't imagine she'd ever been friendly in her life, but I wondered if she might have been less outwardly hostile. Less odd.

I didn't feel as nervous around her as I had on previous occasions, and I realised this was for two reasons. Firstly, I knew that I fitted in better with the assembled company than she did. They wanted me there. They had specifically invited me. But it was also because I felt the power of having something over on her. I'd read the private correspondence between her and her brother, and I knew they'd had a disagreement. I knew there was something she wanted him to keep quiet, and although I had no idea what it all meant, I still felt that gave me an edge.

I gathered from the chat around the table that Brendan owned the bar where I already knew Rebecca worked – Jenny had pointed it out to me as we'd passed it one afternoon – and where it transpired Luke had once worked too. I listened carefully for details I should pick up on, although it sounded like Luke had left the bar some time ago.

Rebecca seemed tense. At one point she ran her eyes over me in a way that made me want to shrink inside my clothes, to pull my sleeves over my hands and retreat from her gaze.

Brendan and Rebecca sat hand in hand the whole evening. It was an unusual sight – Rebecca displaying a sign of affection, no matter how small. After a while though, I noticed Rebecca had tried to wriggle free, but that he'd pulled her hand back into his. I thought she'd try again, but instead her shoulders sank and she looked down, resigned.

It was, I thought, rather like she was scared of him.

Rebecca

Chapter 34

I hadn't wanted to join in with the awful, maudlin occasion at all and I wouldn't have, had I been on my own. I would have said I was busy or too far away or, more than likely, deleted the message from my father without replying. But Brendan had picked up my phone when the message came through. That was a habit of his – picking up my phone as if to pass it to me, then taking the opportunity to scan the essence of the message from its preview on screen. I had tried changing the settings so only the sender's name displayed before the message was opened, but Brendan demanded to know why, what I had to hide, and began one of his dreary wounded-little-boy monologues about trust and intimacy, so it just seemed easier to change it back.

'We should go,' he said, sitting forward on the sofa and looking at his watch. 'If they're all there, we should be there. We're family.'

He vacillated when it came to my family. Most often his habit was to pull me away from them, to moan that they weren't good enough. If I said I was meeting Luke he would sulk and pout and complain that he was a waste of space.

When, though, he sensed he couldn't win that way, he would go to the other extreme. He would insist on coming with me, of staying close to me at all times, of referring to us constantly as if we were one identity – what *we* thought about things, what *our* plans were. It was as if, if I was going to persist in having a family, he had to prove to them – or perhaps me – that he was more important than them now.

So we went, and it was uncomfortable and tedious, but it could have been worse.

There were enough people at the gathering that I quickly realised I could navigate the evening without contributing anything of substance, and hopefully without Brendan doing anything noteworthy either.

Sully was sitting beside my parents and tending diligently to their needs, whether fetching them drinks or listening attentively to the rambling anecdote my mother was telling about Luke trying to catch a jellyfish in an old bed sheet. Charlotte, as ever, was smiling and nodding and spouting whatever vapid twaddle came into her head, completely void of any genuine emotion. Dead behind the eyes.

There was only one moment when we properly acknowledged each other. She leant forward to retrieve an empty glass and pass it to the barmaid clearing the table, and as she did so, the sleeve of her jumper rode up her forearm just enough to reveal a bracelet – a leather cord with a metal bead engraved with the letters SFB.

SFB are the initials of both my father – Stephen Fintan Burley – and a particularly uncouth thrash metal band my brother favoured in his mid-teen years who called themselves 'Shit For Brains'. The reason I was aware of this is because some fifteen years ago, when Luke's admiration of said band was at its peak, he bought a T-shirt from a merchandise stand at a concert. The design on the T-shirt featured the band's logo – which I won't describe, but suffice it to say included a detailed illustration of both elements of the band's name – together with the initials, SFB.

One morning, our father emerged from his bedroom wearing the T-shirt, declaring that he assumed our mother had bought it for him, due to the presence of his initials. Luke – and Mum – found the spectacle highly amusing, and this was further exacerbated by Dad's stubborn refusal to accept Luke's insistent warnings regarding the true meaning of the letters.

The incident became a running joke between Dad and Luke, and at Christmas time, Luke would often present Dad with something from the Shit For Brains merchandise range, which Dad would always hold up with a feigned innocent smile and declare, 'Stephen Fintan Burley! That's me!'

The joke continued long after Luke's appreciation for the band had subsided, and Luke had already told me that for our father's upcoming birthday he had found him a bracelet.

'It's very classy and understated,' Luke had told me with a grin. 'The band have really matured.'

I hadn't seen the bracelet myself, but I found it improbable to say the least that Charlotte could, independently and co-incidently, like the obscure metal band at the heart of the joke enough to wear their products. The obvious conclusion was that this was the bracelet Luke had intended for our father, which left me with the question, why was Charlotte wearing it now?

For the entire duration of the pub outing, Brendan gripped my hand tightly like I was a helium balloon that might break free.

Chapter 35

I was finding it increasingly hard to ignore the unwelcome shift in the dynamic of my relationship with Brendan.

It was true that I had always had to tread carefully. Although we owned 50 per cent of the business each, I knew that if the club was going to be a success, it was essential that I made 100 per cent of the decisions. This had taken careful handling on my part – always making sure that Brendan felt my taking over was to save him the bother and an indication of my devotion to our joint future – but I had managed it well. Back then though, when we first started out, I knew that even when I started withdrawing from Brendan and disentangling myself from our romantic relationship, ultimately, we would still be equal shareholders. We were partners. On a level playing field.

All that had changed though, on the night of 16 December, when The Watch had held its first – and possibly last – Christmas party. Sarah Rubinstein had been found dead in her car before dawn and I knew that Brendan would always have the upper hand. It was no longer just the decision-making power I would stand to lose if I didn't keep him onside; it was my freedom. My life.

Brendan wasn't a stupid man, in the intellectual sense, but he did possess a quite breathtaking capacity for self-delusion. If he'd witnessed our relationship from the start, if he'd watched the interactions between us as a disinterested outsider, I'm sure he would have grasped the measure of the situation quite quickly, but as it was, his ego let him go on believing that I was complicated, troubled, repressed – and that this was my reason for any lack of warmth on my part – but that in spite of these flaws in my psychology, I was quite besotted with him.

Brendan seemed pleased by the evening in the pub with my parents. He tended to get a renewed confidence at times like these, as if our mutual acting as a conventional couple for a few hours had somehow moved us closer to the real thing. As if my flinching when he touched my face was just one of those things every couple goes through.

As I boiled the kettle and waited for him to leave, he buried his face in my neck.

'Shall I stay over?'

I was practised at this, at the gentle extraction of myself from any duties that were just too unappealing to bear. Instead, I said that there was a man coming to measure the bathroom in the morning to quote for retiling. It was a curious technique I'd adopted – citing random administrative and household tasks that needed to be completed as a reason for him to leave. He rarely questioned it, never seemed to wonder why a tiler in the morning meant no sleepover tonight. Thankfully he left.

Feeling a physical sense of release at finding myself free of his clammy hands, I sat on the sofa, opened my laptop and decided it was time I put some dedicated effort into finding out what I could about Charlotte Wright. It wasn't just the bracelet that bothered me, it was her expression when she realised I'd seen it. It was at once defiant and guilty, and I had a strong feeling there must be a reason for that.

I barely used Facebook and had only set up an account to allow me to gather information on other people – most recently to ascertain the character and likely wealth of potential members of The Watch. My mother's page was usually my first port of call for any research related to the family, and opening her profile now showed me she and Charlotte had become connected earlier this week. This irritated me, but did at least mean I was sure the page belonged to the correct Charlotte Wright.

I entered Charlotte's profile now, clicking on the photo of her looking windswept in front of the pier – taken herself, judging by the outstretched position of the arms. I never know why people aren't more ashamed to do that, to photograph themselves in public, letting everyone around them know how pleased they are with themselves.

As we weren't directly connected ourselves, I was limited in what I could see and was disappointed that my research looked like it wasn't going to unearth anything more interesting than a seaside photograph.

I clicked on the 'Friends' tab of the site. She didn't have many, I noticed. Although I was hardly one to gloat in that department, having only amassed around twenty myself, I was surprised. People like Charlotte, with their overfamiliarity and exaggerated expressions and disingenuous warmth, tended to approach recruiting friends like they might collect conkers on an autumn walk – seizing anything vaguely shiny and adding to the basket.

I went back to her main page and scrolled down, not quite sure what nugget of information I was hoping might appear. I found that the page came to an abrupt stop, the last post – or rather, the first – reading 'Welcome to Facebook!!' from someone called Alison Burns. Before that nothing, except 'Charlotte was born: 1990.'

I was surprised by Charlotte's late adoption of social media – I would have had her down as exactly the type to enjoy sharing the banal details of her life with an army of similarly vacant disciples.

I clicked on Luke's profile next. I'd avoided doing so since his accident, largely because seeing the photos of him cheerful and healthy, reading the exchanges between him and his friends, ribbing each other, making plans, was too painful. I knew seeing him side by side with Charlotte, ready for a night out, messing about on the beach, whatever it was they found to do together, would be at once irritating and difficult – painful to know that he'd not shared this development in his life with me – but I felt I needed to. I wanted to try to understand the dynamic between them. I wanted to know when they had met, at least.

Unlike Charlotte's page, Luke's was awash with information – photos, links, comments. Most recently there were notes from friends – some names I recognised, some I didn't – wishing Luke well, expressing concern for his health and instructing him to 'keep fighting'. All of these were addressed to Luke, as if he were in any position to read them, which seemed faintly ridiculous to me, but I suppose their intentions were good.

Further and further I scrolled, opening photos, scouring lengthy messages about curry nights and stag weekends and barbecues, but not once did I come across a photo or mention of Charlotte. Then I looked through his friend lists – which, at 345 people, put me, Charlotte and even my mother to shame – in search of her name. There were three Charlottes, but none of them Charlotte Wright. None of them *the* Charlotte.

I closed my laptop down, frowning at the wall in front of me. What was it about her? What was it about Charlotte that meant Luke wanted to keep the relationship a secret?

Chapter 36

The next morning, Brendan arrived at my flat unannounced. He was carrying cardboard cups of coffee and bacon sandwiches wrapped in brown paper bags, dripping with fat.

This was a tactic of his, I'd noticed. If he arrived without invitation empty handed, then he was aware it was an imposition and as such I was within my rights to tell him it wasn't convenient. If, however, he arrived bearing offerings – like a cat bringing home a decapitated mouse after a night's hunting – then it wasn't an inconvenience but a 'surprise' and I was etiquette-bound to admit him.

'Tile bloke been yet?' he said, dropping the greasy packets onto my worktop.

I picked them up and put them on a plate. 'Later,' I said. 'He's running late.'

As Brendan busied about in the kitchen decanting coffee into mugs, I sat by the window and looked out wistfully at the horizon, as if lost in thought. I was hoping that if I appeared distracted and unresponsive to his attempts at charm, he'd be disappointed or annoyed and leave.

He pulled over a side table and sat on it in front of me.

He put his hands on my upper arms, forcing me to look at him.

'What is it, sweetheart?' he said. 'What's on your mind?'

I paused for a moment, wanting to tell him that the table he was sitting on wasn't designed to be used as a chair and that he should get off it before the legs buckled, but I decided it didn't matter for the time being because there was something else that was annoying me more.

'Luke,' I said, for once not trying to hide my irritation. 'Obviously, Luke is on my mind, Brendan.'

Brendan flinched at the implicit accusation of insensitivity. He did so pride himself on being sensitive and attuned to my feelings.

He nodded slowly. 'Of course, honey. Of course, I know it's Luke. I meant, what specifically? What are you thinking?'

I threw my hands up, exasperated by this obtuse line of questioning. 'Oh, I don't know! When's he going to wake up? *Is* he going to wake up? How long will this go on for? What do you expect me to be thinking?'

Brendan blinked again, but this time his face darkened. I rarely spoke to him like this. I was calm usually. I always fed him the lines he was expecting. It was easier that way. And it was safer.

'Well, don't snap at *me* about it.' He stood up and roughly pulled the side table back to where it had originally stood.

It took considerable self-control on my part not to hit back at this point – to remind him that when my brother was in hospital with a brain injury, the tone of voice I took with Brendan and whether it upset his sensibilities was very far from my main priority. Instead though, I took a breath and let my sense of reason guide my words. 'Sorry.' I wrestled my voice into a conciliatory tone. 'It's just a worrying time.'

I went back to looking distractedly out of the window, and

Brendan came over, put his hand on my shoulder and sat down on the arm of the chair beside me. 'You know,' he began, 'maybe it's for the best, in a way. Try to see the silver lining.'

I jerked my head around to look at him.

'I just mean,' Brendan said, 'all this business he'd started up about talking to Daniel Rubinstein. It was just like him, wasn't it – naïve, childish. Maybe it's for the best, that he's having a bit of . . . enforced downtime. Maybe it's better for all of us that he's not in a position to go running—'

'Shut up, Brendan,' I said. My voice was quite calm, perfectly measured, but deadly serious.

Brendan's brow twitched. He closed his eyes briefly, then he looked at me carefully, his head tilted downwards. I thought he was going to protest, to continue to talk, to hack away at his terrible point, trying to make it sound acceptable. But instead he got up. He put his mug down on my coffee table, and stood in front of me.

'I'm not too happy about you speaking to me like that actually,' he said, in a light, calm voice that was markedly eerier than any of his attempts at menace. 'I've noticed it quite a bit lately. More than I'd like. You're taking me for granted. You're not showing me any basic respect.'

'I don't—'

He cut me off. 'I've tried to be understanding because I know you haven't yet developed healthy coping mechanisms for stress, but I'm only human. I won't put up with it indefinitely.'

'What's your point?' It sounded more aggressive than I'd intended. I intended it as a genuine question; a request for clarification.

'My point,' he said slowly, 'is that you need to remember what you owe me. What I've done for you. Not many men would let their women have the run of things at work that I let you have. And not many men would keep their women's secrets as reliably as I have for you.'

I looked at him. 'What?'

'You always seem to forget that I know exactly as much as Luke knows. You've been so busy fussing about what he's going to do, what he's going to say, that you've forgotten what I could say if I wanted to. I wouldn't, obviously. Because, unlike Luke, I know when to keep my mouth shut. I know what's at stake.' He moved over to the window and looked out, his arms folded. 'But you might want to consider everything I've done for you. To protect you. The lengths I've gone to, to keep your secret.'

He turned and looked at me, giving me a wide, forced smile that didn't reach his eyes. Then he picked up his bag and quite calmly walked out of the flat, closing the door quietly behind him.

When he'd gone, I stepped through my lounge window onto the flat patch of roof I used a terrace, despite being expressly forbidden to do so by the terms of the lease. I sat there for a while, with my hands resting on my knees watching a pair of seagulls scavenge in the bins in the street below. It occurred to me – as it had many times before – that it would be so relaxing to stand up, to take two steps forward, to feel the air rush past, and then for everything to go black.

I went back into the flat and picked my phone up from my desk. I navigated to the *Sussex News* article that I kept bookmarked in my browser, for no reason that I'd yet been able to discern. Its headline read, 'Journalist dies in Christmas party horror crash', and the photograph was dominated by the blue lights of emergency services vehicles. Behind them, it was just possible to see the outline of the figure on a stretcher. The figure of the woman who had, just two hours earlier, been sitting at a table talking to me.

I replayed what Brendan had said. He'd been quite clear: he knew the consequences if the truth about the evening with Sarah Rubinstein came out – perhaps he'd done some legal research of his own, although I found it hard to imagine – and he was keen to protect me from those consequences. I didn't doubt this was true, not because I believed it would genuinely pain him to see me come to harm, but because, if the secret became common knowledge, it would mean the end of our arrangement – our 'relationship' – so his commitment to protecting me was a thinly veiled declaration of his intent to protect himself.

All this I was clear about, so despite Brendan's threat – his 'reminder' – that he too had the power to divulge my secret, I felt confident he never would. In fact, I believed him when he said he would go to any lengths to stop anyone else doing so.

But with the only person with the potential to talk silenced by a blow to the head, I had to consider exactly what lengths Brendan had been referring to.

Chapter 37

At the hospital the following day I was surprised, and somewhat irked, to find that things were positively jolly around Luke's bedside.

Mum was gabbling away about the bizarre music compilation project Charlotte had come up with, which seemed to serve no purpose other than keeping Mum occupied with long and meandering trips down memory lane as she unearthed some new inconsequential happening from Luke's youth, declared it 'a real milestone' and duly assigned it a music clip designed to tap into Luke's deep unconscious.

'Isn't the idea that Luke wears the headphones, rather than you?' I asked, raising what was surely an obvious point. Mum's smile immediately fell though and, as she transferred the ear buds from her own ears to Luke's, Charlotte shot me a look of reproach, as if she had any business passing judgement on how I spoke to my own mother.

Mum muttered something about going to look for the nurse and hurried out, leaving me and Charlotte alone. I had already decided after my foray into her scant social media presence that direct questioning was the only route available to me, and that I should put this into action at the first available opportunity.

'How long exactly have you known my brother?' I said. Then, lest there be any confusion about the type of association I was interested in, I followed it up with, 'How long have you been a couple?'

There was a look of consternation on Charlotte's face as if I'd asked her a question that required a great deal of soul-searching and analysis to answer, rather than the recall of a simple piece of empirical data.

'Well,' she said, turning back to Luke, ostensibly to moisten his mouth with the damp sponge the nurse had given us for the purpose, 'it's hard to pinpoint the exact moment with stuff like that.'

I kept my eyes trained on the back of her head, so when she turned back she would be forced to meet my eye immediately. 'Try,' I said.

But she didn't say anything. She just continued to prod and stroke and fuss over Luke as if I hadn't said anything at all. Then, before I could press the issue, the rotund nurse with the greying ponytail arrived and Charlotte took the opportunity to invent some spurious question to shut down our conversation.

However, in many ways, her lack of response was all the information I needed. When she left the ward with the nurse in search of some piece of apparatus, I sat in the chair at Luke's bedside and considered my position.

Charlotte had irritated me from the outset, but I felt there was sufficient evidence now for me to believe that my issue with her wasn't the result of bad temper or unjustified intolerance on my part. I wasn't happy about the way she had placed herself centre stage with my family – she was living with them, for goodness' sake – but I had known people to

177

foist themselves on others due to an embarrassing lack of boundaries before. That in itself wasn't necessarily suspect. But then there was the bracelet, and the fact that, as far as I could tell, she had only conjured herself into existence a few months earlier. And now her inability to answer what should have been, if the situation was as innocent and straightforward as she claimed, a perfectly simple question.

It was then that I decided: it wasn't just that I didn't like her. I didn't trust her.

Charlotte

Chapter 38

It put me on edge, Rebecca being so directly confrontational with her questions.

I'd established she was cold right from the beginning, and soon after that that she didn't like me specifically. It didn't bother me too much. Number one because I was used to rubbing people like her up the wrong way. I'd known people like Rebecca all my life, who flinched when you tried to touch them, who looked away when you smiled, like they literally had no idea how to respond to basic human friendliness. But it was also because I knew that in our current world – the current world featuring Stephen and Jenny, and revolving around Luke and the hospital – I was ranked higher than her. She may have been a blood relative, but it didn't take a relationship psychologist to see that her place in the family was an awkward one. I suppose that was why, as each day passed, her vendetta against me seemed to grow.

It was worrying though, her choosing that particular question, wanting to unpick the details of my connection to Luke. Jenny and Stephen had asked before, of course, but from Rebecca, it had felt pointed, like she was trying to unsettle me.

It was actually the first time that I'd got the feeling that anyone suspected mine and Luke's relationship was anything other than what I'd said it was. I'd been vague with Jenny and Stephen about the details, so although they knew it was a relatively recent development, they hadn't demanded exact details of specific milestones. Because of this, I'd never stopped to work them out. I'd never, even in my own head, pinned down what I would consider to be our first meeting, or at what point we'd become an official couple. It hardly mattered anyway. Everyone knew that traumatic events like what had happened to us over the last week gave couples a closeness that even those who'd been together for months or years hadn't yet achieved.

I was just tending to Luke to buy myself a few moments to compose a timeline when the nurse came by and I took the opportunity to leave the ward with her, hoping that by the time I returned, Rebecca's interrogation would have lost momentum.

When I came back though, I found Rebecca exactly where she'd been before, and she picked up the conversation as if I'd never left.

'A month?' she said, following me around the cubicle with her eyes as I tidied up. 'Two months? Six?'

'I'm not—'

'Because,' she went on, 'I'm wondering why there's no evidence of your relationship. Not one person who's seen you together. Not a single photo on Facebook.'

'I'm not sure what you're trying to say.' I felt my eyes fill with tears – real tears – at the surprise of being ambushed like that.

Reykjavik, Helsinki, Oslo.

'It seems to me,' she went on, her voice steady and emotionless as ever, 'that you're very at home playing the part of the carer. It puts me in mind of those parents who manufacture maladies in their children simply to place themselves at the centre of attention, to elicit sympathy from those around them. Something warped like that.'

I just stared at her. I just couldn't fathom how she had so quickly, and so accurately, got the measure of the situation.

Tallinn, Stockholm, Moscow. No! Riga.

I felt my only option was to play dumb, to pretend I couldn't compute what she was saying.

'But . . . how could I have made it up?' I gestured to Luke, in his bed. 'He's clearly injured, you can see it with your own . . .' I shook my head in bafflement. 'What do you even *mean*?'

Rebecca rolled her eyes. 'I'm not suggesting the medical situation has been inflated, just the significance of your role in it.' When I didn't reply at once, she seemed to become impatient. 'What I mean is that I think you've significantly overplayed the seriousness of your relationship with Luke because you're enjoying the attention.'

I stared at her, my mouth open. It was such a serious, such a *nasty* accusation to throw at someone – someone who really hadn't done anything objectively wrong – without any evidence of it being true.

I could hear a buzzing sound in my ears, the one I always get when I start to feel things slipping away from me, when I start to feel like I'm losing control.

Moscow, Copenhagen, Vilnius.

When I know I'm being treated badly but I can't work out how to take back the reins, how to get things back on course.

Minsk, Dublin, Berlin.

But then – and I don't know where from – I had an idea. A spark of inspiration that quickly took hold and became a solid possibility. There was a very obvious explanation that would cut Rebecca's suspicions right down.

'There was someone else,' I said. 'Another man.'

Chapter 39

'What?' Rebecca said. She looked irritated. 'What man?'

And so I explained. I explained it all, making up the details as I went, drawing on inspiration from my life, from friends' lives, from books I'd read and snippets of conversation I'd overheard on trains.

I told her that I had been in a long-term relationship with another man – 'someone from school' – but that Luke and I had met, and had a connection immediately, and realised we wanted to be together, but that it had taken some time to officially wind things up in my old relationship, and in the meantime, Luke and I had had to be discreet.

'Why?' Rebecca demanded, clearly unconcerned by the thought that all this might not be any of her business. 'You meet someone new, you end the previous relationship. What's so complicated? You weren't married, were you?'

I sighed and frowned. It was no surprise to me that Rebecca should see everything in such a black and white way. If I hadn't seen Brendan with my own eyes, I would doubt she had ever been in a relationship with anyone more significant than her pinstripe pencil skirt.

'It was difficult,' I said quietly. 'He was . . . sensitive. He had mental health issues. I couldn't risk upsetting him.'

'So where is he now?' she said, looking around us, one hand on her hip. 'Doesn't he wonder where you are while you're loitering around the hospital, making yourself at home with my parents?'

I opened my eyes wide. 'Oh, it's over now. It was over before Luke's accident. But even once it was, Luke and I planned to keep things low-key for a while. I didn't want to splash it all over Facebook. I didn't want to rub Kai's nose in it.'

I took myself by surprise, choosing that name, of all the names I could have plucked from the air. It was interesting – funny almost – that my subconscious had delivered Kai's name to me.

Kai was certainly real, as had been our relationship, although it had long been over by the time Luke entered my life. Kai was a figure very much from my past.

I'd met him not long after I'd decided to leave my home town for good, when I'd moved into a draughty, chaotic house-share, full of other people like me – striking out on our own for the first time, trying to break our way into adult life with what few skills and resources we had at our disposal. We'd had fun at first, in that house, despite the mould covering the ceilings and the steady diet of instant noodles. Kai taught me how to roll cigarettes, an activity I approached as a kind of craft project, never smoking them, just enjoying the feeling of the paper in my fingers, perfecting a uniform cylinder. We'd stay up late watching strange European films I never really understood, and he would talk at length about things like why it was sociologically impossible to create real art if you were being paid for it.

In retrospect, I can see that he wasn't particularly interested in me at all, and really, there wasn't much to like about him, but I'd been lost and lonely and clung to him too hard. He wasn't the kind of man to find any kind of neediness appealing so the harder I'd tried to please him, the further he'd retreated.

I'd tried a few different approaches to reignite his interest in me – initially playing the part of the attentive housewife, hoovering his bedroom for him and delivering a mug of instant coffee to his bedside as soon as his alarm went off each morning. When this didn't work I'd tried to rebrand myself as wild and spontaneous, mixing vodka and sodas at eleven in the morning, painting my entire bedroom scarlet, spending a month's rent on a second-hand saxophone on a whim. When this too prompted sighs of exasperation rather than the declaration of love I'd been hoping for, I decided, in a last desperate attempt to make him see what was right in front of him, to abscond for a few days, hoping that the absence would somehow make his heart grow fonder.

The plan backfired. The frantic search organised by my housemates – who thought I'd come to some real harm, while in reality I sat in a single room in the basement of a Travelodge off the A23 – was the final straw, not just for Kai but for the whole flat, and they asked me to move out. I haven't seen any of them since.

Rebecca offered no real response to my story of infidelity. If she judged me for it, it wasn't obvious from her face. If anything, I sensed she was slightly disappointed that I'd been able to explain away her accusations. I suppose people like Rebecca love to have someone to hate. Love to have a reason to mistrust them.

Whether the conversation between us would have gone any further I don't know, because at that moment, Anne Moriarty, the consultant neurosurgeon, came walking briskly down the corridor, her glasses in one hand, a paper file in the other.

'Good, you're here,' she said without a smile. 'Are Mum and Dad around?'

It made me smile, her referring to Jenny and Stephen in that way, as if those were their actual names.

'They're just downstairs,' Rebecca said.

'Can you call them up?' Anne Moriarty said. 'I'd like to have a little catch-up, to assess where we are.'

Rebecca

Chapter 40

Once my parents had been summoned and Anne Moriarty had herded them into the relatives' room, my mother fussing and clucking about, thinking she'd left her phone in the canteen and then realising she hadn't, and saying over and over again, 'What's happened? Has something happened?', she took a seat in front of us.

'In some ways,' she began, 'there's not much I can tell you. As you've been able to see for yourselves, very little has changed since those first twenty-four hours. I must be honest with you though, the fact that there has been so little improvement after this length of time is worrying.'

Dad sat forward in his chair. 'Worrying how?'

'We still wouldn't rule out the possibility of some recovery,' Anne Moriarty went on, 'but as each day passes the chances lessen.'

'What?' Mum said. 'What do you mean?'

'Yes, what do you mean?' Dad said. '"Possibility", "Some recovery" – what are you saying?'

'If there is only the possibility of recovery, then there is, presumably, the possibility of what?' I said. 'No recovery?'

Anne Moriarty nodded slowly. 'That is one possibility.'

Mum looked at her, open mouthed. 'What, you mean, this is it? That's how he'll stay, just lying in that bed?' I heard the wobble in her voice.

'Are you sure?' Dad said, sounding sceptical suddenly, like Anne Moriarty might have put forward this prognosis as a dark prank. 'It seems clear to me that he's getting better all the time. Just compare the state of him when he came out of surgery that first night to how he looks now!'

Anne Moriarty nodded again. 'Yes, the physical scars from the operation are healing nicely. But the brain, I'm afraid, is more complex.'

No one said anything for a moment. Mum and Dad looked at each other, clearly unable to accept that this message could be true. Charlotte reached out for Mum's hand.

I too was struck dumb. I suppose we had all been labouring under the assumption that we were on an upward trajectory, however shallow, and that the outcome would ultimately be positive. Or an improvement on the current state of affairs, at least. To hear that there was a chance that we'd already plateaued, that we may never emerge from this dark tunnel, seemed almost too bleak to comprehend.

Chapter 41

The evening after Anne Moriarty had delivered her dismal warning, the police sergeant in charge of Luke's case, DS Leech, paid me a visit in my flat.

I assumed – naively perhaps – that, as a member of Luke's immediate family, the visit was a courtesy call to keep me updated on the investigation. However, when my initial queries around whether they had been able to identify any possible culprits or if they had discovered anything at all of relevance over the last week and a half were evaded with vague comments about 'various lines of enquiry', I realised that DS Leech had no particular interest in explaining herself to me. It was then that she revealed the true purpose of her visit.

'Would I be right in saying you're in a relationship with Brendan Scott, who owns the private members club where you work?'

I frowned. It was never something I was keen to admit to. 'Yes, of sorts.'

She looked like she was going to query that qualification but decided to let it go for now.

'And Luke, too, worked at the club, for a time?'

I nodded. 'He left last year.'

DS Leech nodded and looked out of the window for a moment. Then she said, 'And Luke and Brendan didn't get on?'

'What makes you say that?'

'We've heard that relations were frequently strained, and that on one occasion Brendan threatened to kill Luke?'

My initial reaction was to curse Sully for reporting this inconvenient detail to the police, but I then realised it was quite possible that Luke had told a number of his friends about the row, and that any one of them could have passed it on.

I rolled my eyes to demonstrate how trivial the issue was, and how preposterous I found the suggestion that it could have any bearing on her investigation. 'I hardly think that everyone who utters the words "I could kill him" as a display of exasperation should be suspected of violent crime.'

'Perhaps not, but then it's not common for the subject of that casual threat to be hospitalised with a catastrophic brain injury a few months later.'

I didn't say anything. There was a certain logic to her point.

'Anyway,' she went on, her tone breezy now, 'it should be quite easy to clear up. Do you know what Brendan was doing last night Saturday night? The night Luke was attacked?'

I shrugged. 'You'd have to ask him.'

'Yes, we did. He said he was with you.'

I nodded, as if quite unruffled by this news. 'Well, then there's your answer.'

'You can confirm that he was with you?' She wasn't, I noticed, giving any clues as to what Brendan had claimed we were doing together that evening, or where we'd been doing it.

'I would need to check my records.'

She raised her eyebrows. 'You keep a record of when you meet your boyfriend?'

'I have work schedules. I have a diary of appointments.'

'You can't remember what you doing one evening last week? The evening you later got the news your brother was seriously injured?'

I sighed. 'I see Brendan a lot. Every day. I'm sure I saw him that day, yes. I can't remember though, the exact time we met nor the precise duration of our time together. As I say, I will check my records.'

DS Leech nodded. 'OK,' she said. 'When you have, please give me a call.'

As soon as the woman was out of my flat, I sank down against the door and pulled my knees to my chest.

The uneasiness I'd been feeling since Brendan's suggestion that it may a good thing that Luke had been silenced had now been amplified to fear. Why would Brendan tell her he'd been with me? It may have fended off DS Leech for a while, but he surely knew she would report this claim back to me? Was this Brendan's way of letting me know what he'd done?

Was this an indirect admission on his part, one that only I would understand?

Chapter 42

That night I checked my mother's Facebook page as I'd begun to realise that I could glean more about Luke's condition, and my parents' reaction to it, from her daily posts and the subsequent conversations with the commenters below than I could from attempting to speak with them directly. On this occasion, my review was cut short when I read the most recent post Mum had made that day.

Not many blessings to count lately but one blessing I'm truly grateful for is Charlotte Wright. That girl is keeping us going.

'Idiot!' I said out loud, slamming my laptop shut. What was it about my mother that made her so shallow? So seduced by bright smiles and pink lipstick? Couldn't she at least pretend to look a bit further below the surface? To dedicate the same effort to her blood relatives? The people she'd known their whole lives?

It was several hours later, as I lay awake, watching my

bedside clock march steadily from one a.m. to two to three, that the idea came upon me.

There was, I realised, a clear strategy that would allow me to kill two birds with one stone. Or if not kill, then perhaps cause some useful damage.

It was clear I needed to divert the police's attention away from Brendan. Although it still wasn't clear whether his intimation that he was responsible for Luke's attack was just one of his mind games or something I should take more seriously, what *was* clear was that I needed to remove him from the police's spotlight. Any line of investigation that placed Brendan at its centre would be sure to look for his motives, and that carried a very real risk that my own misdeeds may come to light.

If, of course, it transpired that Brendan *had* had anything to do with Luke's attack, then I would make quite sure he was punished – and far more thoroughly than the official channels may be able to manage. It had occurred to me recently that it would be quite possible to make a man like Brendan disappear altogether and that very few people would notice, much less care. But first, I needed to divert DS Leech away from him.

One option was to play along with Brendan's false alibi, but I sensed an afterthought corroboration from his girlfriend may not be enough to extinguish the police's suspicions entirely. What I really needed, I decided, as the idea began to crystallise, was to set the investigation on another path altogether. To hand them a different suspect to distract them from looking too closely at Brendan. And what better suspect than this woman who, as far as I could tell, had materialised from the ether on the very night in question?

It was merely a bonus that any suggestion by the police,

however unfounded, that Charlotte was a person of interest in their inquiry would be sure to lower her in my parents' regard as well. Even if she was subsequently cleared of any wrongdoing, my parents would realise they barely knew her at all, and that the sensible course of action would be to cool relations.

'There's no smoke without fire,' my mother was fond of saying, so all I had to do was conjure up a little smoke.

Chapter 43

I woke up on my sofa, having attempted to send myself to sleep with the all-night news channel, to find that at some point, Brendan had let himself into the flat, and was slipping himself onto the sofa, gently placing my feet in his lap.

'Hi,' he said when I opened my eyes. 'I didn't mean to wake you.'

I pushed myself up groggily. 'What are you doing here?'

He had taken the liberty some weeks ago of cutting himself a key, and frequently took the further liberty of using it whenever he chose. I had yet to risk tension by raising my objections to this.

'Just wanted to see how you are. Thought I should stay for a bit.' He nodded at his leather holdall on the floor. 'Keep an eye on you, make sure you're OK.'

I hadn't contacted him since he'd stormed out on Sunday. The fact he was back now, acting in this conciliatory way, suggested that he was starting to grow anxious about this. He generally liked to wait for me to come to him, to make it very clear that if there were olive branches to be extended, it was my role to be extending them. But if I held my nerve and bided my time – or if I'd other, more important things on my mind, as I did this week – he would start to panic and begin creeping around again.

Usually I was relieved as I really couldn't afford to have him offside and, if he initiated the reconciliation, it was one less thing to have to sort out. Today though, although I knew it was for the best that he was keen to move past our row, I just couldn't bear the thought of him there. I was overcome with a feeling of suffocation, like a weight on my chest. The thought of him loitering in the flat all day, trimming his toenails with my kitchen scissors. The thought of him in my bed all night. The way he always smelt like sour milk in the morning.

'No,' I said, standing up. 'No. I don't want you here.'

He frowned, offended. 'Why, honey? I just want to be here for you. I know you've had a tough time. I just want to be—'

'No,' I said again. Then – something I rarely do – I shouted. '*No!*'

His expression contracted quickly, from surprise to anger. He stood up slowly, nodding, like he was taking my views on board.

Then he turned to me and said, in a low quiet voice: 'Why do you always have to be such a little bitch? Why can't you be normal?'

He took a step towards me. Instinctively I moved towards the wall.

'I covered for you. I was willing to lie for you even when your own family wasn't. You've got no idea how far I've put myself out to keep your secret. No idea.'

He picked up his holdall and walked to the front door. I followed him to the hallway.

'What did you do?' I said. 'What did you do to Luke?'

He put his hand on the handle.

'What did you do?' I said again, my voice louder this time.

200

He looked up at me, spit gathering at the corners of his mouth, but he didn't reply. Instead, he left, letting the door slam behind him.

Charlotte

Chapter 44

What Anne Moriarty said about Luke's recovery – or lack of – marked a real change in atmosphere in the family. I'd been shocked myself. I hadn't expected the official message to take such a dramatic downward turn.

Up until that point we'd been making progress, we'd been moving forward. That had been the belief anyway. It was true there had been little discernible change in Luke's condition but I think all of us had been under the impression that behind the scenes, behind those closed eyes, his body was busy healing, repairing itself, and one day his eyes would flicker open, he'd wake up, sit up and be a person amongst us once again.

We hadn't discussed the timescales or specifics of this miraculous recovery but we all – Jenny in particular – spoke of a future Luke who was, to all intents and purposes, exactly the same person as the Luke she had always known.

I had been aware that we were erring on the side of optimism, and I could tell from the doubtful look on Stephen's face when Jenny spoke brightly of plans for the future that he knew this too. But really, in the absence of any solid information to the contrary, it had seemed the best way to be. Now though, Anne Moriarty had pulled all of our heads roughly out of the sand. We could no longer ignore the grim possibility that things might never get better.

Or, at least, that's what I thought she'd done.

Jenny though, within ten minutes of the meeting's abrupt ending, shook off her shock and replaced it with something else. Something defiant.

The interpretation of the doctor's words she had obviously chosen to run with was that they had begun to lose patience with Luke. That they had set a limit on the length of time they would give him to show progress, and that as this was beginning to expire, they weren't prepared to keep expending resources on him. The way she spoke was as if she imagined there to be someone in a glass-walled office somewhere on the top floor of the hospital, studying a spread sheet of cost/benefit calculations, and that Luke's row in the table had turned red. He was no longer a good investment.

'I know my son,' Jenny said. 'No one knows a boy like his mother. And that counts for more than any of their scans and textbooks and beeping bloody machines!'

It was clear that this reaction was a simple defence mechanism on Jenny's part. It gave her a new role to play – that of protective mother, fighting the system to look after her son. I sensed Stephen doubted the wisdom of this stance but that he felt he didn't have any option but to support his wife, or risk finding himself in the firing line too.

All of this went unspoken, a silent undercurrent running beneath the day to day conversations about how and when we were going to meet, collecting groceries for the house, anecdotes about the hospital and about any small events – a twitch of a finger, a flush of colour to the cheeks – that could be wheeled out and inflated until it could be held aloft as evidence that progress was being made, despite what the doctors said.

At first, I went along with all this, knowing that my role in the situation was to support Jenny. If she was already feeling panicked and powerless, siding with the hospital in their gloomy prognosis would only make her feel worse.

As time went on though, as Jenny began to show me articles covering court cases where relatives of the gravely ill had challenged doctors' decisions, as she began to stay up late, trawling through articles on her iPad about Chinese medicine, Reiki, anything at all that suggested there was still something to fight for, I began to realise that I should stop taking the path of least resistance. I realised that siding with Jenny, indulging her indignation and determination, probably wasn't beneficial to her in any real sense.

Since the beginning of the whole situation, the reason I'd been able to hold my head up despite the white lies I'd told them was because I felt my unique position allowed me to play a valuable role in helping carry them through this nightmare. With this in mind, wasn't it exactly my role to step in with advice when I could see my slightly removed standpoint made me best placed to give it? When I could see that they were too close to the situation, to Luke, to see clearly?

I wanted to bring up the subject with them gently, to open the door for them to begin to consider that Anne Moriarty might have said what she had in good faith. That they might need to start to think realistically about how the situation was going to unfold, and how they were going to cope with it, rather than simply denying that things might not turn out as they hoped.

I was nervous though. I knew that as fully as Jenny had embraced me as part of the family, we hadn't known each other long. I was worried that if I showed any signs of dissent, I would be ejected, and I'd find myself once again alone – not to mention homeless.

Chapter 45

It was Sully, in the end, whom I turned to for advice.

'He might never wake up,' I said, within a few minutes of us sitting down on the bench outside the Aquarium where we'd agreed to meet. 'That's what they think. Some people don't. They can keep him alive with the machines – breathing for him, pumping food directly to his stomach – but there's a good chance he'll never be Luke again. Not really.'

Sully blinked and swallowed. 'Shit.'

I gave him a moment to take this in. 'I know.'

'How are Jenny and Stephen?' he asked.

I shook my head sadly. 'Angry. I think it's denial. Jenny's using this kind of . . . rage at the hospital to keep her going.'

Sully nodded thoughtfully and stirred his drink with his straw. 'Probably not really who she should be angry at.'

'How do you mean?' In a brief flash of paranoia, I thought perhaps Sully was about to accuse me of something.

'I mean, what are the police doing? Be angry at them, maybe. They haven't come up with any answers yet. But then, no actually – be angry at the wanker who did this to him. That's who they're really angry at. They need a name, a face, to blame this on. Then they can stop being mad at a bunch of doctors and nurses who are just doing their best.'

'Yeah.' I sighed and sat back in my chair. 'I guess you're right.'

The police and their investigation had taken a relatively low profile in the post-accident life of the Burley family. I myself had visited the police station and gone through the formal process of recording my statement about how and where I found Luke, confirming that I had seen no one in the area, nor had seen anything that I suspected could be a discarded weapon nearby. I'd heard reports from Stephen – who checked in with them from time to time – that they were talking to other potential witnesses, checking CCTV footage, but nothing of any substance had been discovered – as far as we knew anyway.

I suppose I'd assumed this would be one of the many crimes that go unsolved and that, anyway, given that the culprit was likely to be found to have been some down-and-out, someone after Luke's phone to sell for drugs money, I wasn't sure what difference it would make to anyone to know which particular down-and-out it was. Now, though, talking to Sully, it suddenly occurred to me that maybe it *would* make a difference. Not practically, in terms of Luke's health, but to Jenny and to Stephen who perhaps, as Sully said, needed someone to blame more than I had realised.

'I just assumed they'd get him. The one who did it,' Sully went on. 'But I suppose real life isn't like that. The good guy doesn't always make it. The bad guy doesn't always get caught.'

I nodded sadly, and we sat in silence for a while.

'The only thing is,' Sully said carefully. 'The thing I keep thinking . . .' He stopped and looked out to sea, his eyes narrowed.

'What?' I prompted.

He turned to look at me. 'A while ago, a few months – maybe even before you met him, I don't know – Luke and I went out one night, just for a few beers. And when we got back, he was being weird. He was saying he had this secret. Maybe he didn't use the word secret at first, but he said there was something. Something that was eating him up. I think those were his words. He was drunk, but not that drunk, so it was weird. Anyway, I said, "What are you on about, mate?" but he was being all vague and mysterious. And then he seemed to think better of it, saying like, "Forget I said anything" and all that. And the one thing he did say – and I remember this – was, "It's not my secret to tell anyway."'

I nodded slowly. 'When was this?'

'Sometime around February, I think. Anyway, so I had no idea what he could've been talking about. But then Rebecca told me the other day, about you and . . .' Sully seemed awkward suddenly. 'Like, not judging or anything, but about you and your other boyfriend, who you were still seeing when you met Luke.'

I could just imagine Rebecca running to Sully with this little piece of gossip, no doubt pleased with herself at being able to pass on news of my bad character.

'And so I was wondering,' Sully said carefully. 'Maybe *that's* what Luke had been talking about, when he said he had a secret, but that it was someone else's? Was he going to tell me about you, but he decided that the secret was really yours because you were the one . . .'

'Cheating?' I finished for him.

'Well,' he said. 'Yeah,' He looked down, embarrassed. He pushed his hands into his anorak pocket.

I processed this piece of information for a moment. Obviously, I knew that Luke's secret wasn't anything to do with me, but was there any benefit in letting Sully think there was? No, I decided, there wasn't. I was curious to know what secret Luke had been referring to as much as anyone, and we'd never be able to work it out if Sully wrote it off as a simple reference to our secret relationship.

I shook my head. 'Things hadn't . . . begun in February,' I said. 'He wasn't talking about me.'

Sully pushed his lips together and nodded slowly. 'Yes. That's what I thought.'

'Really?' I was surprised. I'd assumed that's exactly what he'd thought. 'Why?'

'Because later, when I was just leaving, and he'd had another few drinks by then, a good few rums actually, he said something like, "Sorry, mate. Sorry to be weird. It's just Rebecca, you know, she's my sister. She'd kill me." And I was like, "You what, mate?" but then he just wandered back into the flat and I went home and well, that was that really. We never spoke about it again.'

'So you think his secret was about Rebecca?' I said, still frowning. 'He thought she'd *kill* him?'

Sully just shrugged. 'Nah. No. Not really. It's just an expression, isn't it, "she'll kill me" – doesn't mean literally kill, does it? But it just made me think: I wonder if Luke was involved in something I didn't know about. I wonder if he was in trouble.'

Chapter 46

When I arrived back at the house, Stephen was in the front garden, wearing a pair of grubby gardening gloves and snipping away at a large camellia bush.

'Oh hello, love,' he said when he saw me. He nodded towards the bush. 'Just doing a bit of nip and tuck for Arlette. Seems the least we can do is keep the place in order.'

I let myself in through the gate.

'Jenny's just inside,' he said. 'She's just back from the hospital. I'm sure she'd welcome a tea, if not something stronger.'

It was gin Jenny requested, when I found her standing at the window looking out at the back garden.

'A proper strong G and T,' she said, pulling off her jacket and putting it on the back of a chair. 'I'm going to sit on that bench, in that patch of sun, and pretend just for five minutes that none of this is happening.'

I nodded, directed her to go and take her seat, and told her I'd bring the drink out to her.

As I poured the gin into one of Arlette's tall, gold-rimmed glasses, the ice from the dispenser on the front of the huge fridge jangling in the glass, I stopped for a moment and stood perfectly still. The kitchen radio was on, turned down low, playing some kind of easy-listening soul music. Out the front of the house I could hear the clink of Stephen's secateurs, the rustle of the black sack at his feet as he filled it with debris.

I went to the utility room to fetch the tonic and as I came back into the kitchen, I heard voices in the front garden. With Jenny's drink still in my hand, I crept closer to the window, hovering behind the curtains so I could hear what was going on without being seen. I couldn't see her but I didn't need to; there was no mistaking Rebecca's crisp tone.

'I think you're being very unfair, Becs,' Stephen was saying in reply.

'I think I'm being perfectly rational and responding to the facts as I see them. Unlike Mum, I know that it takes more than a bright smile and clean hair to prove a person's integrity.'

I felt my heart thud. It was obvious who she was talking about. Although Rebecca had made no secret of the fact she had little time for me, I'd never heard her voice her objections out loud before – I'd never heard her report them to Jenny or Stephen.

Stephen sighed. 'It's not really like that. Your mum's no fool. Charlotte's been very good to her, to both of us, through all this.'

Rebecca made a snorting noise. 'I would like to believe that Mum's no fool but unfortunately sometimes she makes that very hard.' She paused and lowered her voice. Then she said: 'I don't trust her, Dad. And really, what makes you think *you* should?'

'Why wouldn't I, Becs? What exactly is it that she's done to rub you up the wrong way? If there's something you think we don't know, by all means show us the light.'

'Do you not think it's a coincidence that she just happened

to stumble into the alley where Luke was found? Doesn't it strike you as a little far fetched that she just *happened* to turn up, immediately after he'd been attacked, the timing exactly right for her to be able to intervene to save his life, but without being able to provide any useful information on what had happened to him to get him into that state in the first place?'

'Now, listen,' Stephen said, his voice louder now. 'You're the one being far fetched. You're talking absolute nonsense, throwing around accusations with nothing whatsoever to base them on. Your mum doesn't need this, on top of everything. I don't need it. You either go inside, be civil to Charlotte, be supportive of your mum, or you go home. And come back when you can be reasonable.'

'Fine,' Rebecca responded, as cool and as calm as ever.

The crash of the front gate closing behind her told me which of the options she'd chosen.

Chapter 47

Despite my shock – my indignation – at hearing Rebecca accuse me so explicitly of being dishonest, at having it confirmed just how deep her contempt for me went, as I headed through the house and out of the back door to deliver Jenny her drink, I actually felt buoyed.

Yes, Rebecca couldn't stand me, and yes, she was keen to turn people against me, but I already knew that. What mattered was the way Stephen had defended me. I'd had accusations thrown my way before in my life, but it had always fallen to me to defend myself. Rarely – never perhaps – had anyone spoken up for me, fought my corner, felt I was worth defending. And to side with me over his own daughter . . . well, that was really something, wasn't it?

I felt upbeat all evening after that, humming to myself in the kitchen as I made macaroni cheese for the three of us and helping myself to a generous glass of the half-full bottle of white wine from the fridge.

Over dinner, Jenny and Stephen seemed in relatively good spirits too, better than they had of late, anyway, Stephen giving us a rundown of his work in the garden, Jenny reporting back from a phone call she'd had with a friend from home who had passed on good wishes from various neighbours and community acquaintances. When conversation turned to Luke, as it always did once other business was out of the way, Jenny's demeanour seemed more positive than it had the day before. The reason for this shift was an article a friend had emailed to her, about a man who had been in a coma after being kicked in the head by a horse, and even though medical professionals had lost hope and were advising the family to say their good-byes, he had, against all the odds, begun to breathe unassisted, and later had woken up and been able to communicate with his family.

'There weren't any photos or anything to say exactly where he is now, if he's living back at home or with his parents or where, but the point is, the doctors were wrong. That's what the article kept saying – "Much about the exact workings of the unconscious human brain remains a mystery to science," and that basically, treating injuries like Luke's involves a lot of guesswork.'

Even Stephen, who tended to be more cautious than Jenny, seemed hopeful. 'I'll have to have a look at it after dinner,' he said. 'But yes, as you say, I get the distinct feeling no one really knows anything very much. Disappointing really,' he added, 'when you build these people up in your mind to be like gods.'

As we sat watching Arlette's television that evening, I found myself imagining how the scene would look if Luke were there. I found it very easy to picture him with his parents, I realised. Not just what they'd look like – I'd seen photos to know he towered over his mum, that he had his dad's colouring – but how they'd interact. I could quite clearly imagine how it would be – Jenny doting on him, fetching him drinks and snacks, whilst at the same time scolding him for leaving his shoes lying around, Stephen asking about his work, his bike races, the two of them affectionately teasing Jenny together. I wondered, though, what would the dynamic be between Luke and me, if he were there? Would he be sitting close to me, stroking my hair as I rested my head on his shoulder? Would Jenny look for my support against the boys' gentle ribbing?

But obviously the reality was that if Luke were there then I wouldn't be. Or at least, I'd be sitting there awkwardly, not able to meet anyone's eye, while he looked at his parents in confusion, asking them who this strange woman was they'd invited into their lives. I knew that as much as Luke waking up might bring happiness to Jenny and Stephen's lives, it would mean the end of my part in it.

And I couldn't pretend that wouldn't come as a very harsh blow indeed.

Chapter 48

I had worked out on my first evening in the White House that there was a particular spot on the landing, where the airing cupboard backed onto the bathroom, where I could hover and listen in on Jenny and Stephen's pre-bedtime end-of-day chat, whilst looking as if I was on the way into the bathroom should they come out of their bedroom unexpectedly. I had begun pausing there every evening, when we had all turned in for the night, to do just that. Not only did I find it a useful way to keep abreast of any developments which I might not otherwise be privy too, but I found the interactions comforting. The familiarity of it. The mundane details. 'I've made you a hot water bottle, love.' 'I got your heartburn stuff from Boots. Why don't you have a swig now, save you waking up in the night?'

The evening after his disagreement with Rebecca in the front garden, as I hovered in my usual spot, I noticed that Stephen seemed to be talking to Jenny more intently than normal, and it was as if he was making an effort to keep his voice low – which wasn't something they usually bothered with.

'And I don't know if she meant it to sound like that, but it really was like she was trying to say Charlotte could be behind the whole thing.'

'What whole thing?' Jenny whispered.

'The assault!' Stephen hissed. 'The mugging!'

I felt my skin prickle. The impression I'd got when I'd overheard the argument was that Stephen had disregarded Rebecca's wild accusations entirely. But maybe, I thought now, maybe that was just what I'd wanted to believe – because here he was now passing Rebecca's theory onto Jenny, opening it to the floor for discussion.

'What?!' Jenny said, her incredulity making her forget to keep her voice down. 'How's she worked that one out?'

'I have no idea.' Stephen sighed. He sounded exhausted. 'I have no idea.'

There was a pause. I wasn't sure if they were both lost in thought or just busy continuing their bedtime preparations.

'It's almost like,' Jenny said eventually, 'like all that . . . that *jealousy* . . . she's always had about Luke . . . It's like now he's how he is, now she's . . .'

'Transferring it,' Stephen finished. 'On to Charlotte.'

'Yeah.' Jenny sighed. 'Like that. Don't you think?'

'I don't know, love,' Stephen said. 'I think there's probably something in that. She's always been so highly strung, hasn't she? There's always been something . . . something I've never quite understood.'

'What did we do to make her like that, Steve?' Jenny said. 'What did we do to get it so wrong?'

'Nothing, love.' I heard him kiss her then. 'We did our best for both of them. But they go their own way, in the end, kids.'

I crept back to bed, relieved that Stephen and Jenny weren't giving any credence to Rebecca's ideas.

Jenny's explanation of Rebecca's behaviour – that she was

jealous – was interesting. I'd never seen Rebecca and Luke together to know how things were between them, but hearing how Jenny and Stephen talked about him, contrasted with the way they spoke to and about her, it certainly made sense that she'd be jealous. And if jealously was a weakness of hers then I suppose it wasn't too much of a stretch to see how she might also believe she had grounds to be jealous of me. It was all plausible enough psychology, but it was still unnerving to realise the extent of her vendetta against me.

I wondered how far she'd be willing to go to prove her point.

Chapter 49

The following Saturday, it reached 22 degrees outside before ten a.m. The weather had shifted from breezy late spring to glorious early summer over the course of a few days, adding to my feeling that this situation, my part in the Burley family, was a long-standing arrangement. It seemed a very long time ago that I'd splashed through the puddles to the bar to meet Emily – or not to meet her, as it turned out – and later found Luke lying on the pavement, his clothes damp from the drizzle.

That evening, I went to the hospital alone. Although I enjoyed the time I spent with Stephen and Jenny in the White House, I was beginning to tire of the hospital visits. I always came away feeling grubby and irritable from sitting in the windowless cubicle under the harsh strip lighting. I'd feel nauseous from the cheap bland sandwiches that the hospital café sold, and from the smell of chemicals that clung to my clothes.

The reality was that spending time with someone who was unconscious was really very boring and, I increasingly believed, completely pointless. I felt obliged to work especially hard to prove my devotion to Luke as I knew Rebecca would pounce on any signs of waning enthusiasm as evidence that I didn't truly care for him. It was frustrating to feel constantly assessed when I hadn't done anything wrong, but the situation was complicated – and that was something I knew was my own fault, really. I knew I was lucky, all things considered, to have been welcomed into the family, so I tried not to resent my duties too much.

That evening, as I was sitting in my usual chair, a porter trundled by, pushing a trolley of bottles and whistling. He stopped outside Luke's cubicle and I looked up from the game I'd been playing on my phone.

'Knock, knock,' he said in a Caribbean accent, poking his head through the curtains.

'Hi,' I said.

The porter took a couple of bottles off the trolley and put them into a tray on a shelf inside Luke's cubicle.

'You all right there?' He left his trolley where it was and came and stood at my shoulder. 'How's he doing?' he said, nodding towards Luke and lowering his voice.

I shrugged. 'I don't know really. They say he might not get better. Any better than this, that is.'

The porter nodded slowly, rubbed his chin, then folded his arms. 'You know, my sister's boy, Aaron, he was seventeen when came off his bike. This was back in 2004. Long time now. He had the same, a bump on the head. They said: "He's never going to get better, you know. He'll never wake up, so maybe its kinder to let him go." But at the time, my sister says: "No, not having it. We'll do everything. Whatever it takes. I'll look after him." And he did get a bit better. He couldn't walk or talk, but he could point at letters on a card. He could communicate a little. And in a way that was a miracle – they never thought that was possible – but it was no life, compared to what it had been. He lasted three years like that, before he got an infection, slipped away. I don't know if it was for the best or not, those three years. Maybe it would have been kinder to let him go sooner. Would've been better for my sister, I'm sure of that. But who's to know God's plan?'

I didn't say anything. I just looked at Luke.

'The docs know best,' the porter said, going back to his trolley. 'They see this every day, you know. Trust them, don't fight them.'

I nodded and the porter ambled off, the bottles on his trolley clinking as he went.

His story reminded me of the account I'd read in the pamphlet that first night in the hospital, in A&E, about the woman who had instructed doctors to do whatever they could to keep her daughter alive, but who had later regretted it. Who wished she'd let her die with dignity much earlier.

I imagined then, Luke, the man I'd seen in the bar, in the photos on his bike, lying in a bed, not able to lift his head, not able to feed or wash or move himself around, reliant on – who? Me? His mother? – was that any life for a young man? I thought about how I would feel in his position, if my choice was that or death. I was sure I'd choose death every time.

I thought then about what the porter had said, about the pointing on the letters on a card to communicate, and I wondered, if Luke were to manage that, what those letters would spell out.

'Who's that woman?' perhaps.

Chapter 50

Sully asked to meet for a drink the following day, for an update on Luke's progress. He didn't say as much but I sensed he found it difficult to be around Jenny and Stephen. Perhaps it was their shared history that made things particularly painful, but he seemed to prefer to get his news on the situation via me.

'No change?' he said, looking at me over the top of a pint of Guinness. 'Jenny still wanting to fight the doctors?'

I thought about this. 'Not really,' I said eventually. 'Not as much. She's more . . . hopeful again.'

Sully frowned, confused. 'What's the reason for that though? If nothing's changed?'

I shrugged. 'Just . . . easier to be like that, I suppose.'

Sully nodded and sipped his drink.

'The thing is,' I said, 'is that Jenny and Stephen, and Rebecca actually, think it's up to them to decide everything.'

'And you feel left out?'

'Oh! No!' I said, jumping in quickly to correct the misunderstanding. 'I don't mean that. What I mean is, I looked it up and it's up to his doctor – this Anne Moriarty – to decide what's best. And the role of the family is just to help the doctor work out what *Luke* would have wanted. Rather than say what *they* want, if you see what I mean.'

Sully nodded slowly. 'And you think Jenny is confusing what she wants – for Luke to be kept alive at any cost – with what Luke would have wanted?'

I paused, not wanting to say the wrong thing. 'Perhaps,' I said eventually. 'You can hardly blame her for it but . . . yes. I think that's what she might be doing.'

Sully squinted, looking off into the distance. 'There's no way Luke would want to live like that. If that really is what we're looking at.' He shook his head. 'I mean, I don't think anyone would really, but Luke particularly. A long rehabilitation is one thing, learning to walk, to talk again . . . but to just lie in a bed day in, day out, being fed and changed like a baby. No way. I can imagine him here now, saying it. Can't you? Saying, "No way, man. Kill me. Put a gun against my head."'

'Yeah,' I said quietly.

And I could imagine it. I really could.

Chapter 51

Later that day, Stephen came into the kitchen and said the doctor had called, and suggested that the next time we were all in the hospital that we had a meeting to discuss things.

Jenny spun around from where she was standing at the sink. 'Has something happened? Is there news?'

Stephen shook his head. 'I don't think so, love. That wasn't the impression I got. It's just a . . . catch-up. That's all they said. We shouldn't get our hopes up.'

Jenny nodded, but I could tell from the faraway look in her eyes that she already was.

An hour later, Rebecca had been summoned and the four of us sat opposite Anne Moriarty in the relatives' room, where I was starting to feel like I'd spent more time than in some of my more short-term flats.

'I wanted us to gather together for what we call a Best Interests meeting about Luke,' she said. 'The purpose is – as the name suggests – that we try to reach some agreement about what course of action is in Luke's best interests.'

'I don't follow,' Stephen said, looking at Jenny for support. 'We all know what's in his best interests, don't we? It's best for him if you carry on looking after him? Giving him whatever he needs.'

Anne Moriarty nodded slowly. 'Of course,' she said. 'Of course, our primary focus is to care for him. But what we need to determine is, what is the most caring thing that we can do.'

'What do you mean?' Jenny said. I could see she was beginning to get agitated.

Anne Moriarty cleared her throat and folded her hands in her lap. 'Let's take a step back a moment, shall we? The thing people often don't realise is that, with the remarkable things we can do with modern medicine, it's very possible to keep the body alive – lungs functioning, vital organs supplied with blood – for a very long time. Years, in some cases. But sometimes, the temptation can be to let this go on longer than is really . . . desirable.'

'What do you mean? We—' Jenny started up again.

'Let her speak, Mother!' Rebecca snapped. I too thought Jenny would be better to let the doctor speak rather than to keep asking questions but, as ever, Rebecca's tone was uncalled for.

Stephen gave her a reproachful look and put his hand on Jenny's knee. Jenny looked down at the floor, but she didn't try to speak again.

Anne Moriarty continued. 'We know Luke's brain is very severely damaged. And as we discussed before, although there is a slim chance of some recovery, we need to be realistic about what that recovery might look like. We need to ascertain the type of life that would be acceptable to Luke.'

'So what you're saying is that you want our permission to let him die?' Rebecca said.

Jenny made a sort of whimpering noise, like an injured pony.

Anne Moriarty's voice remained as calm as ever, only the

227

slightest twitch between her eyebrows letting on that she was finding Rebecca's manner trying.

'My job, as Luke's clinician, is to make sure that any decision I make is in his best interests. Your role, as those closest to him, is to help me discover what those best interests are. It's not really a matter of permission, as such, in that the responsibility to make the most appropriate decision lies with me. In reaching any decisions regarding his treatment, I need to establish the type of life Luke would want to live.'

'So really, you're going to do exactly what you want, regardless of our feelings on the matter?' Rebecca said, folding her arms and looking at the doctor without blinking.

Stephen joined in this time, surprising everyone in the room by raising his voice for the first time. 'I'm not sure how you're trying to spin it that leaving him to die is in his best interests!'

Anne Moriarty frowned and closed her eyes briefly. I sensed she felt the meeting was getting away from her.

'I think we should all calm down,' I said, as gently as I could. 'The doctor is only trying to help us. We need to let her.'

I avoided looking at Rebecca at this point, knowing how furious it seemed to make her when I spoke in any of these meetings, which she clearly still felt I had no business being part of.

'OK,' Stephen said, swallowing hard. 'OK, I'm sorry. So what are the facts? What are the specifics? In terms of recovery, what's the best case?'

Anne Moriarty nodded like she appreciated the direct question. 'OK. Sure. So, given the level of damage to the brain, I'd say it's likely that the best case we're looking at is maybe some low-level consciousness. He may, for example, be able to squeeze your hand.'

Jenny made the injured pony sound again, and Stephen put his hand on hers. 'And that's best case . . . is it?' he said.

Anne Moriarty nodded slowly. 'Yes.'

'And worst case?' Rebecca said, one eyebrow arched.

'As I say,' Anne Moriarty said, 'the machines can keep a body alive for a long time. At the moment, they're doing everything for him.'

'You mean he stays like this indefinitely,' Rebecca said.

Anne Moriarty nodded. 'Once a patient's condition remains unchanged for four weeks – and we're not too far off that now – it's what we term a continuous vegetative state.'

No one said anything for a moment. Anne Moriarty looked around at the faces in the room, giving us time to absorb this news.

'I was talking to Sully,' I said carefully. 'I know, it's like you said, the question isn't what *we* want but what Luke would want. And Sully and I were saying, we just don't think Luke would want to live in a vegetative consistent . . .'

I looked at the doctor for help.

'Continuous vegetative state, or permanent vegetative state if it continues for twelve months or more,' she supplied.

I nodded. 'When Sully and I were talking we were saying we were pretty sure – I'm mean, Sully was really, really sure – that Luke would not want that.'

'Oh, well if that's what you and Sully have decided then we must flick the switch at once!' Rebecca said, throwing her hands in the air and twisting in her chair to look at me. 'You've known him for, what, five minutes? So clearly you're the best person to be speaking up. Really, the rest of us should just go home, shouldn't we?'

'Becky . . .' Stephen said, in the warning tone he seemed to have to roll out for Rebecca on an almost a daily basis.

'No,' Rebecca said, standing up suddenly. 'This is just not

acceptable. I have absolutely had enough. What is wrong with you?' She turned to her parents now. 'Why are you so taken in by her? This is about your son! Fight for him, for Christ's sake!'

Then she picked her bag from the floor and barged her way out of the room, letting the door slam after her.

Jenny flinched as the door shut and Stephen turned to watch Rebecca go, but neither of them called her back. Neither of them tried to stop her.

'Sorry,' Stephen said, turning back to Anne Moriarty. 'Sorry for the . . . outburst. Rebecca has always found it—'

I don't know what he was going to say – 'difficult to be normal', perhaps? – but Anne Moriarty held up a hand to stop him. She shook her head. 'No need to apologise. I completely appreciate what a horrendous thing this is to have to contemplate. Please, take some more time.'

Jenny nodded slowly, her eyes wide and unfocused.

'What I will say though,' Anne Moriarty said as she rose from her chair, 'is that Charlotte is right when she says we need to try to work out what Luke himself would want. That must be our focus here.'

Rebecca

Chapter 52

It was so familiar to me, that slow burn of rage. I could physically feel it, expanding in my stomach to the point of bubbling
over, in need of an outlet to escape.

Injustice. That's what's always provoked it. The kind that
makes you want to scream, 'But that's not fair!' But you don't,
because you know the phrase is overused and sounds petulant,
and at any rate, always prompts that most frustrating of replies:
'Life's not fair.'

The irony though, about my most recent outburst, was that
previously it had almost always been something Luke had
done – and the ensuing reaction to his behaviour – that
prompted the feeling. Luke being given a car for his seven-
teenth birthday when I, on a point of principle, had been
forced to save my wages from my Saturday job for two years
to buy my own. Luke being excused from household chores
on the flimsy reasoning that he was 'more of a hindrance than
a help'. Luke being given money to pay for hotels all around
the country so he and Sully could take extended drunken city
breaks in whichever part of the UK they felt like, under the
pretext of attending university open days, even though both

my parents knew he had no real intention of enrolling on a course, while I had had to get up at four a.m. and pay ninety-seven pounds to take the train to Manchester on my own, my mother refusing even to accompany me because it clashed with a pastry-making workshop she wanted to attend.

And what was the reason for this continued preferential treatment? Nothing more significant than the fact that he had dimples, long eyelashes, a warm laugh. He smiled and beguiled, and bought my parents off with cheap tricks like letting them overhear him speaking well of them to his friends or occasionally turning up with a bunch of cut-price carnations from the petrol station for Mum. Because he asked their advice and pretended to act on it, and made them feel important. He knew how to charm people and my parents had always been inclined to value charm over substance. As I saw it, that was their shortcoming, not his.

And now, here they were, falling for it again. Only this time, Luke's role in the situation was quite different.

Charlotte, with her voice like a toy music box and her pantomime facial expressions, had sat there, making her threat to end someone's life sound like a plan to make a blackberry pie. I could just imagine her voice now – 'Let's just pop the machine off, shall we, see what happens. Oh dear, whoops-a-daisy, off he goes to heaven!'

I knew that if the circumstances had been different her relationship with Luke would never have lasted for any length of time. Charmers hate the charming. It becomes a competition.

When I was outside in the hospital car park, and as the fire of my fury began to subside, I realised how dangerous it was that I'd left Charlotte there, enjoying the doctor's undivided attention, setting out her warped agenda and manipulating everyone into her way of thinking. Surely, I thought, surely

Mum will argue with her, even if Dad can't manage it? But then she'd look so defeated in that room, as if Charlotte had ground her down.

From the road outside the hospital I phoned the direct line Anne Moriarty had given us – I didn't want to risk going back up to the ward and seeing them all again – and, when she assured me that no decisions would be made today, I decided to go home, to collect my thoughts and assess the situation I found myself in.

As I walked home, I forced myself to detach from my emotions and consider a rational analysis of what had just happened. I had already known, as I think we all had, that at some point the doctor was going to let us know that ending Luke's life support systems was something we may have to face. But although my emotions carried an undercurrent of grief, it was Charlotte who had incited the rage that had spilled out of me. I had to consider how I could use her actions against her.

The fact that Charlotte had so explicitly advocated a course of action that I knew – until recently, at least – my parents had found abhorrent, could prove useful, I felt. This incident could be packaged together with other evidence to make a clear case that she was not to be trusted.

What I needed, though, was that other evidence. So far, the cornerstone of my case was the lack of publicly held informa-tion about Charlotte and my own subsequent suspicions, and I knew I was going to need more than that to persuade my parents to lower her from her pedestal.

At home, I turned on my computer and opened Charlotte's Facebook page. I wanted to build up a picture of Charlotte's life outside my family. What was her network? Who were her friends? Where were her family?

I opened the 'Friends' tab and scrolled through the list,

looking out for any clues to suggest that one of them might be particularly close to Charlotte.

They weren't a terribly diverse group. Mostly in their twenties and thirties, from what I could gather. As I scrolled through the list, the one factor I noticed that was mentioned across several of the profiles was the name of a workplace – Good Stuff Ltd. A search for the name told me the company was some kind of vegetable subscription service for people who lacked the time or imagination to buy their groceries in the shops like everyone else. I don't think Charlotte had ever divulged to me the exact nature of her work, and at any rate she rarely seemed to be there, but a cross-reference with her own profile told me that she, like many of her contacts, was an employee of the company.

Near the bottom of the list of faces I noticed there was a name that sounded familiar: Emily Hender. I retrieved my memory stick from my bag, plugged it into the computer and opened the spread sheet of password-protected client data I kept in order to manage membership of The Watch. I ran a search for Emily Hender and found a row under that name, on the list of people who had taken a one-month trial membership but had never become fully paid-up members. On further exanimation, I saw that the mobile phone number she had provided matched the one shown below her name on the 'Our people' page of the Good Stuff website. It was the same person.

When Emily answered the phone, I introduced myself as the manager of The Watch and waited the moment it took for her to place the name.

'Oh yeah, I remember,' she said. 'It's just the thing is, I'm not really interested in paying full membership. I mean, no offence, the place is fine – it's great! – but I just can't afford to be paying money for that sort of thing at the—'

'Yes that's fine,' I said quickly. I didn't want her to think I was harassing her into signing up and to hang up before we got any further. 'That's completely fine. That's not why I'm calling.'

'Oh. OK.'

'As we're getting busier and membership is more in demand,' I said, trying my best to deliver naturally the script I'd prepared, 'we only accept members through referrals. Which means if someone wants to be a member, they have to include in their application the name of someone known to us who can vouch for them.'

'Oh. Right. Has someone given my name then?'

'Yes.'

'Really?' She seemed to find this amusing. 'Who?'

'A . . .' I paused and shuffled a few papers on my lap to make it sound as if I was looking for the name on a list. 'A Charlotte Wright?'

There was a pause. 'Really? She gave my name?' She didn't sound so amused now. There was a sigh, then she added wearily, 'Jesus.'

I sat up straighter. 'So, you do know Charlotte Wright?'

She sighed again. 'Yeah, but I wouldn't exactly say she's someone I could vouch for.'

I could have stayed in role. I could have remained formal, asked Emily to confirm she was refusing the referral, but I wanted to go deeper. I wanted to ask more questions. I knew the current pretext limited me though; further questioning would sound odd. Instead, I took a gamble. 'Actually, I think I know her too.'

Emily sounded confused. 'Oh, really? So, why . . . ?'

'It's a rather complicated situation,' I said. 'I wonder, would you be able to meet me? Tomorrow? I promise I won't take up too much of your time.'

Chapter 53

I arranged to meet Emily at eleven-thirty the next day in a pub that was tucked away down Duke's Lane. I'd specifically selected it for the privacy it would afford us. It was large but dimly lit, the tables set apart from each other in secluded booths. I was early, so I took my seat and watched the door.

Emily was wary of me, of my request to meet. I could tell that as soon as she came into the room. We were the only two people in the pub, apart from a pair of young male students playing pool in the far corner, so she was able to head to my table without hesitation, but as our eyes met, she gave me a tight, nervous smile.

'Rebecca?' she said when she reached me, and when I confirmed, she gave a brief nod and took a seat opposite me. She put her bag on the floor but I noticed she kept her jacket on.

'Do you want a drink?' I said. I couldn't really be bothered with the niceties, but I knew I should offer.

Luckily she clearly had no desire to make this into a social occasion either. She looked round at the bar briefly but then shook her head. 'I can't stay long.'

'Thank you for coming,' I said.

She nodded again, then said: 'So what's this about? What's Charlotte done?'

I raised my eyebrows. 'What do you mean "done"?'

She waved the idea away with her hand. 'Oh, I don't know. I just mean . . . how do you know her?'

I wasn't ready to show my hand just yet – I knew that interviewers garnered more valuable information when they didn't lead their subject – so I met her question with one of my own. 'She's a colleague of yours, isn't she? And a . . . friend?'

Emily crinkled her nose briefly. 'I used to work with her.'

'You left the company? Good Stuff?'

Emily shook her head. 'She did.'

I was surprised. Charlotte had definitely used the present tense when she spoke about her work. She said she'd been allowed some time off to tend to Luke, but there had never been any suggestion that she'd moved on entirely. 'How long ago?'

'Four or five weeks.'

I frowned and nodded. 'Right. OK. And when she worked with you, what did you . . . what did you think of her?'

Emily sat up straighter, as if backing away from me. My questioning had made her suspicious. 'Sorry. How did you say you know her?'

'She's my brother's girlfriend.'

Emily pulled a face, bemused almost. She put her head on one side. 'Really?'

I nodded. 'You seem . . . surprised?'

Emily's mouth turned down at the corners. She looked out of the window for a moment, thinking. 'Yeah. I am a bit. How long has she . . . ? How long have they been together?'

'I'm not sure of the exact timelines at this stage.'

'It can't have been long though,' Emily said.

'No?'

'I am almost one hundred per cent certain she didn't have a boyfriend five weeks ago. But . . . I don't know. They say things can move quickly when you've met the right person. Or something.' She shrugged. 'But I don't get it – why did you want to meet me?'

'As I said, the situation is far from straightforward, but I'm obviously keen to protect the interests of my little brother.'

I had made very deliberate use of the word "little" there. It wasn't terminology I would make a habit of employing, but I felt that playing the part of an over-protective older sibling might seem sufficiently nonthreatening to convince Emily to let down her guard a little.

'I just wanted to know a bit more about who he was with now,' I went on. 'You know men can sometimes be reluctant to talk about these things.' I cringed inwardly at this tedious all-girls-together angle, but I was having to think on my feet. 'I'm just curious, I suppose.' I forced myself to smile for the first time. 'I just want to know a bit about her.'

'Right,' Emily said. She was looking at me out of the corner of her eye. She was clearly unconvinced by my reasoning but prepared to give me the benefit of the doubt. 'Well, I wouldn't say I knew her well. She only joined the company in November.'

I raised my eyebrows again. 'So, she was only there a few months in total? Was it a temporary position? Maternity cover?'

Emily shook her head. 'No. It just . . . didn't work out.'

'Why was that?'

Emily took a breath. I could tell that she was being as hesitant as I was about saying the wrong thing, about giving too much away. We were like two nervous dogs, circling each other. 'I know she's dating your brother and everything, and

240

I'm sure she's a good person. Probably. She could just be a bit . . . much.'

I leant forward. 'In what way?'

'She was very . . . young.'

I frowned. 'She's twenty-seven, isn't she? That's what she said.'

Emily shook her head. 'Oh, I don't mean literally. I mean, in herself. A bit teenage. Intense.'

'I see,' I said, although I still wasn't clear what she meant.

'Right from the beginning, she was a bit eccentric,' Emily explained. 'On her first day at Good Stuff, for example, she turned up with a box of cupcakes – enough for everyone. So that seemed immediately quite keen but . . .' She shrugged. 'People are often keen on their first day, aren't they – it can be hard to get the tone right. But what made it all a bit weird was, she'd got all the little cakes handmade with our photos on. She must have sent a sheet of photos to the bakery and got them to print them on edible paper or whatever they use. There was one for every single person in the office. Forty-two, that is. Forty-two people. Forty-two personalised cakes.'

'I see,' I said. 'Quite a lot of effort to go to.'

'Yes.' Emily winced, as if the incident made her physically uncomfortable. 'And the strangest bit was, she'd got most of the photos from the staff page on the website, but not everyone has a picture on there yet. Some people just have their name. So for those, she'd actually gone onto their Facebook, trawled through holiday photos, wedding photos, all sorts, to find a picture. For this one guy, he didn't share his pictures publicly, but she'd gone back *two years* and found one post where he'd mentioned his daughter winning a county swimming championship. Then she'd searched local news websites, cross-referencing the name of the daughter, the swimming club and everything, until she found a photo of him that way – standing next to the kid, holding up her swimming medal. It was . . . an odd thing.

'And to start with, we just, sort of, let it go. I mean, some of the guys in the office joked about her behind her back but I defended her. I said she was just trying to impress us and she was nervous. And I don't know, maybe that was true. For a while.'

I nodded. 'But then . . . ?'

Emily shrugged. 'We were friendly for a bit, me and her, and some of the others. She was always quirky, but mostly it was just her being a bit OTT. She would invite herself along to social things even when it wasn't quite appropriate, or make slightly too-personal comments to clients. But it's like I say, she just seemed young. Naïve, I suppose. We used to joke it was because she was from the country, that she was dazzled by being in a city sometimes.'

Emily was quiet for a moment. She looked out of the window again, that pained expression returning to her face, like she found the whole business of Charlotte Wright quite confounding.

'And she could be really kind,' she added eventually. 'She would do things for people – run errands, fix things. Sometimes she did more than she needed to. Like once I was moaning that I needed this particular type of light bulb for a lamp, and then, at the weekend, she got the train all the way to this shop in East Croydon that sold them and brought it into work for me on the Monday. That kind of thing was a bit weird, but I just felt sorry for her. She was always vague about her life before Brighton and I thought maybe it hadn't worked out. I knew there was a boyfriend before who had messed her around so maybe it was that.

'She never talked about her parents or family. She was

chirpy, but then sometimes you'd look at her and her eyes seemed sad, like she was covering something. So anyway, we got to be quite friendly. As I say, she would invite herself to things – after-work drinks, sometimes weekend things too. It seemed cruel to tell her she wasn't invited, and unnecessary too, because at the beginning she was no trouble really.'

She paused and lowered her voice a little.

'But then it did start to get annoying. She would turn up at our flats – mine, this other girl from work, Meredith's – at strange times, and just sort of invite herself in to watch telly. And sometimes she'd pick up on the most random detail of a conversation and get completely carried away. One afternoon at work, my friend Alison just made some comment about always wanting to live in the kind of house with roses around the door, and the next thing we know, Charlotte's turned up at her house with these two enormous rose bushes and about half a tonne of manure! Just dumped it all in her drive!' Emily shook her head in bafflement. 'After nights out she would always invite herself to stay over even though she had her own flat. She'd say "Let's have a sleepover!" and she'd want to buy all this junk food, like we were thirteen or something and God . . . I don't know.'

Emily shook her head again and sighed.

'Anyway, it was sort of annoying and sort of . . . creepy. So Meredith and Alison and I – we were the main ones she'd attached herself to – we decided to consciously step back from her. We didn't want to be rude about it, so we weren't going to actually say anything. We just thought we'd . . . remove ourselves from the situation a bit.'

'And did that work?'

Emily shook her head. 'It seemed to make her worse, really. It was like she realised she wasn't being invited to things, that she was being pushed out and . . . it made her panicky and she'd end up being there even more, even harder to get rid of.

'So one evening, we decided we'd have to do something.'

Chapter 54

Emily hesitated, and I worried she might be having second thoughts about her candour.

'Go on,' I said in what I hoped was a breezy, gossipy tone.

'Well, she turned up at my flat when Alison and I were just having a quiet evening in – she'd obviously overheard when we were arranging it in the office – and just sort of sat herself down on the sofa, made herself comfortable. And we'd agreed that next time she did anything . . . weird, we'd say something. So we did.

'And we were absolutely as nice as we could be about it – we just said she should try and branch out a bit, and stop trying so hard to impress. Honestly, we didn't just say, "Back off, would you," or anything harsh like that. But she just went very, very quiet. And then she asked if she could stay over, one last time, and I looked at Alison like "is this girl for real?" and Charlotte saw the look and basically pleaded, said it would be the very last time and then she would leave us alone; her landlord was hassling her and she didn't want to go home. So we just relented. Said she could sleep on the sofa.'

'And did she leave you alone after that?'

'Well, yes. But wait, there's another bit first. That night, in the early hours, I thought I heard her creeping about – I knew it was her; Alison had gone home – but assumed she was just going to the loo or whatever. Then, the next day, she was gone before I got up. She was at work as normal, but she was strange. Sort of aloof and cold.

'I assumed she was just hurt from our confrontation and decided to give her some space – hoping that finally she'd got the message – but then, around mid-morning, our boss, Marcus, called me into his office. He says, "I'm guessing you haven't seen this" and turned his computer round for me to look at. And it takes me a minute to realise what I'm looking at but, when I do, I see it's a photo of me, in bed, with my arse hanging out and everything, and it had been uploaded to the front page of *the company website.*'

Emily gave me a moment to process this development.

I frowned. 'So you think . . . ?'

Emily nodded emphatically. 'Charlotte. I knew it straight away. I mean for one thing, content management of the website was her job, so totally easy for her to do it, but I knew it was from the night before by the clothes that were on the floor in the photo, and it all just made sense – her creeping around, all of that.'

'But . . . why?' I said. 'What was she trying to achieve?'

Emily shook her head and breathed out hard. 'Honestly? I do not know. I thought it was just simple anger, revenge. Her just getting her own back on me for humiliating her, or something. But then when I confronted her – I asked Marcus to let me speak to someone before I told him I knew it was her, to kind of have it out with her, woman-to-woman type thing – she was so . . . *light.* It was insane. She was grinning like it was all just a hilarious bit of mischief. She almost seemed to be making out that I was overreacting by trying to have a serious conversation about it.'

'So what happened then?'

Emily sighed again. 'Well, when I couldn't get any sense out of her, I just told Marcus it was her, that we'd had a falling out and that's probably why she'd done it. Her contract was ended then and there – there was no way Marcus was going to put up with some playground argument tarnishing his brand – and she was marched out.'

'So, that was it? You never heard from her again?'

'Well, I've not really seen her,' Emily said. 'Not properly. She kept calling me for a while, so I blocked her number. Then she got a new one, so I had to block that as well . . .'

I nodded slowly. 'Unnerving behaviour.'

Emily nodded grimly. 'Indeed. I just think she found life a struggle. I heard she took on a flat way nicer than she could afford and was always in trouble for not paying her rent. I just don't think she knew how to be a grown-up yet . . .' Then her face cleared, apparently remembering the connection Charlotte had to my family and making a late attempt to reassure me. 'But I do think it was probably just a case of poor social skills. I don't think she ever meant to do anything malicious. She was sad, not bad, if you know what I mean. And actually, maybe a boyfriend is exactly what she needed. I think she just wanted to be loved.'

I nodded again, but didn't say anything.

'What do you make of her then?' Emily asked. 'There must be something that's bothering you, for you to have asked to meet me?'

I shrugged. I still didn't want to give too much away about my opinion on Charlotte, largely because I wasn't sure how the information I'd gathered in the last twenty minutes fitted in with my own impressions.

'I'm not sure,' I said eventually. 'But my brother is in poor health at the moment, so I just wanted to gather a little more intelligence on the people around him.'

Emily nodded. 'I see. Well, as I say, Charlotte was always so keen to help. She's probably come into her own, if she's got someone to look after.'

'Perhaps,' I said, vaguely.

Emily said she had to get going and I thanked her for her time and her honesty. Then, as she stood up, a thought occurred to me:

'I don't suppose you know who her other friends are?' I asked. 'Perhaps people from outside of the company?'

Emily shook her head. 'I never met anyone. I don't think she knew many people in Brighton, anyway.'

'She mentioned a holiday she went on at the beginning of the year – to Goa – that must have been when she was at the company still? I don't suppose you know the names of the people she went with?'

Emily frowned, then she laughed, and shook her head. '*We* went to Goa – Alison and me – I always got the feeling she wanted to come, but we'd only just met her and it was all booked up. I can't imagine she went, at the same time, with someone else, and just never mentioned it to us.'

I pursed my lips and nodded. 'There must have been some confusion.'

One of Emily's eyebrows twitched, but she just nodded. 'Anyway.' She tucked her chair under the table. 'Good luck.'

After Emily had left, I remained in the pub for some time longer, contemplating everything I'd learnt. It was interesting, and it was perplexing.

Although in some ways I felt vindicated to hear that someone else found Charlotte as unsettling as I did, Emily's story had also led to a shift in my feelings.

My rage had cooled, and instead, I felt pity. That wasn't something I'd considered before – to feel sorry for her. It was as Emily had said: perhaps she was sad, rather than bad.

There was one thing it didn't change though: I was still more than a little wary of her. I still didn't trust her. I still didn't like how close my mother was to her, or the influence she had over my family. And it was because of this that I knew I had to stay focused.

It was, I reasoned, quite beneficial to my cause for it to emerge that Charlotte had some kind of instability about her character. It would be all the easier to convince people that it was she – not Brendan, and not me – who should be looked at closely, if and when it was decided that Luke's assailant may be someone closer to home.

I paused for a moment to consider my conscience: if Charlotte wasn't an evil opportunist, but a sad lonely girl taking advantage of my parents' warmth to feel included, did that change how I felt? Was I still happy to see her investigated – potentially punished – for a crime she didn't commit, just to prevent my own misdeeds from coming to the fore? Yes, I decided, with some sadness. Yes I was.

Not *happy* as such, to see that happen, but certainly willing.

Chapter 55

I had already planned to head to the police station after meeting Emily, although I was prepared to keep an open mind and adjust that plan if what Emily said had some bearing. I decided though, that although her story had put Charlotte's character on an interesting contextual backdrop, there was no reason not to continue.

At the police station, I asked for DS Leech but I was informed by a surly young policewoman on the front desk that she was unavailable, and that I should come back at another time, preferably with an agreed appointment. However, it had taken not inconsiderable resolve to progress my scheme this far and I didn't want to leave without accomplishing anything at all.

I asked if I could speak to someone else in DS Leech's stead, and after keeping me waiting for nearly forty-five minutes, a police officer who couldn't have been more than about nineteen years old took me into a side room and asked me what I wanted to talk about.

He introduced himself as 'Roy' – although I wasn't clear if that was his first name or if it was 'PC Roy'. Confidence was not inspired when I told him my brother's name and gave him a brief summary of the case in question and he seemed to have no knowledge of either. Still, he promised he'd record what I had to say and make sure it 'got to the right people'.

'I'd like to report a suspect in that case.'

Roy looked at his notepad then up at me, with an exaggerated confused frown, like a schoolboy learning to tie his shoelaces. 'Sorry, do you have some new information?'

'Well yes, that's what I'm saying. I have a new suspect for you to consider.'

'And who's that?'

'Her name is Charlotte Wright and she's already taken part in the investigation in her capacity as first on the scene and as the victim's partner.'

He raised his eyebrows. 'She's your brother's girlfriend? And you think she . . . committed the assault?' He paused, his pencil hovering over his notepad like he wasn't sure how to record this information.

'I think that it's an avenue you should be exploring, yes,' I said, refusing to engage with his scepticism.

'What makes you think that? Is there a witness? Someone who saw her with the victim? If you have a name, we can talk to them directly.'

I sighed. 'That's not the point. The point is, there isn't anyone else. DS Leech, whoever is in charge here, has been looking for other witnesses, other culprits, and there aren't any. It seems clear to me there was no one in that alley at the time my brother was attacked because if there had been, they would have found some trace of them by now.'

'Absence of evidence isn't evidence of absence, you know.'

'I didn't say it was. All I'm saying is there is one person we *know* was there. Charlotte was the only person we can prove was in that alley at the same time as Luke, so it's quite clear

251

she should be the prime suspect. And they shouldn't be discounting her just because she . . . she has blonde hair and blue eyes.'

Roy gave me a funny look. 'Well, I don't think they will have done that.'

I continued to look at him as if he hadn't said anything at all.

He looked up at the clock on the wall and said, 'OK, well I'll certainly pass on your comments,' in the manner of a waiter recording a complaint from a diner that he intended to forget as soon as the conversation was over.

'Yes,' I said. 'Do.'

I knew Roy was far from convinced by my suggestion, but I didn't believe that in itself was too much of a setback. I believed that he would pass my theory on and that that would be enough to sow a seed. It would be enough to get the ball rolling.

And, with any luck, chasing that ball would keep the officers sufficiently busy that they wouldn't have the time to look too closely at Brendan.

Chapter 56

Early the next morning, my father called me.

He sounded strange on the phone. Uncomfortable. Disgruntled, perhaps. He asked me if I would call by the house 'at my earliest convenience' – those were his actual words. It was an unnatural turn of phrase for him. It was strange.

'Fine. But why?'

'Your mother and I would like to speak to you. To have a few things out.'

'What things? Is it Luke? Has something happened?'

'Not Luke, no. Not directly. Let's just talk in person, when you come.'

'Talk about what?'

'I'm not prepared to go into it on the phone, Becky. But we'll be at the house between nine and two today.'

I was anxious about what it could be and, despite Dad's assurances that there was nothing specific to worry about as far as Luke was concerned, I made my way to the house immediately to get to the bottom of the situation.

As I arrived, I encountered Charlotte in the front garden.

She was wearing a grey fleece that I knew belonged to my father and had a bag slung across her chest.

She greeted me coolly, and I responded in kind.

I assumed that would be the end of the encounter, but instead of continuing on her way, she said: 'You know, they're going to need both of us, after Luke's gone. We're on the same side, really. There's no reason we should be enemies.'

I ignored the second part of this statement, and addressed my response only to the first.

'Luke may yet make some recovery. Only time will tell.'

She closed her eyes briefly, like I was a difficult school pupil testing the teacher's patience. 'It's not fair to anyone to keep him in limbo like this. We all know it, however hard it is to deal with. The sooner we let him go, the sooner your parents can begin to rebuild their lives. I know you don't think much of me, but think of them, at least.'

Charlotte didn't wait to hear my thoughts on this and continued down the path to the gate. As I waited at the front door for my parents to let me in, I turned to watch her let herself out into the street. As she did so, I saw an envelope slip from the pocket of her fleece and onto the path. She didn't notice – and I didn't call out to tell her – so it remained there as she made her way down the road and out of sight.

When she was gone, I walked down the path and picked it up. It was addressed to a Miles Sampson, at an address in Bath.

I took my phone from my pocket, opened Charlotte's Facebook page and scrolled through her list of friends. None of them was a Miles Sampson. Through the glass, I saw my father approach the front door, so I slipped the envelope into my bag for further investigation later.

'Ah, you came.' Dad seemed relieved, if not pleased, to see me. 'Your mum's upstairs having a lie down. I'm just trying to fix a leak in the shower, then I'll be with you. Put the kettle on, why don't you?'

With Dad temporarily occupied and Mum in bed, I took the opportunity to take the card back out of my bag, and using the steam from the kettle, I gently eased open the flap. Inside was a greetings card featuring an uninspiring photograph of a seagull picking at a tray of discarded chips, the pier out of focus in the background.

I opened it and read the message inside.

Dear Miles,
  Happy birthday! Last year as a teenager - enjoy it!
  Sorry I've not been in touch much - crazy busy with work, but I will write properly soon!!
  Lots of love,
  Hester

I read the message through again, then closed the card. If Charlotte was posting the card on behalf of someone else – or if one of my parents had asked her to – then who, exactly, was Hester?

I went upstairs to put this question to my father.

'Hester?' he said, struggling to twist a spanner. 'I don't know anyone called that. It's quite unusual, so I think I'd remember. Why?'

I decided not to tell him where I'd seen the name. A thought had occurred to me.

'The music compilation that Mum and Charlotte are making for Luke,' I said. 'They're keeping a list, aren't they? When they think of new songs? They're writing them down some-where?'

Dad nodded. 'Yep. It's on the dining table.'

'I just want to check something,' I said vaguely as I headed back downstairs.

The blue cloth-bound notepad that I'd seen Mum and Charlotte pass between them to take it in turns to carefully record any piece of music Luke may have heard in his life was on the table. I flipped it open and looked at the scrawled list of songs, which, by this point, covered several pages.

I recognised my mother's handwriting easily, so it was clear that the other hand must be Charlotte's. I barely needed to, but in the name of rigorous investigation, I slipped the card out of my bag and compared it side by side with the book. I carefully compared the more distinctive shapes – the way the tails of the Ys looped back on themselves, the horizontal line of the Z. It was obvious they were a match.

I was left then with two questions: who was Miles Sampson? And why was Charlotte writing to him and signing herself off as Hester?

Chapter 57

An internet search for Miles Sampson returned nothing of significance.

There were a number of profiles listed under that name, but none suggested any immediate association with Bath, and more importantly, none provided any link to Charlotte.

I considered the information I had: a name and an address. It seemed the most direct, decisive course of action at this juncture was to simply go there. I would have to find out whatever it was that Dad wanted to discuss later.

Heading west from the south-east had never been straightforward and the three hours – including a thirty-five minute wait at Southampton Central and a twenty-minute delay in the middle of a nondescript patch of English countryside – dragged painfully slowly. During that time, I considered what I was going to say when I arrived at the house. It was impossible to devise an accurate script with so many unknown variables to take into account. The only pieces of information I had to guide me were three names: Miles Sampson, Hester and, of course, Charlotte Wright. Everything else I was going to have to improvise.

During the journey, Brendan called my phone. I could tell

by the tone of his voice – he has four stock variations that he switches between – the type of call it was.

'Hey, stranger.' This was his wheedling voice; the one he employed when he'd sensed a distance between us and wanted to close it down.

'Hello, Brendan.' Usually at this point I had to choose whether to placate him or to make him work for the reconciliation. On this occasion though, I was too distracted to make any effort either way.

'What have I done, honey? Why are you being funny with me?'

I sighed. 'Because I'm tired.'

'You work too hard. I always say that.'

'Not physically tired,' I said. 'I'm tired of you playing games with me.'

'What games?' He sounded wary. Defensive.

'The game where you deliberately keep the truth from me to try to retain the upper hand. Where you make insinuations without explanation.'

'I don't know what you mean, honey. Honestly, I don't.' The voice had shifted now to another of his favourites: wounded. It was all as predictable as the tides.

'Just tell me –' I lowered my voice and turned my back to the couple at the far end of the carriage; they both had earphones in so I thought I was safe '– did you have anything to do with what happened to Luke? Were you there, that night? In the alley?'

'Honey,' he said. 'Becs.'

'What?'

'I would do anything for you, you know that.' I felt my skin prickle. I closed my eyes and rested my head against the window. 'What would you say if I had?' he went on. 'If I'd done that, for you, to protect you from him?'

'What would I say?!' I was exasperated at even the question.

'I mean, I know you'd be surprised, but you would know that it was for you that I'd done it, wouldn't you? They've never been good to you, your family. Not Luke, or any of them. And I think deep down, once you really thought about it, you'd be pleased.'

'Brendan!' I had to force myself to keep my voice low. 'No, I would not be pleased. What is *wrong* with you? He's my brother. I . . .'

Brendan began to chuckle. 'Calm down, angry lady,' he said. 'Obviously, I didn't do it. I didn't do anything to your brother. My point is, all I was saying, is: I would. If you had wanted me to. I'd do anything for you.'

'I don't even know what to believe.'

'Believe?' Brendan's amusement evaporated. He sounded anxious again. 'You believe me. You believe what I'm telling you. What else is there?'

'Why did you tell the police you were with me that night? If you've got nothing to hide, why did you invent a false alibi?'

He paused. 'It was hardly a false alibi. They just asked me where I was and I didn't particularly want them to know, so I made something up.'

'That's exactly what a false alibi is.'

He didn't say anything. His silence made me anxious.

'Why didn't you want them to know where you were?' I asked. 'Please just *tell* me, Brendan.'

A further pause, and then he said quietly, 'I went to see Joanne.'

Joanne Waite was a woman Brendan had had a brief relationship with, not long before he met me. I didn't know much about their time together, except that his particular breed of persistent romance had resulted in her seeking a restraining order against him. I had met her myself once, when she had waited for me outside the club to tell me she'd heard Brendan and I were 'involved' and wanted to warn me what I was letting myself in for. I'd thanked her for going out of her way to call by, but assured her I would be fine, believing then that, as I had no intention of getting emotionally attached to him, he would never have a psychological hold over me as he had her. Little did I realise there were other ways he would find to ruin my life.

'Joanne?' I said. 'Joanne Waite? Why would you see her?'

He seemed to misread the confusion in my voice as shock and immediately began to reassure me. 'Honestly, honey, it was really nothing. But we went through so much stuff together and it all ended so suddenly we never got to close things off properly. I just wanted to talk.'

I was tempted to ask Brendan if in the 'stuff' they went through he was including the time he cut her passport into strips with a bread knife or the night he locked her out of her own flat when it was minus two outside to punish her for going for a post-work drink with two male colleagues.

'And she was pleased to see you, was she? When you – what? – turned up at her flat?'

'Well,' he said. 'It was never going to be easy, but she wanted closure too.'

'Right.'

'But I didn't want the police to know I'd been there because—'

'Because of the restraining order?'

He cleared his throat. 'Because it's none of their business. You won't drop me in it, will you, honey? You can just say we were in, watching TV, all evening?'

'I have to go now,' I said. 'I've got a lot to do.'

Chapter 58

The Miles Sampson address was some four miles outside the centre of town, so I took a taxi, which drove me to a long meandering road, where the houses were set back from the street, and largely shielded by substantial conifers.

'That'll be number twenty-eight then,' the driver said, as he delivered me outside a property whose hedge was markedly more dishevelled than the others.

I stood in the opening to the driveway. There was an assortment of discarded objects lining the gravel path to the front door – a rusted washing machine, a pile of tyres. What looked like the steering wheel from a ship.

I picked my way through the items to the front door. There was no bell, so I rattled the cast-iron knocker and waited. I knew it was perfectly possible that I wouldn't find anyone at the address, that no one would answer the door at all. My contingency plan for such an eventuality was initially to wait and, failing any developments after an allotted passage of time, branch my investigation out to neighbouring houses, to see if someone could tell me who Miles Sampson was, or where I could find him. After a few moments though, the door was opened by a woman in a shapeless black woollen dress with long greying hair, hanging straight down either side of her face. Her skin had a yellow tinge and was pulled taut across her severe features. Behind her, I noticed the hallway was filled with boxes, stacks of paper and rusted hand tools, piled so high against both walls that there was only the slimmest of walkways down the centre.

She stood and looked at me, her face expressionless. She said nothing at all.

'I'm looking for Miles Sampson,' I said.

She continued to look at me for a moment and I noticed that one of the items behind her was a glass tank, and inside it, curled around a log, was a thin orange snake. Instinctively, I stepped backwards.

'No,' she said eventually.

'He isn't here?'

'No,' she said again.

A man emerged from a door off the main hallway. He too had greying hair – his wild and unkempt. He was wearing a waistcoat but, strangely, no shirt beneath it.

'Miles?' he said with a frown.

'Yes. Miles Sampson,' I repeated.

'He's—' the man began, but the woman cut him off.

'No!' she said again, sharply this time, and closed the front door.

I stood for a moment, wondering if perhaps they would open it again, but they didn't, so I retreated up the drive.

It was then, as I stood where the gravel bordered the pavement and looked back at the house, that I noticed the pale face of a young man at an upstairs window.

Chapter 59

I didn't have a specific time frame in mind when I decided to wait, but once I'd waited forty minutes, it seemed a waste not to reach the full hour mark. Then, once I'd been there that long, there seemed no reason not to wait another half an hour. And so on it went until, when I had been sitting on a bench a few metres down the road, shielded from sight by a tree, for just over two hours, I saw the woman and the man leave the house, both of them pushing a wheelbarrow. When they had rounded the corner and were out of sight, I approached the house once more and again rattled the knocker. I knew he must still be in there, the pale-faced boy, but I wasn't at all sure he would be willing to come to the door.

My first attempt to attract his attention went unanswered, but shortly after my second, I saw the shadow of a figure behind the glass of the door.

I tapped on the door again and the figure flinched, but still didn't step forward.

I opened the letter box. 'Can I talk to you?'

The figure didn't move.

'Miles?' I tried.

He hesitated for a moment, but then he stepped forward and opened the door.

The person standing in front of me was a tall, very thin, young man with sunken eyes and lank dark blond hair sticking to his forehead.

'Miles Sampson?' I said, trying hard to keep my voice unthreatening. The boy seemed nervous and I didn't want him to panic and slam the door shut.

He nodded slowly. I noticed he'd taken the orange snake from its tank and it was weaving in and out of his fingers.

'This is William,' he said, holding the snake out to me. I nodded but pulled my head away from it. The thing was only small, but it had a sinister look about it.

'Miles, I need to ask you a question,' I said. 'Do you know someone called Charlotte? Charlotte Wright?'

He shook his head.

'What about Hester?' I said. 'She might use that name. Do you know someone called Hester?'

He froze, and looked at me, wide eyed.

'Hester?' I said again. 'You know her?'

He nodded, then he said: 'My sister. My sister Hester.'

'Your sister? Are you sure?'

I reached into my pocket and took out my phone. I quickly navigated to Charlotte's Facebook page. I found her photo and clicked on it to make it fill the screen – carefully obscuring the fact that it was labelled 'Charlotte Wright', so as not to confuse things. I turned the screen to face Miles.

His mouth twitched – almost a smile – and he touched the screen with his forefinger. 'Hester,' he said again. 'My sister.'

There was a sudden noise behind me and he jumped and stepped back into the house. I turned around. The greyed-haired man and woman were back, pushing their wheelbarrows, which were now filled with what looked like scraps of dirty carpet.

'Oi!' the woman said, picking up her pace as she approached me. 'You! Get away! Go!'

She dropped the wheelbarrow then and marched over to me, putting her hand on my arm.

I pushed her hand away. 'Get off me, please.'

'You get off!' She shouted, her long hair swinging around her face. 'You stop harassing my son, he's not well. Clear off my property!'

The man stood by, looking at the floor like he wished he wasn't there. Miles had retreated inside the house and was nowhere to be seen. It seemed I had no choice but to leave, as it was clear the woman had no qualms about demonstrating her apparent objections to my presence with physical force.

I turned out of the drive and headed back down the road, with no clear plan about where to head. I returned to the bench I had been sitting on a few minutes earlier but found there was now a woman in a red anorak in my place. As I passed her, planning to locate an alternative waiting position while I considered my next move, she called out to me.

'You got off lightly!'

I stopped and looked at her.

'When the bloke from the council came round about the rubbish out the front, she shut the door on him so fast she broke his thumb.'

'Do you know them? That family?'

The woman nodded and sighed. 'Oh yeah. Well, as well as anyone does, I suppose. They're not exactly the friendly type, as you just saw. Lived here for years though.'

'Do you know Hester?'

The woman's eyes widened slightly. 'Hester? Yeah. Yeah, used to. Long time since she's been mentioned though.'

'Can you tell me anything about her?'

The woman shrugged. 'Depends what you want to know.'

Charlotte

Chapter 60

I'd decided that the most positive way forward was for me to make every effort to be the bigger person where Rebecca was concerned.

From the way Jenny and Stephen spoke about her, I knew they already thought her petty, jealous and vindictive, so I knew that by going out of my way to be magnanimous and pleasant I could solidify my status as the better, more mature, woman.

I'd put this new approach into action when I bumped into her in the front garden on my way to post Miles's birthday card and, even though it was clear she'd fully intended to ignore me, I greeted her pleasantly and reminded her that we were on the same side. Unsurprisingly she seemed irritated by the gesture and as I let myself out of the front gate, I knew she would be seething on the doorstep behind me.

I realised when I got into town that I must have left the card in the house. I considered going back for it, but I decided it was easiest to just buy another one and write it there in the street, next to the post box.

I carried with me a constant feeling of guilt about Miles. I had since I began living with Frieda, as soon as I realised I'd never go back to that house, that I would never live in a house with my parents again. I'd thought about going back for him, but I just couldn't imagine how I could factor him into my new life – any of my new lives – and I don't think he wanted to be part of them anyway. His world was small, focused around his attic room, his work on his train and his snakes. I couldn't picture him outside of that bubble, interacting with other people, starting again somewhere new. Even with me for support.

It was when I'd posted the card and was looking in the window of a delicatessen, wondering if Stephen and Jenny would prefer tomato and pepper chutney or chilli jam with the lunch I planned to offer to make them when I was home, that I bumped into Emily. She passed so close behind me on the narrow stretch of pavement that I smelt her before I saw her, if that doesn't sound too strange. She always wore a distinctive musky perfume; you could always tell when she'd been in a meeting room.

When I turned around and we found ourselves face to face, her mouth fell open, as if she'd completely forgotten that we shared a town. I imagined that she felt guilty, and probably embarrassed, that she hadn't returned my calls or explained herself for standing me up that night all those weeks ago. Perhaps if I hadn't been so occupied in the weeks since then I might have felt more disgruntled, but as it was, it all seemed a long time ago.

'Charlotte,' she said, blinking. 'Hi.'

'Hey, Emily,' I said, and for once it was nice to hear the coolness in my voice. I've always found fallings-out uncomfortable, so tend to do more of the heavy lifting when it comes to the patchings-up. Now, though, with my priorities firmly shifted to my new responsibilities, my new relationships, I

wasn't as anxious to get Emily back on side as I might otherwise have been.

'Uh, how are you, then?' She fiddled with the cuff of her
jacket.

I nodded. 'Good. Fine, thank you. Busy.'

I wondered if she'd heard about my problems with Yanis
and the flat. I hoped she hadn't. It was embarrassing to be a
grown adult and to have got in such a muddle about finances.
I guess I'd just been bowled over by the place and had signed
up without doing my sums. The problem with debts is once
they've started, they can suck you into a downward spiral
until you've got no feasible chance of escaping them in an
honourable way. I'm not making excuses, but everything is
that little bit harder when you don't have any family to act
as a safety net, to help pick up the pieces when you make
mistakes.

'I heard you . . . you're seeing someone. Boyfriend type
thing.'

I was surprised. I couldn't think how she would know that.
Although I couldn't say I wasn't pleased. They did always make
me feel quite patronised, Emily and the others, just because
I was new in town and didn't know as many people as they
did. It was nice to have them know I was capable of meeting
people on my own. That there were actually people out there
who wanted to spend time with me, even if they didn't.

'Yeah,' I said. 'Luke. But how did you—?'

'I met your . . . his sister. Rebecca,' Emily said.

My bubble of satisfaction burst immediately. 'Rebecca?
When? What did she say?' Panic gave my voice an aggressive
edge and Emily stepped back from me.

'Nothing.' She shook her head. 'She didn't say anything.'

I saw that my hand was on the sleeve of Emily's jacket.
'What did she say about me?' I said again.

Emily pulled her arm free and stepped into the road to move past me. 'Nothing,' she said again. 'Sorry, I've got to go.'

As always, I realised too late that I'd acted inappropriately. 'Sorry!' I called after her. 'Call me soon, yeah?'

Emily waved her hand vaguely behind her but she didn't look back. I was left on the pavement outside the delicatessen with a sensation that had become familiar to me over the years – the feeling that I was standing on an unstable cliff edge and the rocks had started to fall, and that quite soon the whole ledge would crumble away underneath me and I would be in free-fall, with nothing to grasp onto.

Why, I wanted to shout. *Why me?* I had made one small error of judgement that Emily had overreacted to, and Rebecca had taken an instant dislike to me for no discernible reason, and now, these two women with their quite separate, equally unreasonable grievances, seemed to be colluding, to be coming together to take away the tiny pocket of happiness I'd managed to carve for myself.

Chapter 61

When I got home, I found Stephen sitting in the garden reading. He said Jenny had gone for a walk to get some fresh air, so he and I were alone.

I was glad to see there was no sign of Rebecca. When I asked if she'd stayed long when she'd called by earlier, he sighed and shook his head. 'No. No she didn't. She upped and left before we'd had a chance to say a bloody word to her. Didn't even say where she was going.'

'Oh.' I sensed there was more to the story but I wasn't sure how to ask him about it. 'Was she . . . OK?'

He put his book down and looked at me. 'It's not been easy. Parenting a girl like Rebecca. She's so . . . closed. She keeps everything inside. And it's especially hard for Jen because she's so . . .' He scrunched his hands up into fists then opened them in a burst, his fingers splaying outwards like a firework. 'She wears her emotions on the outside. Heart on her sleeve and all that.'

'I see,' I said. I wasn't really sure that I did see, but I sensed Stephen was just thinking out loud rather than arguing a specific point.

'And the thing is,' he went on, 'when you keep everything inside, it has to go *some*where. You can't just keep things bubbling away inside without something . . . spilling over at some point.'

'Yes,' I said. 'I suppose.'

He paused for a moment and picked his book back up and I thought perhaps that was the end of the conversation, only he kept the book there on his lap, closed, so I stayed where I was for a moment, in case there was more.

'You know, when the kids were little – Luke was two, so Becky would have been ten – we won this prize. It was a raffle at work, for some charity, I forget the details. Anyway, the prize was a trip to a water park. It was the talk of the town, this place. It was set in a big lake, with inflatable obstacles to scramble over, and a big slide with water coming down and oh, all sorts. And there weren't many places like that, where we lived back then, so it was quite a big deal, all of us going for a proper day out. And Becky was excited I suppose, told her mates about the trip and everything.'

I found it hard to imagine Rebecca being excited about anything, much less scrambling over inflatable obstacles. And actually, I found it hard to imagine her having friends to tell.

'But then that morning, we were trying to get ready, getting all the gear in the bag and Jen's making pasta to put in a tub for lunch because you know the prices of the food at these places, but, Luke – I mean, he's two years old, you know what two-year-olds are like – he spent the whole morning kicking off and screaming and you can't just put a kid in that state in the car. It's just asking for trouble. So it was getting later and later, and Becky was just sitting there quietly at the kitchen table and I remember Jenny saying, "We can't go with him like this, it's going to be a nightmare, it's just not worth it" and I remember looking at Becky, thinking she was going to pipe up, to whinge, like you'd expect a kid to when they were about to be disappointed, but she didn't. She just sat there, looking at her hands, on the table, spread out in front of her like she'd never seen them before.'

He spread his own fingers on his lap in front of him and looked down.

'Anyway, Luke was playing on his mat on the kitchen floor and Jenny was upstairs trying to get something down from the top of the wardrobe and she called me to help, so we left them alone – Becky at the table and Luke on the floor. And the next thing we hear this scream, this yelp like you wouldn't believe, so Jenny and I come thundering down the stairs and there's been this saucepan on the side, boiling the water for the pasta and it was on the floor next to Luke, and Luke's sitting on his mat which is soaked and his leg is red – you know, like scarlet – and already it's blistering. And Becky's just standing there, her bag in her hand and she just says, "I think it's time we were going" as if nothing had happened at all.'

Stephen looked at me, signalling he'd reached the end of his anecdote, but I didn't know how to respond. This account of the creepy child version of Rebecca made me feel uneasy. As an adult, her coldness was strange, but in a child, it sounded chilling.

'So,' I said tentatively, not wanting to jump to the wrong conclusion. 'Do you think . . . What do you think? That Rebecca . . . ?'

Stephen rubbed his face with his hand. Then he crossed his arms over his chest and shook his head sadly. 'I don't know. We don't know. Jenny rounded on Becky – it was, I've always thought, the thing that set their relationship on a downward spiral – and asked her what the hell she was doing. I don't *think* she tipped the pan on purpose, but I can imagine that she saw Luke climbing up, reaching out for it, and just . . . let him. Didn't care either way what happened.'

'Because she was angry at him for . . . ruining a day out?'

Stephen just shook his head. Then he said, 'He needed a skin graft, on his leg. I'm sure you've seen the scars. I don't know if he told you the story of how he got them.'

'He never told me,' I said, truthfully. 'He never told me that story.'

'But that's what I mean, anyway,' Stephen said, cracking open the spine of the book. 'She just lets her feelings bubble away under the surface. But she can't pretend they're not there.'

'And you think . . . she's going to boil over again?'

Stephen pushed his lips together. 'Maybe,' he said. 'Unless she already has.'

I went inside and busied myself unloading the dishwasher, Stephen's story going over in my head. It made sense suddenly, how nervous they seemed around her. A capacity for violent rage is always there, surely, however rarely it surfaces? Were they thinking – had they been thinking since the night they got the call from the hospital – that the person who'd put Luke in hospital was closer to home than anyone would have liked?

And, I thought, pausing with a glass measuring jug in my hand as all the pieces seemed to fall into place, Rebecca must *know* that's what her parents might suspect, which is why she was creeping around, trying to put me in the frame, trying to suggest to her parents that I was the one who couldn't be trusted, that I was the one with questions to answer about what happened to Luke before I found him. She was using me to divert attention from herself.

I put the jug down and shook my head, hardly able to believe the absolute nerve of the woman.

Chapter 62

That evening, I went ahead of Jenny and Stephen to the hospital, planning to meet them on the ward later. After twenty minutes or so of the boring business of sitting in a chair next to a comatose man, I decided to give myself a change of scene and go and buy a drink from the café. As I opened the double doors from the ward out into the corridor, I came so close to walking straight into a woman that she had to hold her hands up to physically stop us colliding.

'Oh God, sorry,' I said at the same time as she made her own apologies.

I was about to go on my way when a glance at her earring sparked the tiniest glimmer of familiarity and made me look back at her. My double take caused her to pause and take another look at me too, and we seemed to make the connection at the same time.

'Oh, it's . . .' She looked at me, bemused.

'Yeah . . .' I said. 'Hi. Again.'

It was Kelly, the woman Luke had been on a date with the night I'd found him. The woman I'd escorted to a taxi, relieved of a glove puppet and packed off home.

Initially, I assumed her presence in the hospital was purely coincidental. It was a big place with hundreds of patients. However, I had thought of Kelly a number of times since I'd been part of the Burley family – specifically how I might explain things if the police discovered that Luke had been on a date with her that evening, when, according to popular belief, he was already very much spoken for.

Still, I'd felt confident as the weeks went on that an explanation wouldn't be needed, as the police had made no mention of Luke's date and no one seemed to know that it had occurred at all.

Here, though, was Kelly. And here was I. And just a few feet away, there was Luke, unconscious in a bed.

I knew that the easiest, cleanest thing here would be if Kelly remained ignorant of everything that had happened, so immediately began preparing my own justification for being in the hospital in my head – something to do with an elderly relative, and definitely nothing at all to do with that handsome young man she'd been in a bar with several weeks earlier. But before I could begin to deliver my lie, she put her hand on the double doors to the ward and said, 'Is that Intensive Care?'

'Uh, yeah,' I said, 'but I don't think . . .' I wasn't even sure what I was going to say, something about restrictions or visiting times or needing a security pass – anything I could think of to stop her wandering in there and spotting Luke in his bed. But before I could say anything she looked at me and said: 'Do you remember that guy I was with, in the bar? The young one?'

I blinked. 'Yes. Yeah.' I couldn't think of anything else to say.

'Well, apparently,' Kelly said, her voice low and urgent, 'he was mugged. Literally that night, after he left.'

'Oh!' My surprise was completely genuine, prompted not

by the news of the mugging, but by the realisation that Kelly knew about it. 'Mugged?'

Kelly nodded, her eyes anxious. 'The police told me.'

'The police spoke to you?' I remembered then that there had been a few missed calls from DS Leech, along with a voicemail requesting a 'chat', that I hadn't yet got around to dealing with. This explained what she wanted to talk to me about.

Kelly nodded. 'Literally just now. Earlier today. They're trying to work out who did it. Who hit him round the head.'

'Do they have any idea?' I asked, still trying to make my interest in Luke – in the whole business – sound casual, no more than simple politeness.

Kelly shrugged. 'I told them what I thought. For what it's worth.'

'What was that?'

'I'd been getting these texts. From this guy – the one I told you about, the one who wanted me to take his speeding points? He was saying about wanting me back and that. He said he'd fight for me, do anything to get me back. And I just thought he was talking bollocks like they all do, but now the guy I was on a date with is in hospital. Coincidence maybe . . . but I don't think so. I don't think so.'

I was surprised. I assumed the police were still working on the assumption that it was a random mugging. I had no idea they were now considering it might have been more targeted. 'You think your ex attacked Luke? Out of jealousy?'

She shrugged again. 'I mean, I don't know anything for sure. But he's beat people up before, Flint has. He once punched a guy in the face for touching my arse in a club, so . . .'

I nodded, turning this over in my mind. I had been quite happy to accept the police's vague hypothesis that it was some down-and-out behind the attack. The truth was, I didn't much care who they thought did it, as it wasn't going to make any material difference to where we found ourselves now. But now, with Rebecca making it clear she wanted her parents – maybe even the police – to believe I had something to do with it all, perhaps it was a good thing if the police were setting their sights on someone more specific than an addict looking for drugs funds. Perhaps this Flint and his violent past, his motive to want to hurt Luke, was useful.

'I wanted to see him,' Kelly said. 'Well, his family really. It felt the right thing to do, if I really was the last person to see him before . . .'

She looked towards the double doors again and I followed her gaze. Then I turned back to her.

'It's none of my business but . . .' I paused, for effect mostly – to get her attention. 'But do you think that's a good idea? To meet his family?'

She looked at me, confused.

'I just mean,' I said quickly, 'if what you're saying is true and this guy, this Flint, whacked Luke on the head because he was jealous – jealous about you then . . .'

Realisation crept over Kelly's face and she nodded slowly. 'They'll think it's my fault.'

I pulled a face like I was finding the conversation uncomfortable. 'Yeah. Kind of. I mean, I know that's not really fair or reasonable or true. But when people are in the middle of a trauma, they don't always make sense. They look for someone to blame.'

Kelly nodded. 'Yeah. I guess that makes sense.'

'I mean, it's just my opinion,' I said. 'I might be wrong. I just think if I was you, if I was in your shoes, I'd save myself the hassle and steer well clear.'

Kelly hesitated. She looked at the doors to Intensive Care

one more time, then she sighed. 'Yeah. You're right. I shouldn't be here.'

She pushed her hands in her jacket pockets and turned for the stairs. Just before she headed down, she stopped and turned back to look at me.

'You know – he had a girlfriend, apparently. That's what they said. Came out on a date me with me even though he had a missus waiting at home.'

'Really?' was all I could think to say.

'Yeah.' She raised one eyebrow and shook her head. 'Men, eh?'

I just nodded.

'Anyway, see you around.' She headed off down the stairs.

Rebecca

Chapter 63

'It's not an entirely straightforward matter,' I said. I looked back towards the house, half expecting to the see the wild-haired woman round the corner begin pursuing me with a carving knife, or similar.

The woman in the anorak crinkled her nose. 'I get you,' she said conspiratorially, although I didn't see how that could possibly be the case. 'Want to pop inside? That's my house, there. With the green door.'

I looked over. Given my experiences so far on the road, I wasn't sure I wanted to go inside a stranger's house. But then I'd come in search of information, and this woman seemed quite keen to divulge some, so it seemed foolish to turn down the offer.

'I'm Barb,' she said as we crossed the road and made our way up her driveway. 'Barbara, but they all call me Barb.'

I wasn't sure who 'they all' were, but I didn't much care.

'Rebecca,' I said, considering too late that it might have been prudent to use an alias.

Barbara fussed around for a while, brewing tea in a pot and sorting letters from the sideboard in the kitchen into a rack on the wall. She directed me to sit at the kitchen table so I did as she said, although I kept my jacket on so I would be ready to leave at short notice if I had to.

'So, what brings you here asking after Hester?' she said when she eventually took a seat opposite me at the table. 'Not often that happens. Not often anyone goes calling at the Sampson house, to be honest.'

'It's complicated,' I said, because it was, and also because, as I understood it, that was the accepted vernacular when wanting to remain ambiguous.

She frowned. 'Right-oh.'

I could see I was going to have offer something to grease the wheels of conversation, to get the story going, so I said, 'When did you last see her? Hester?'

'See her? God, I don't know.' Barbara thought for a moment, her hands curled around her mug. 'It would have been eight years, I suppose. When she called back, just for a short visit. To see Miles, I think. But before that I hadn't seen her for three years, after she got took away. But I didn't *see* her see her – as in, bump into her in the street, say hello – since she was a kid. Fourteen or fifteen anyway.'

'Right,' I said, trying to shuffle this deluge of statistics into some kind of narrative. 'But what do you mean "taken away"?' I hadn't meant to correct her grammar, but I couldn't have repeated her own choice of words without sounding as if I was mocking her.

Barbara suddenly seemed suspicious. 'If you're saying you know her, then you know exactly where she went. What do you want with it all anyway? Are you from the papers? I thought they'd got bored of this years ago.'

I shook my head. 'I'm not a journalist. I know someone who sometimes uses the name Hester. And who sometimes . . . doesn't. I know a woman who has a connection to that house, to Miles. I'm trying, in the first instance at least, to confirm that it is the same person.'

I remembered then the photo on Charlotte's Facebook page. I showed it to Barbara and she nodded. She seemed weary almost. 'Oh yeah. That's her. Hardly changed.' She squinted at the screen. '"Charlotte Wright", that's what it is now, is it?'

'What is?'

She took a sip of her tea then nodded her head at the phone. 'What she's calling herself.'

'So, Charlotte Wright isn't her real name?'

Barbara pulled a face. 'No, darlin', it's Hester. Thought you knew that much. Do keep up.'

'So, just to recap where we are,' I said, the drink in front of me untouched, 'Hester lived here as a child. At some point – around the age of fifteen or sixteen? – she was taken away. She then returned, briefly, and went away again. She now lives under an assumed name, which is something she has done on more than one occasion? Is that all correct, so far?'

Barbara nodded. 'That's about the size of it.'

I frowned. 'So why was she taken away? And why would she use a false name now?'

'Oh, well I would've thought that was obvious.'

Chapter 64

This is the story Barbara told me, in long animated sentences with barely a break, aside from the occasional pause to check I was keeping up:

The aggressive woman with the grey hair and the old man who seemed to cower in her presence were Dorit and John Sampson. They had lived in the village longer than Barbara, since their early twenties she believed, and had always been 'a funny lot'.

'For one thing, they collect all sorts of junk,' Barbara said. 'You saw for yourself and that's just the driveway. They go out with those wheelbarrows and collect it. Sometimes you'll see John tinkering about with it – "Fixing it up" he says, but you never know what he's actually doing – then every so often, they'll hold a kind of garage sale. Lay it all out on the front lawn with price tags on. Radios with the wires hanging out. Guitars with no strings. All absolute rubbish, all of it. They never sell a thing of course, so then they just have to wheel it all back inside again at the end of the day.'

I asked how the couple had been able to survive given their choice of living was so clearly unprofitable. Barbara said she didn't know, but that it was widely believed that Dorit had inherited money from somewhere and that the sum involved meant their unconventional business model didn't need to prove fruitful.

After some years of living in the house, the couple had a baby girl – Hester – and then, when Hester was eight, a boy, Miles.

'The boy was always odd. Backwards or special or whatever they call it. But the girl, Hester, people always used to say it was remarkable, how she turned out, given what she'd come from. I didn't know them well – I don't think anyone did – but my friend Paula – she was a teacher at the primary and I used to do her nails – she used to teach Hester. Twenty years ago it must have been. And she always said she was a sunny little thing. Not a genius, but a tryer, you know? Tried to do her best. Didn't seem to mind – or notice – that the elastic had gone on her skirt or that she never had any socks on.'

According to Barbara, despite the community's doubts over the fitness of the Sampsons to be parents, much of Hester's childhood passed without event. It was when she graduated from middle school and moved onto upper school, at the age of thirteen, that the problems began.

'I suppose in some ways it was just usual teenager bullying. She was different, the girl, there was no getting away from it, and kids pick up on that. It was clear she was lonely, at school. She would hang around the rec – Branson Recreation Ground, on the corner there – just avoiding going home, I think. So that's how Frieda came to know her.'

Barbara explained that Frieda was a woman who had lived at the far end of the street and, as well as having three children of her own, she fostered teenagers. They all lived together in a big house that had become something of a refuge for lots of local young people – not just her own children and her official foster placements, but their friends and their friends' friends.

'Everyone round here knew Aunty Freed,' Barbara said. 'That's what they called her. You know how you just get those people who everyone calls aunty? She was one of those.'

I said I did, although I did not. I thought briefly how my mother might have enjoyed playing this role in her own community, had she known such a position was available.

Barbara said that one way or another, Hester began spending time at 'Aunty Freed's' and by the summer of 2005, when Hester was fourteen, she was sleeping in the front bedroom of her house so often that she could be considered to live there.

'It was nothing official – I'm sure Dorit would have kicked up a right fuss if any social workers or whatever had got involved – but Hester just chose to spend more and more time there. And Frieda wasn't one to turn people away.' Barbara took a sip of her tea. 'But it was when she'd been there about six months that things started to get strange.'

Chapter 65

'By this point, by the January, Hester basically never went near the Sampson house at all. God knows what Dorit and John were saying about it, behind closed doors. But they didn't seem to be bothered about getting her back.'

Barbara told me that although she never heard Hester do so herself, there were stories in the village that Hester would routinely claim that Frieda was her biological aunt, and occasionally even her mother. On one occasion, to which there were several witnesses, Hester apparently became angry when another teenager referred to her as a Frieda's foster child.

'As the story goes,' Barbara said, 'she was ranting and raving that Frieda was her mum, would you believe! And you must remember –' Barbara gave me a hard look over her mug '– she wasn't, in actual fact, even a foster child of Frieda's. She was nothing really, nothing official. But here she was bumping herself up not one but *two* levels – claiming to be a blood relation! Kin!'

Barbara shook her head and sighed, then refilled her mug from the pot. I shook my head when she offered it to me and I saw her slightly frown when she noticed I hadn't drunk the first cupful.

'And a little while after that, I bumped into Frieda in Tesco and she had a trolley absolutely loaded up with loaves of bread and Coco Pops, like she always did. I made some joke about feeding the five thousand and all the waifs and strays she had in with her, and at some point I mentioned the Sampson girl, Hester, and she seemed quite tense at the remark. I can still see it now, the face she pulled. It must have been weighing on her mind, the whole business, because she confessed to me then and there how she felt about it.

'She said the girl was starting to make things uncomfortable in the house, that the other children were wary of her because she was so possessive of Frieda, wanted her attention all for herself. Apparently, she'd started to invent ailments – all sorts of health things – and persuade Frieda to take her to hospital to get them seen to, and get quite cross if Frieda suggested they didn't go. And she would make up other stories too, about things the other children had done, to get them in Frieda's bad books – odd things, like killing a squirrel with a stone – that just didn't sound right to Frieda. And I can tell you, as she stood before me in Tesco that January night, that woman was at the end of her tether with the situation. So she was about to act, I'm sure of it. She was about to call someone in, to have the situation taken care of. And I think Hester knew it too, she knew things couldn't go on for ever.'

'So what did Frieda do?'

'Oh, well nothing in the end. She never got the chance. Because it happened that night. Right after I'd seen her in Tesco. That's when the fire started.'

292

Charlotte

Chapter 66

Jenny and Stephen didn't stay long at the hospital that evening, and the three of us were back at the house before eight, Jenny absorbed in her online world, and Stephen and I watching one of the quiz shows we all enjoyed. My phone rang just as the closing credits began to roll.

I immediately tensed when I noticed the Bath area code of the number on my screen. It was almost Pavlovian, the reaction I had to any mention of that place. I knew I'd have to answer it though, or spend the next week puzzling about who it could have been, driving myself mad with theories.

'Hello?' I stood up, crossed the lounge and headed out of the French doors to the garden, hoping that Stephen and Jenny would interpret this as a reluctance to disrupt their viewing, rather than as a sign I had anything to hide.

'It's Miles Sampson please can I speak to Hester Sampson.'

'Miles?' It had been a long time since I'd heard Miles's voice. It was a little lower, I noticed, than I remembered it.

'It's Miles Sampson,' he repeated.

I wasn't sure I had ever spoken to Miles on the phone before. I kept him up to date with my frequently changing mobile numbers and although he didn't have a phone of his own, he was able to text me from a website on his computer that let you send messages directly to mobiles. As long as I asked specific questions he would reply, writing me long unpunctuated messages detailing his doings. 'I am healthy I have one new bridge for my train set I have new black gloves William ate a mouse.'

'Where are you? Where are you calling from?'

'I am one metre away from the rec.'

I squinted, picturing the local park in my mind. 'You're in a phone box?'

'Yes I am in a phone box.'

'Are you OK?'

'Yes. There was a lady with a black coat and brown hair and she said, "Do you know Hester" and she showed me a picture of you on her phone.'

My heartbeat quickened. 'Someone was looking for me?'

Miles didn't reply. The intonation wasn't enough for him to realise it was a question.

'What else did the lady look like?' I said. 'And what else did she say?'

'Her hair was thirty centimetres long. She had a white shirt with black buttons. She said, "Can I speak to you?" She said, "Miles Sampson." She said, "Do you know someone called Charlotte Wright" and she said, "Do you know someone called Hester". I showed her William.'

I wasn't able to visualise lengths and dimensions as clearly as Miles, but when he recounted the details of the shirt buttons, I closed my eyes and felt my shoulders sag. As he said my name – my two names, Charlotte Wright, Hester – I sat down heavily on the bench. Rebecca.

'What did you say to her? Did she come in the house?'

'I said you were my sister and then she went back to the

pavement and then she talked to Barbara and then she went in Barbara's house.'

'Barbara?' I stood up again. I knew Barbara would love to find someone interested in her stories about the road, and that she could spend a whole afternoon setting out her theories, detailing her analysis of all the characters involved, if she had a willing audience. And as Rebecca had gone all the way to Bath to find out whatever it was that she had gone to find out, I felt sure she would be exactly that.

'If the lady comes back,' I said to Miles, 'don't say anything to her at all. Just close the door and wait till she goes, OK? The same if anyone asks for me. If anyone says "Hester" or "Charlotte" just close the door. OK?'

'OK,' Miles said, and then he put the phone down.

I considered calling the number of the phone box back but I knew there was little point. I stayed on the bench, looking at my phone's blank screen, my heart still racing.

Reykjavik, Helsinki, Oslo.

I tried to slow my breathing.

Talinn, Stockholm, Moscow.

'Are you all right, love?' I looked up to see Jenny standing in the doorway to the lounge. 'The lottery's about to start. You coming in?'

They'd started playing the lottery enthusiastically since I'd met them. They never had before, they said, because they never thought they'd win, but Luke's attack had caused them to reassess their view of probability. 'We never thought something this bad would happen to our family either, so maybe something good is owed us too.'

I sat on the sofa and pretended to watch the television whilst thinking hard to try to work out where Rebecca was now, what she knew and what she would do with the information.

297

It didn't matter, in the end, how hard you tried. I was learning that now. What was the point in trying to reinvent your life when you were only ever as good as your lowest moment, your worst mistake?

I looked around the room. Stephen had gone into the garden to pick fresh mint to make us all mint tea. Jenny was pressing buttons on the remote, frowning as she tried to find the one that adjusted the brightness of the picture. The French doors were open and outside the early summer birds were singing as the sun set. On the side in the kitchen was the bag of pasta and vegetables that I would soon offer to prepare for dinner. That was all it was. It was just normal. A normal family on a quiet evening. And yes, Luke's situation overshadowed it, but that was only temporary. Once he was gone and the grief was over – and really, it had already begun, the grief, we all knew what was going to happen – things would settle and we would have this. And it was all I wanted. It was all I'd ever wanted. To be allowed to stay. It seemed such a small desire, a life that so many people took for granted, that it seemed so unfair to me that wherever I went, whatever I did, people would collude and conspire and work to take it away from me. Why couldn't they just let me stay?

I didn't realise I was crying until Jenny noticed and came to me. 'Charlotte love, what's the matter?'

I looked at her, and reached up and touched my face. 'It's just . . .' How could I answer that? 'It's just too much, some-times. I'm just a bit overwhelmed. That's all it is.'

Jenny shifted along the sofa and pulled me into a hug. She kissed the top of my head. 'I know, my love. I know.' She got up and went out into the hall. 'Let me get you a tissue and you can tell me everything going on in your head.'

As I heard her climb the stairs to the bathroom, the flashing screen of her phone that she'd left on the arm of the sofa caught my eye. I leant over to read the name on the screen: Becky.

As the call rang off, the display was replaced with:

Becky: 2 missed calls

I held down the power switch until the screen went black, then I slipped the phone into my pocket. Stephen had left his phone on the mantelpiece, so I did the same with his, noting as I did so that Rebecca had tried him a number of times as well. I wasn't stupid, I knew there was a good chance my time in this family was running out, but I was going to do everything I could to preserve it for as long as possible.

When Jenny returned with my tissue I wiped my eyes and then my nose and generally made a show of pulling myself together. Then I apologised for the display, said I had to go to the shop for 'a few bits' and went to the hallway to collect my bag. Hanging from a row of hooks by the front door, next to the car key and the key for Luke's flat, was a single silver key on a green fob labelled 'Becky.' I put it in my pocket with Jenny's phone.

I reasoned that I had one thing in my favour. Now, more than ever, Jenny and Stephen needed a daughter in their life. They needed someone to look after and someone to look after them, and it was abundantly clear that Rebecca was neither willing nor able to be that person. But she had time on her side – she'd had years to foster a relationship with them – and I knew that to overcome that I was going to have to give them more reason to be wary of her than her bad temper and prickliness. I needed to give them a real reason to cut her out.

I needed to prove to them what she was capable of.

Rebecca

Chapter 67

The fire had begun on 8 January, in one the back bedrooms of Frieda's house.

'It was Frieda's eldest's bedroom, where they said it started. She was seventeen and had candles all over the shelves, how they do at that age. They said it was them that started it. But the thing is – ' Barbara leant forwards on her elbows ' – and this is just the first weird thing about it all – she wasn't in at the time.'

'Who wasn't?'

'Leah. Frieda's eldest, whose room it was. She was out at a pal's. Which was a blessing obviously, but it does make you wonder: who lit the candles? Because she hadn't been there all afternoon. They've always said she must have left one lit before she went out, but she's always swore blind she didn't.

'Anyway, it tore through that house, this fire. And it was Hester who – as the story goes – smelt the smoke, jumped out of bed, rounded everyone up – all the kids, all the overnight guests – and got them all out before the fire engines were even on the scene. Everyone that is, apart from Frieda.'

'How did she get out?'

Barbara's eyes widened. 'Well, she didn't! That's just the thing. She didn't get out. She died, right there in her bed, from the smoke.'

I stared at her. The whole story of the strange couple and their damaged daughter had been unsettling, but this was shocking. 'Frieda *died*?'

'Yep.' Barbara nodded in a manner that could almost be considered triumphant. 'But it's as I say, there was something funny about it all. Not just the candles. Other things too.'

'Such as what?'

'The smoke alarms for one thing. Where were they? I mean, they were there, in the house. But why didn't they go off? Fire brigade said the batteries must have been flat but I don't buy that. All of them, all four of them, flat batteries? And Frieda wouldn't have had that. She was hot on that kind of thing. You have to be, when you foster. And then there was Frieda herself.'

'How do you mean?'

'Well, why she didn't wake up, with all the smoke and the hollering and the bedlam going on around her? They took her away, for investigations – her body, I mean – and they said it was sleeping pills. But again, it doesn't ring true to me. Frieda didn't take sleeping pills. I know because I do – terrible insomnia I get – and on more than one occasion, when I said about it to Frieda, she said, "You want to try looking after eleven kids all day. That'll cure anyone of insomnia."'

'Did anyone say that at the time? Did anyone mention they felt the taking of sleeping pills was out of character?'

'Oh yes,' Barbara nodded. 'Yes, we did. But they spoke to the GP and it turned out that Frieda did have a prescription for them.'

'I see. So I suppose it transpires—'

'But,' Barbara cut me off, 'the prescription was done over

the phone. And guess who toddled off down to the chemist to pick them up? Guess who collected the pills?'

I just looked her.

'Hester!' she said, tapping her hand on the table. 'Hester got them.'

'How did Hester behave after the fire?'

'Oh, she was beside herself! Grief stricken. Sobbing and sobbing. I mean, they all were, all the kids, but Hester was the worst. Eventually, she stopped talking altogether. She went completely silent. And she refused to go back to the Sampson house of course, so I don't think they knew what to do with her. So that's when she got took off – took to the clinic or hospital or whatever it was. They just didn't know what else to do with her.'

'But you think . . .' I hesitated, reluctant to say anything that was putting words into Barbara's mouth. 'You believe that Hester . . .'

Barbara nodded slowly. 'I believe there was more to it than the official report. Officially, it was an accident. Officially, the smoke alarms, the pills . . . it was all just bad luck. But it's too much of a coincidence for me. For a lot of people round here. Everyone knew Frieda was going to have to tell Hester to sling her hook sooner or later, and . . . yeah. That's how it looks to us. Hester couldn't deal with it. She was angry, and hurt. So she decided to finish Frieda off for good. Revenge, pure and simple.'

Chapter 68

Barbara paused in her story at that point to offer to refill the teapot. I sensed though that she could go on a good while longer on this topic. I wasn't averse to hearing more and under any other circumstances might have stayed a while longer to probe further, but I knew that I'd heard enough to confirm my suspicions – my suspicions that Charlotte – Hester – was someone to be very wary of indeed.

As Barbara delivered each part of her story, as she painted the picture of Hester's character, I found I was able to slot the pieces together with the fragments of what I had discovered of Charlotte – her demeanour, her relationship with my parents – and what Emily had told me about her time working with her, to create a clearer image than I'd ever had before. And whilst there were still gaps in that image and questions I couldn't fathom the answers to, what I did have made me very uneasy. And very certain that I needed to get back to Brighton – to my family, to Luke – and that I needed to do so without delay.

It was nearly forty minutes later by the time I managed to extricate myself from both Barbara's kitchen and then the passenger seat of a talkative taxi driver's cab and, as I anxiously checked the departures board at the station, call my parents. But neither of them answered and eventually both began redirecting straight to voicemail. I sent them both messages asking them to call me as soon as possible but there was no saying when they'd pick the messages up, or how quickly they'd act on them if they did. There was nothing I could do but board the next train, and go to them in person as quickly as I could.

As I waited for the train to pull out of Bath station, I considered how my view of Charlotte's character had shifted once more since the revelations Emily had recounted the previous day. 'Sad, not bad,' Emily had concluded, and at the time I'd felt that judgement to be sound. Now though, I was worried that although 'sad' may have been an accurate diagnosis, it didn't preclude her from being bad, and it definitely didn't preclude her from being mad. And a cocktail of all three could be very dangerous indeed.

I wished – as I had countless times since Luke's admission to hospital – that I could speak to him, that he could explain to me the exact nature of his and Charlotte's relationship. Was he completely smitten, charmed by the pretty face, the earnest way of talking? Or had she pursued him, clung to him like she had that woman, Frieda, and he'd been trying to work out a way he could untangle himself from the situation? That would certainly explain why he hadn't mentioned her to anyone – not my parents, not Sully, certainly not me – in the time before he was attacked. He was hoping she wouldn't be a feature in his life for long enough to make it worth it.

It was sometime later that it occurred to me that, perhaps, it wasn't Luke at all that Charlotte wanted. It was something more general than that: to be part of something. To be accepted. Rejected by her own mother, she had attached herself first to Frieda, and now to my mother – and quite possibly to any number of other people in between. Emily's story, certainly, suggested a similar pattern of behaviour.

I tried both my parents twice more, but still not even a ringing tone from either. This made me nervous. I knew there was a good chance they'd be angry with me for my sudden departure from the house before they'd had the opportunity to air whatever grievance they had, and so may be avoiding my calls, but why would both phones be switched off? My mother didn't like being disconnected from the world under any circumstances, and especially not with the situation with Luke as it was. I had to hope that they were simply in the hospital, phones switched off, as per the signs that most people ignored.

I looked at my watch. I would be home in two hours and forty-five minutes. I told myself to think rationally. Charlotte had been worming her way into the centre of my family for several weeks. Nothing had happened – as far as she knew anyway – to threaten her position or to give her any cause to do anything dramatic. Nothing would change in a few hours.

With my fears about Charlotte and what she may be capable of wrestled into submission, my mind was laid open for other thoughts to spill in. Those thoughts, I found, were centred on Luke, and the last conversation we'd had. I felt a swell of guilt as I remembered the earnest look in his eyes, the consternation he felt at having to bury our secret. How he truly believed that honesty was the best policy, that no real harm could be done – and more than that, pain could be eased – if only people were honest. The frustration I felt at the naivety of this belief was still there, but it seemed dwarfed now by the longing for him to wake up. The longing to have him back.

I remembered too, how I had treated Brendan to an uncharacteristic display of raw emotion, the day after Luke and I had rowed. How I'd listed point by point how grave the consequences could be if we couldn't persuade Luke to stay away from Daniel Rubinstein. How I'd made clear my desire that we should find a way to convince him not to talk. And how, despite Brendan's claim to have been with his ex-girlfriend, Joanne, the night Luke was attacked, this story seemed suspect to me and that meant I wasn't able to completely discount the possibility that Brendan had lied to both the police and me, and that he had followed Luke into the alley that night. I realised there was one quite simple way to test his story.

I reached into my purse, took out the business card Joanne had given to me the night she'd warned me off Brendan and wrote her a message.

Dear Joanne,

My name is Rebecca Burley, you paid me a visit some time ago to discuss your ex-partner, Brendan Scott, and to suggest my involvement with him was unwise. For reasons I'm not able to go into at present, I need to find out where Brendan was the night of 28 April. He claims to have been with you, but given your feelings towards him when we last spoke, I doubt the veracity of this statement. Please let me know as a matter of urgency.

Best,

Rebecca

If Joanne contradicted Brendan's version of events, then I would know Brendan had lied. That in itself wasn't a definitive answer to the question of whether he'd been involved in Luke's attack, but it would certainly raise some very difficult questions. I had to hope that, however unlikely it seemed, Joanne confirmed that she and Brendan had been together.

When the message was sent, I noticed I had a new email from Dad. That was unusual. He would send me text messages or call, but rarely – if ever – had he emailed me.

Becky,

I wanted to speak to you in person, but you obviously had somewhere more important to be. I don't want to cause a drama, God knows we've got enough of that at the moment, but I've been talking to your mum and you should know you're really upsetting her with all these insinuations that Charlotte may know something about what happened to Luke. The police said you've even mentioned it to them, which I must say I'm very disappointed to hear. I know it's hard for you that your mum and Charlotte get on so well when you've struggled to feel part of the family but you're just going to have to accept that your mum really needs Charlotte right now. I don't want you to have to stay away from the house but if you can't be pleasant I think it's better that you do, just for the time being.

Love

Dad

I hit the reply button and began to write back.

Charlotte Wright is not her real name. You can't trust her. You need to—

I stopped. I needed to tread carefully here, I knew. My parents weren't going to want to hear what I had to tell them, so they would be looking for any reason to discount my version. I knew that a series of hastily typed startling accusations ran the risk of sounding unhinged. I needed to speak to them properly. I deleted the incomplete message, closed my inbox and once again dialled my father's number.

As I watched the English countryside glide past, I thought of Aunt Frieda, sedated, choking to death in her own bed.

Charlotte

Chapter 69

I was still formulating the plan even as I began putting it into action, walking quickly down the road, my hand in my pocket to hold firmly onto both phones and the key to Rebecca's flat.

First, I headed to the hospital. As I entered the main lobby, I made sure I looked up at the CCTV camera to give it a clear view of my face. I did the same to the camera in the corridor between the lift and the doors to ICU. On both occasions I resisted the temptation to smile – I knew that would give the impression I was quite mad.

Once inside, I walked to the far end of the corridor, through a door marked FIRE EXIT ONLY and down the cast-iron steps at the side of the hospital that led to the walled-off area where the bins were kept. This way there'd be no record of my leaving at all so if any questions were asked about my whereabouts during the next hour or so, I would be able to claim I was paying Luke an impromptu visit.

Stephen had once pointed out Rebecca's flat to me, in one of the grimy squares set back from the sea to the west of the city centre, and I had no trouble finding it again. I let myself in through the main door that led to a narrow staircase covered with a cheap brown carpet and made my way to her flat on the fifth floor.

Inside, it was exactly as I imagined Rebecca's home would be. Cold. Uninviting. Bare. The front door opened directly into a lounge room with one sofa pushed against the wall and a coffee table in the centre with a laptop on it. There was no carpet and no curtains. There was a large cactus on the floor by the window, although even that seemed an oddly frivolous object for someone like Rebecca to own.

The window was an old-fashioned sash type and it led directly onto a flat piece of roof. Lots of the flats in Brighton had these, I'd noticed. Not officially roof terraces, but a little square of unfenced outside space, where those desperate enough for fresh air – or for a cigarette – could sit and look out at the world below.

'Right,' I said out loud. 'What am I doing?'

What I was doing was gathering evidence. Finding something to prove to Jenny and Stephen that Rebecca was more than just cold – that she was cruel and twisted and dangerous. That she would hurt her own family. That they couldn't trust her.

The laptop seemed the obvious place to start, especially with there being little in the way of actual physical objects in the flat to examine. I opened the lid and booted it up.

I launched a browser and was immediately taken to the login screen of an email account. Unlike me, Rebecca didn't leave her inbox signed in and although I toyed with the idea of trying to guess the password, I knew my chances of getting it right – even with unlimited chances – were less than slim. Instead, I opened Facebook. This time I had more success; I was taken directly to Rebecca's profile.

I almost laughed when I saw the state of it. She barely had any friends – even fewer than me, and I'd only set mine up a few a months ago – and her entire timeline was dominated by the posts, photos and likes of her own mother. There were also lots of messages about Luke – sending her and the family best wishes, asking to be kept updated on his condition. It came as no surprise to notice she hadn't bothered to reply to any of them.

I knew the place I was likely to find material of interest though wasn't in her public interactions but her privates ones. I opened her personal message inbox.

The vast majority of her messages were from Brendan. Scanning through these was quite an amusing experience – Brendan frequently and enthusiastically declaring his love, how beautiful he thought Rebecca was and how he couldn't wait to see her, Rebecca either not responding at all, or writing simply, 'Thanks.'

Further down though, a conversation from Boxing Day the previous year was far more interesting:

[Brendan]: Don't worry baby you didn't do anything wrong.
[Rebecca]: We did, and now a woman is dead because of it.
[Brendan]: You couldn't know that would happen.
[Brendan]: Look baby only three people know what happened. I'm not going to tell. You're not going to tell. And Luke can be persuaded. There are plenty of ways to keep him quiet.

I read the message over three times. I could hardly believe my luck. I found I was actually grinning with the sheer perfection of it. It was so nice to be right about something for once.

I took Jenny's phone from my pocket and turned it back on. I typed out a brief message and sent it to Rebecca.

Meet me and your dad at your flat ASAP. Love Mum x

Rebecca immediately called the phone back but I cancelled

the call and turned the handset off again. Then I climbed out of the window and sat crossed-legged on the warm patch of roof to watch the sun set over Brighton while I waited.

Chapter 70

It was a very pleasant twenty minutes or so, sitting there in the fresh air, the seagulls calling overhead, the sound of some kids skateboarding in the street alongside the block. I felt I would have liked a drink really, something short and sophisticated, to toast my success. To enjoy the fact that this was my moment.

In a way, it wasn't just about Rebecca but about all of them: my parents; the kids at Aunt Frieda's who thought they were better than me; Kai and all of them in the house share; Emily; Meredith. How cruel they'd been when they'd cast me out. And how *smug*. I'd told them I would find my people one day, people who got me, who appreciated me, who didn't think I was 'a bit much'. And I now I'd found them, I was going to fight for them.

I really felt as if I'd grown, matured, and that was to be reflected in how I planned to handle my upcoming meeting with Rebecca. In the past, I'd been fiery and impetuous and emotional, and that had always got me into trouble. But sitting there, waiting for her to come back to her flat, I felt really quite calm. Rebecca would admit what she had done, Jenny and Stephen would realise they'd lost not just one but two children the night Luke was attacked, but I would be there to support them, to help pick up the pieces.

It was pleasing to see her come into the flat, from my vantage point on the roof, to watch her put her keys down and take her jacket off, all the while looking around her like she wasn't sure what was going on or who she was going to find. When she saw me, sitting out on the ledge outside the window and looking in, she froze momentarily. 'Where are my parents?'

'Look,' I said, pointing vaguely down into the street. 'Look, here.'

She frowned and eyed me suspiciously.

'Look,' I said again, more urgently this time.

She stepped through the window and onto the ledge and sat down next to me – it really wasn't the kind of surface you'd want to be standing up on – and looked down to where I had pointed.

'What?' she said, and then again, 'Where are my parents?'

'It's just a lovely view, isn't it?' I said, turning to smile at her. 'Not sure about Jenny and Stephen though. At home, I think?'

She frowned for a moment, puzzling about why her mum had sent her a message to ask her to meet here, and then not shown up, so I thought I should help her out. I took the phone out of my pocket and laid it on the roof between us.

'You sent that message?' she said, reaching for the phone.

I nodded and snatched the phone back before she could take it, so I could make sure it got safely back to Jenny.

I could see the thoughts compiling behind her eyes. It was like watching a robot compute new data.

'You're mad, aren't you, Hester?' she said eventually. She sounded calm about it though. I saw her watching my face, waiting for signs of alarm or shock at the use of that name.

318

But of course, I was quite prepared for that, so I barely reacted at all. That annoyed her, I expect. I didn't say anything, so she changed tack. 'How did you get Luke to like you? Who did you pretend to be to him?'

'I was exactly what he needed.' I hadn't planned that answer, but I was pleased with it.

Her phone beeped then and I waited while she took it from her pocket and read the message on her screen. She closed her eyes, just for a second, after she'd done so. Whatever it had said, she clearly wasn't too happy about it.

'You won't be able to pretend for ever. My parents won't want you living with them when they realise who you are.'

I was ready to give her a telling off, because she really needed to remember that thing they say about people in glass houses not throwing stones. 'I think they'll probably be a bit more cross with you than me, don't you think?' I laughed. 'When we lay everything side by side, I think they'll know who's been worse.'

She looked at me, her face almost bemused now. She seemed to have no idea what I was talking about. It really was satisfying to be leading her around by the nose like this. 'What you and Brendan did to Luke!' I explained. 'I can't really see them forgiving you for that, can you?'

I'd spent enough time in my life bluffing my way through tricky situations that I knew the best way to cover up any gaps in your knowledge was to simply pretend they weren't there. Pretend you know everything, and soon you will. They should put that on a fridge magnet, shouldn't they? Anyway, it worked beautifully here. It didn't matter that I wasn't exactly sure of what I was accusing Rebecca of. I'd got to her. I could tell by the way her eyes were moving quickly from side to side, like she was frantically trying to read instructions on what to do next from a manual inside her skull.

I picked up my own phone, and from the photographs I'd taken of her laptop screen, I read the exchange between her and Brendan.

'"There are plenty of ways to keep him quiet."' I repeated that line twice. 'You'd have to say that a bloody great whack on the head was quite a good way, wouldn't you? He's certainly very quiet now!' I laughed and shook my head.

Rebecca stared at me, expressionless. 'He's going to wake up,' she said quietly.

I rolled my eyes. 'Oh, for goodness' sake, be realistic. And also, could you stick to the point? You've been busted! I got you! Just admit you're wrong for once in your life!'

And I laughed again – a proper joyful laugh, because it was so nice to feel like I was winning for once.

Rebecca

Chapter 71

My phone beeped and as reluctant as I was to take my attention away from Charlotte when we were sitting precariously on the edge of a rooftop like that, I was badly hoping to see it was a reply from Joanne.

It was.

Hi Rebecca. One word: NO. I'd hope from what I said when I came to see you that you'd know he's the last person I'd want to spend time with! I wasn't with him that night, or any other night for that matter!!

I deleted the message, and closed my eyes, just for a moment. I knew it was inconclusive that Brendan's claim had transpired to be another lie, but once again, I was no nearer to knowing the truth.

I was just so exhausted by it all. Of trying so hard to manage things, to stay in control, to stay afloat when nothing would remain in my grasp.

I was so tired. So, so tired.

'You won't be able to pretend for ever. My parents won't

want you living with them when they realise who you are.'

'I think they'll probably be a bit more cross with you than me, don't you think?' she laughed. 'When we lay everything side by side, I think they'll know who's been worse.'

I had no idea what she was talking about.

'What you and Brendan did to Luke!' she said, impatiently. 'I can't really see them forgiving you for that, can you?'

She picked up her phone and – somehow – it displayed an exchange between me and Brendan that we'd had shortly after Sarah Rubinstein's death.

'"There are plenty of ways to keep him quiet,"' she repeated. 'You'd have to say that a bloody great whack on the head was quite a good way, wouldn't you? He's certainly very quiet now!' She laughed and shook her head.

I stared at her. I had no idea how to respond to this truly bizarre behaviour. 'He's going to wake up,' is all I could think to say.

She rolled her eyes. 'Oh, for goodness' sake, be realistic. And also, could you stick to the point? You've been busted! I got you! Just admit you're wrong for once in your life!'

She laughed again. Never has a sound been more alarming. She was looking at me, twisting a strand of hair around her finger like a mischievous child. How had it happened, that the tables had turned so quickly? I had so much on her. I knew her past. I knew who she was and what she'd done, yet she was looking at me for an explanation. She was accusing me of having some involvement in Luke's attack and I couldn't formulate the case for the defence when I knew there was a substantial chance I didn't have one.

'I would never deliberately hurt my brother,' I said, fighting to keep my voice calm, trying to think of a way to safely manage her madness. 'There is no one I care about more in the world than him.'

'Liar,' she said. She wasn't smiling any more. 'You've always been jealous of him. Your parents told me. They love him more than you because he's normal and you're ... what *is* even wrong with you? I don't know what it is, but you hate him because of it. You're jealous and you resent him. You—'

'It's not him I resent, it's them!' I hadn't been able to stop myself from shouting. 'They think I have a problem with Luke because they're too stubborn, too stupid, to look at themselves. But it's them who are the problem! It's always been them! Them who have made me feel like an unwelcome guest, an imposter. A freak. It's all them.'

Charlotte stared at me, fascinated. 'So you attacked Luke to . . . get to them?' She seemed genuinely curious.

'I didn't attack him.'

She waved her hand. 'Well, Brendan then. Whatever. So was that the only reason he did it? Just to get revenge on your parents for you? Or because of this "keeping him quiet" business? What *were* you guys trying to keep quiet anyway?'

She pulled her knees up to her chest and wrapped her arms around them, staring off over the rooftops to the sea for a moment. Then, quite without warning, she reached across the roof and wrenched me forward by my jacket, and held me, suspended in the air, a five-floor drop below me. 'Tell me!' she shouted suddenly. All signs of amusement were now gone.

And so I did, partly because I was in no position to negotiate, but also because at this point, it hardly seemed to matter any more.

Chapter 72

There had been a party, just before Christmas, at The Watch. Luke and I were both working. He had been behind the bar and I was acting, as usual, as general manager, tending to guests and instructing staff as well as managing Brendan, trying to stop him interfering and embarrassing himself and our business.

That evening we had a special guest in attendance. She was Sarah Rubinstein, a journalist who wrote reviews and opinion pieces for the culture, food and drink supplements of national newspapers. I had read her work before but didn't particularly care for it. She favoured a tiresome contrarian approach, taking whatever angle was most at odds with public opinion, as if to make clear she felt herself better than the masses.

Brendan had invited her to the party in the hope of a good write-up for The Watch in a cultural review piece, but I thought the endeavour was ill advised; Sarah Rubinstein distributed praise sparingly, if at all, and, I knew that it was quite likely our special guest would simply avail herself of the free food and hospitality then write a damning article about how stilted and snobby the place was, no doubt with some unflattering references to my and Brendan's appearances thrown in for good measure.

I was confused at first by Brendan's sudden interest in the club's publicity strategy, but then I realised his keenness that she should attend was largely driven by the hope of some personal fame for him. I think he had visions of a photo of himself in a national newspaper, a double-page spread about the man who'd turned a grimy attic bar into one of Brighton's most exclusive nightspots. I knew that fawning fan pieces were really not Rubinstein's style, but had to admit that even an unenthusiastic but balanced piece, setting out the basics of what The Watch could offer, could only help our fortunes.

Both our hopes were dampened, however, when it was clear from the outset that Sarah was less than enthusiastic about the occasion and made it quite clear she would be leaving as soon as possible.

She'd arrived late, talking on her phone as she crossed the club, and had positioned herself on a far table, away from the other guests. She ate the food put in front of her seemingly without either seeing or tasting it and ignored Brendan's attempts at conversation, refusing the offer of a tour of the club, or to listen to Brendan's boasts about the big names we'd recently signed as members.

Brendan was frustrated, and he began to focus this frustration on one thing, which he claimed to be at the heart of the problem: Sarah's refusal to accept a glass of wine. She insisted on drinking glass after glass of lemonade, her eyes glued to the screen of her phone, which seemed to be playing the highlights of a tennis match.

'This is ridiculous!' Brendan said, joining us behind the bar, where Luke was preparing drinks and I was serving them to guests. 'She could be anywhere. She's acting like she's sitting in her own kitchen at home. This is meant to be an occasion! She's probably not going to write anything up at all at this rate. She hasn't asked me any questions at all! Why won't the woman have a drink and just get into the party spirit, for God's sake?'

Luke and I looked at each other, neither of us with any idea what Brendan expected us to do about the situation. Brendan looked around the bar, his cheeks pink, sweat patches forming under his arms. Then he took out one of the expensive glass bottles of organic lemonade we kept in the fridge and pushed it towards Luke. 'Give her this,' Brendan said. 'And put a decent glug of that in it.' He nodded towards a bottle of vodka.

'She hasn't ordered that,' I pointed out.

'This is a bar not a burger joint,' Brendan said. 'You can't write a review of a bar if you haven't even had a drink. Give her a proper drink and then give her another one and another one until she opens her eyes and starts to appreciate where she is.'

'Can you do that?' Luke said, after Brendan had gone. 'Spike someone into giving you a good review?'

'I don't see that it will work,' I said.

'She'll be able to taste it, I reckon,' Luke said.

But nevertheless, he poured the drinks and I served them, and Sarah Rubinstein didn't register any sign that she was aware of the new ingredient. In fact, there was barely any change in her demeanour at all. Brendan's vision that the vodka would transform Sarah into a rosy-faced easy-going partygoer, full of enthusiasm and joie de vivre, never transpired. Instead, she finished her meal, took her coat from the hook and made her way into the night.

It wasn't until some days later that we found out, through the local press, that Sarah never made it home that night. She crashed her car into a tractor parked on the verge of the A272. She died instantly, along with the ten-week-old foetus she was carrying. Her husband, Daniel, was at home, preparing for the family lunch they had planned for the following day, when they intended to share the news with their families.

When the toxicology tests showed a high – although not astronomic – level of alcohol in her blood, Daniel's protestations that Sarah wouldn't have gone near alcohol and risked the pregnancy were written off as the blind faith of a devoted husband. Chemistry doesn't lie, was the general attitude. And not all pregnant women abstain entirely, even if they tell their husbands they do.

In the end, Sarah was written off as just another reckless partygoer who'd had one drink too many at Christmas time, thought the rules didn't apply to her and paid the price with her – and her unborn child's – life.

Chapter 73

When Luke and I heard the news, we said the same things to each other over and over again: Sarah Rubinstein was forty-three years old but we'd assumed she was older. We hadn't even considered the possibility that she could be pregnant. And the road had been icy that night. It was an accident black spot. She hadn't seemed drunk when she left. She may have had the accident anyway.

But we both knew there was every chance she may not.

Brendan was quick to reduce – erase – his own role in what had happened. Luke had poured the drink and I had served it – all of which, not insignificantly, had been captured by The Watch's CCTV.

Still, despite Daniel's protests, there was nothing to suggest that Sarah hadn't ordered the drinks herself. There was nothing to suggest any wrongdoing on our part. That is, except Luke's desire to bare his soul.

Initially, I'd thought our liability was simply moral. I'd been physically sick when I'd realised what we'd done. What kind of person did it make me to have forced alcohol on a pregnant woman? It was true that we had had no way of knowing that she was pregnant but then we hadn't stopped to consider the possibility. We hadn't stopped to think about Sarah Rubinstein as a person at all. She was, to us, simply a means to an end. A tool to be used in our quest for success. In our desire to appease Brendan. And without the alcohol in her bloodstream, would her reaction speed have been just a fraction of a second faster? And would that have made the difference between her swerving to avoid the tractor, and her ploughing, as she did, into the back of it?

I replayed the evening over in my mind, trying to pinpoint the one moment that sealed her fate: was it when Luke handed me the first laced drink with a helpless shrug? When I'd set it down in front of her? When she exited the building, her hand rummaging in her bag, when it hadn't even occurred to me she may have been reaching for her car keys?

It was only later that I started to consider the legal position. I knew if what we'd done came out it would mean the end for the club – the spiking of the drinks alone would no doubt have ensured that, even without the car accident – but the more I looked into it, the more evidence I found that our actions – mine and Luke's, as those were what had been recorded – were criminal.

Quickly I realised that administering alcohol – a poison or 'noxious thing' – to someone without their consent was an assault in itself. The fact it had then, quite possibly, played a part in that person's death meant there was a good case it could be considered manslaughter. It didn't matter, as Luke was fond of saying, that 'we had no way of knowing what would happen'. The prosecution would argue, I was sure, that we *should* have known. Or at least, realised there was a risk that it might, which was enough.

I read pages and pages of newspaper archives and legal journals on the various situations that had led to manslaughter convictions. There were many where you could quite imagine that the accused would have protested, as we would, that their actions and the resultant consequences weren't sufficiently linked, that the death wasn't sufficiently inevitable, for them to be truly considered blameworthy.

There were burglars held responsible for the deaths of elderly homeowners who had heart attacks hours, or even days, after their break-ins, so shaken up were they by what had happened, in some cases never having set eyes on the perpetrator in person. There were student flatmates who had killed their friends by adding what they thought were harmless prescription pills to their drinks for a juvenile prank. There was a man who'd smuggled cocaine in a bottle of rum intended entirely for his own use but who was held responsible for the death of a man he'd never met into whose hands the rum fell and who drank it, quite unaware of its added ingredient.

In all of these cases, you could quite imagine the defendant pleading their case: 'But I never meant for anyone to die!' And in all of them, you could also imagine the judge's reply: 'Be that as it may, someone did.'

Despite the weight of the secret that I'd been carrying around for months, to convey the bare bones of the story took only a few minutes. Charlotte loosened her grip while she took it in.

'God. That's so bad!' she said, her commentary as inane as ever.

I didn't say anything.

Her gripped tightened again. 'So Luke was going to talk so you tried to kill him! That's so messed up!'

'No,' I said. I twisted around to look at her. 'Perhaps Brendan. I don't know. But I would never hurt Luke. He's everything to me.'

Charlotte crinkled her nose. 'Well, I don't see that that

makes any difference really. Your weirdo boyfriend did it. For you!' She laughed again.

As I teetered on the edge of the roof, I looked out at the town I called home and realised I'd never really felt at home there at all. Or anywhere, in fact. And at this point in my life, it seemed unlikely I ever would.

The future stretched out in front of me, a series of onerous tasks to be completed and misfortunes to divert. It all just seemed so daunting suddenly. Insurmountably challenging and *exhausting*.

I realised then that I'd been battling the inevitable my whole life and it had got me nowhere at all. Brendan's claim that he'd been with Joanne had turned out to be as absurd as it sounded and I knew that with this second lie as to his whereabouts exposed as a nonsense, we were edging closer to the appalling conclusion that he was responsible for Luke's condition and therefore, as I knew my family would see it, so was I. They wouldn't believe that I had known nothing of Brendan's intentions, just as they hadn't believed – or cared – that I wasn't responsible for that pan of boiling water that so horrifically scarred Luke's leg, that he'd climbed up and pulled the pan down before I'd even had a chance to look up, much less intervene to stop it falling. They'd already decided who I was and anything I did to counter that conclusion was futile.

And now, really, with Luke slipping away, what was even the point in it all? What was I carrying on for? And who?

'I know about Frieda,' I said, but the fight was gone from my voice. Seeing how Charlotte would explain herself was just a matter of idle curiosity at this point.

Charlotte seemed unimpressed. Bored almost. 'Yeah, I know. You went all the way to Bath. You nutter.'

'Do you even care if Luke lives or dies?' I said.

Charlotte seemed to be thinking about this. 'Jenny and Stephen will be very sad if he dies, at first. But I think they'll be happier in the long run. They're my priority now.'

I laughed weakly at the pure absurdity of the girl. 'You've known them less than a month! You're virtual strangers!'

She pulled on my jacket to force me to turn and look at her. 'I have been more of a daughter to them in the last four weeks that you have in your whole life. They don't even like you!'

'I'm quite aware of that,' I said quietly.

'How have you even managed that?' she said, shaking her head, bemused. 'Parents are supposed to automatically love their kids and you've managed to make them hate you! How?'

'I don't believe yours were so fond of you either. They seemed quite unconcerned about your departure anyway.'

She narrowed her eyes. 'They were not parents.'

'It's not going to last, you do know that, don't you? Whatever happens with Luke, he's their son. You're just a . . . distraction. A space-filler. When they realise who you are, they'll cast you aside. They'll have no qualms about doing that, I'm sure. They're really quite callous, despite the public image they so carefully curate.'

Charlotte's chin jutted out defiantly. 'They would never kick me out. They need me. I'm the daughter they never had.'

In anyone else this would have been an obvious slight, a dig. But with Charlotte, it wasn't like that. It was as if she'd forgotten to whom she was talking, as if she truly believed in what she was saying.

'You're pathetic,' I said. 'Just desperate. Nothing more interesting than that.' And I said it wearily, because I was just so weary of it all – of people believing whatever they wanted to believe, of people being so hoodwinked by superficiality and

334

nonsense. Of being misunderstood. I sighed. 'Just desperate and mad.'

And then, without warning, she jerked me backwards, and then propelled me forwards, sending me over the edge of the roof.

There was a moment – just a fraction of a second – when I could have reached out for the guttering, or for Charlotte herself, and perhaps prevented myself from falling, but I let the moment pass.

And so I fell. And I was facing backwards and looking up at the sky, and at Charlotte silhouetted against the evening clouds, and I felt the most enormous sense of relief.

Charlotte

Chapter 74

I took the precaution of wiping everything in Rebecca's flat down with an anti-bacterial wipe I found under the sink. I was quite thorough – you probably could have carried out surgery in the place by the time I'd finished – but it was simpler, I thought, if they never knew I'd been there.

I was just considering what to do with her phone when a message came though. It was from someone called Joanne Waite.

> Hi Rebecca, it's me again. I've just found out that Brendan was here the night he said he was but I didn't know about it. Apparently, he was sat outside in his car for hours. My boyfriend didn't tell me coz he didn't want to upset me but I think you should know. I don't know what he thinks he's playing at. I stand by what I told you before: get rid of him.

In the end, I tossed the phone over the edge of the roof and watched the glass smash as it hit the pavement next to Rebecca's body. She wouldn't be needing it now anyway.

When I got back to the White House, Stephen and Jenny seemed relieved to see me.

'Oh there you are, love!' Jenny said. 'We couldn't think where you'd got to. We started dinner without you – there's some on the side for you.'

'Sorry,' I said. 'I bumped into a friend, and she asked if I wanted a chat, and well, I did really. I should've let you know though.'

Jenny waved her hand. 'We tried to call but neither of us could find our bloody phones!' She turned to Stephen. 'Did you try the drawer in the dressing table? I sometimes put things in there without thinking when I'm tidying up.'

Stephen sighed and he put his hands on his knees to stand up.

'I'll go,' I said, giving him a smile and a pat on the shoulder.

Upstairs, I took both phones from my pocket and switched them back on, then I took them back downstairs and delivered them to Stephen and Jenny in the kitchen.

'Oh! There!' Jenny said, taking hers from me and shaking her head. 'What an idiot I am.'

'They were just up there, in the drawer, together, were they?' Stephen said, turning his phone over in his hands as if inspecting it for signs of criminal activity.

'Yep,' I said.

Stephen frowned at the screen. 'Missed called from Becky. I'll call her back.' He held the phone to his ear for a few moments before giving up and setting the handset on the table in front of him. 'Voicemail,' he said quietly. He didn't leave a message.

Stephen and Jenny stayed at the table with me while I ate the dinner they'd saved for me and Stephen asked me about the friend I'd been to see that afternoon.

'Oh, it was just a girl I used to work with,' I said.

'Has she got a name?'

'Emily.'

'And you just bumped into her, did you?' Stephen was looking at me strangely.

'For goodness' sake, leave her alone Stephen,' Jenny said. 'It's none of your business.'

After dinner, we retired to the lounge to watch television, although I was struggling to concentrate after everything that had happened that day.

It was about ten p.m., just as I was about to head up to bed, when the doorbell rang. It had taken longer than I'd imagined for them to come.

I heard Stephen talking to someone in the hall, then he appeared in the doorway to the lounge with two police officers standing behind him, their hats in their hands.

'Jen, it's the police.'

She spun around to look at them. 'Is it Luke? What's happened?'

Stephen shook his head. 'No. They say it's about Becky.'

Chapter 75

The days after the news of Rebecca's suicide were hard, as I knew they would be.

Jenny and Stephen withdrew into themselves so much it seemed they were barely functioning for a while. I had to gently steer them through each day, making drinks, preparing meals, running baths and suggesting they got in them. They didn't really engage with me at all in this time. If they spoke, it seemed to be more to voice their internal dialogue, to diarise. It didn't require much response on my part. They'd always been quite considerate about how I was feeling, and that seemed to be forgotten temporarily, but I knew I shouldn't blame them for that.

I knew they weren't ready to hear it, so I didn't voice the thought out loud, but it was clear at once that it was better that Rebecca was out of the picture. She was – and had always been, as far as I could tell – a toxic presence in their lives. A canker that needed to be gouged out, as it was beginning to infect everything around it. They needed to focus on Luke, on the decisions they needed to make, and Rebecca had only ever made that more difficult.

'I did love her,' Jenny said to me one evening, a few days after the police's visit. 'She wasn't what I thought my daughter would be like, but I did love her.'

'What did you think your daughter would be like?' I asked. I waited to hear a description of myself but perhaps it wasn't needed.

'I don't know,' she said eventually, and wandered off into the garden.

Coroner's inquiries – like many of life's boring administrative matters – take ages. The police were quite clear from the beginning that it was all just a formality, and the verdict would almost certainly be suicide. I had no qualms about this. It was like Stephen remarked once, when he and I were spiralising a courgette in the kitchen, 'Becky just never felt at home in this world.' In this way, I felt her death was suicide, if you took into account the wider context. There had been barely any fight in her as we tussled on that rooftop. It took just the slightest nudge from me for her to surrender to her fate. It put me in mind of those people who brandish guns at the police and wait for them to retaliate, to put them out of their misery. Suicide by another hand is still suicide.

Once the immediate shock and rawness had begun to subside a week or so after her death, we knew we had to turn our attention back to Luke.

As I had known she would, DS Leech had continued trying to get hold of me – both on the phone and in person – since her discovery of Luke's date with Kelly the night of the attack. I'd so far evaded her though. There was something about her voice in the messages she'd left me that sounded smug. Triumphant, even. Like being about to pull this information about Kelly out of the bag and watch my confusion made her feel like she had done something impressive.

That was the thing about police. They thought that any

discovery, any peeling back of the curtain to reveal a truth, was a win. No matter who it hurt. I knew I would have to speak to her eventually, but I was still formulating my response. At first, I thought I had no option but to tell her I knew nothing about Kelly and couldn't imagine why Luke would be on a date with another woman when he was very much mine, but I didn't like how that account made me look. I didn't want to be the deceived, oblivious fool. That wasn't me. Instead, I'd begun to create an alternative explanation, where I claimed to be completely aware that Luke saw other people from time to time, it being an option I also exercised myself.

'Total monogamy's so old-fashioned, don't you think?' I'd tell Leech witheringly. 'You'd have to be pretty insecure, wouldn't you, to insist on being the only person your boyfriend ever spoke to.'

Staff at the hospital had seen the tension in the family during the last attempt at a best-interests meeting and had allowed things to continue for a while without intervention on their part to give us time to accept our situation. They extended this approach once news of Rebecca's demise reached them, so we had, all in all, been given a good while longer than we would have otherwise. But we all knew that we had to face up to reality at some point. The reality being, as Anne Moriarty gently reminded us one afternoon eight days after Rebecca's death, that it was her responsibility, and not ours, to decide how to proceed with Luke's care.

'As I explained last time we met, a scenario where Luke recovers to his previous state is not really a realistic hope at this stage. And, as I know we've discussed at length, a continuous vegetative existence is not a life that would ever be acceptable to Luke.'

She paused. I knew she was giving us space to draw the obvious inference without her having to spell it out.

Stephen took a large intake of breath then blew it out slowly. 'So. What happens? When, and . . . ?'

'Tomorrow morning we'll withdraw the ventilator and breathing tube. You can be with him. It will be quite peaceful.'

Jenny let out a sudden sob, and held her hand tightly over her mouth as if attempting to physically hold in her grief.

That evening at the house Jenny moved about as if in a trance. On several occasions I had to intervene – to stop a sink overflowing, to retrieve a pair of slippers from the fridge. In the end I positioned both of them in the lounge and delivered them their meal on their laps. They barely ate, staring without expression at a documentary about Indian railways. When the programme ended, Jenny switched the television off but the two of them continued to sit, looking at the blank screen. After a few minutes, I started to find the silence a bit uncomfortable, and was just working out what I could say to chivvy them along, when Jenny suddenly said: 'Both of them. All of my children. Gone. How has this happened?'

Stephen turned to look at her. He opened his mouth as if to speak, but in the end he just shook his head.

I stood up and crossed the room to Jenny's sofa. I sat next to her and put my hand on hers and squeezed. 'Not all of them,' I said quietly. I squeezed her hand again.

Stephen's head jerked around to look at me. He had a strange look on his face, as if he'd just encountered a gruesome piece of rotting meat. It was one of Rebecca's favoured expressions, actually. It must run in the genes.

Chapter 76

Later that evening, when I'd managed to pack Jenny off to bed, I found Stephen standing at the window, a glass of Scotch in his hand.

'I emailed her,' he said, without turning to face me. 'To tell her to pull her socks up. I was going to do it in person, but when she didn't give me the chance, I sent her an email – telling her off. I was angry that she'd run off when I'd asked to talk to her. That she didn't seem to have time for us. But now . . .' He shook his head. 'It must have been the last straw.'

'You think she . . . because of what you said in an email . . . ?' I wasn't sure exactly what this email could have said, but I suspected mild-mannered Stephen might have been overestimating the power of his words. I tried to make this point, as gently as I could. 'I think it would take more than . . . more than one thing. One disagreement.'

'Perhaps.' He didn't sound convinced. 'Don't mention it to Jenny though. I don't think any good can come of that.'

Half an hour or so later, I found that he'd moved to the kitchen, and was hunched over the big blue leather-bound photo albums from which Jenny had taken the family photos that adorned the kitchen walls. He was turning the pages slowly, tracing his fingers over the images.

'Trip down memory lane, is it?' I said brightly, flicking the kettle on.

He didn't reply, but continued to turn the pages.

I stood at his shoulder and looked down at the pictures. The page he was on seemed to feature photos from about twenty years ago: Luke a gangly ten-year-old, his hair sticking straight up, a skateboard under his arm; Rebecca standing behind him, leaning against the radiator in a bedroom.

'Luke's tenth birthday,' Stephen said, not looking up from the page. 'Rebecca gave him that skateboard.'

'Is that his bedroom?'

'Rebecca's,' Stephen said. 'Wouldn't have been able to see the floor in Luke's, for all the Lego and computer games and everything else.' He chuckled. The same certainly couldn't be said for the bedroom in the photo, which looked to me not dissimilar from a cell in a high-security psychiatric hospital.

'She wasn't one for bits and pieces, was she?' I said absently, taking two mugs out of the dishwasher and setting them next to the kettle.

'How do you mean?' Stephen asked.

'Oh, you know,' I said. 'Just that she didn't like things. Homey things. I don't think she had a single picture on the wall in her flat! Just white walls. White, white, white.'

Stephen didn't say anything. He just kept turning the pages of the album.

I put his mug down in front of him and he looked up at me. 'When did you see?' he said.

'See what?'

'When did you see Becky's flat?'

I hesitated for just the briefest of moments. Then I said, 'Oh, I didn't. Not myself. Jenny told me. Jenny said, "Not a

347

single bloody photo in the whole place! It's like she's ashamed of us!"'

I was quite pleased with my attempt at Jenny's accent. It was so something she would have said, anyway. In fact, I couldn't be sure that she hadn't said it, at some point.

Stephen frowned and looked back at the album.

'Couldn't say the same for here though, could we?' I smiled and nodded at the wall of photos Jenny had created next to the oven. Stephen followed my gaze, but he didn't say anything.

I stood up and went over to them, putting my mug down on the side. I looked at each one in turn, the smiling faces, the arms linked together. It seemed to me, suddenly, that it was all such a lie, such a sham, that Jenny had created here. This one, for example, with Jenny and Rebecca side by side in some kind of English country garden, as if mother and daughter would frequently take to strolling through shrubbery, chatting about life and men and whatever else. When the reality was, they couldn't stand each other. They made each other's skin crawl.

And one here of Luke, his arm slung around Stephen's shoulders, each of them with a pint in hand, like two old friends. Surely what was closer to the truth was that Luke had been humouring his dad by letting him come out with his friends. No doubt an ungrateful young man like Luke, who had always taken his parents' love for granted, had been counting down the minutes till the old duffer would bugger off home so he could have a proper night out with his mates.

I felt protective of them suddenly. Defensive. I hated these photos. In every one of them their children, their pride and joy, were clearly tolerating them at best – at worst, mocking them. And Jenny and Stephen were so blind to it they'd put up this whole wall of images, making it clear for everyone to see what a laughing stock they were. I suddenly couldn't bear it any more.

I pulled one of the photos from the wall, the Blu-tack giving way easily. 'I think we should take this down,' I said. 'It's not good for Jenny, for any of us, to have all these bad memories around us.'

Stephen spun around in his chair. 'They're not bad memories.'

'I'll take them all down now, before the morning.' I pulled another two from the wall and added them to the pile.

'Leave them,' Stephen said.

'That way Jenny won't have to face them when she comes down.' I added another to the pile. 'Tomorrow will be hard enough as it is.'

Stephen stood up suddenly, roughly pushing his chair back across the slate floor. 'Leave them!' he said again.

As I reached up to take one particularly objectionable image – Jenny and Stephen sitting crossed legged on the grass, Rebecca looming behind them like she was preparing to garrotte the pair of them – Stephen reached out and grabbed my wrist. He pulled hard, wrenching me away from the wall. 'I said, leave them the hell alone!' he shouted.

I froze and stepped back from him, my mouth open. He stood opposite me, breathing hard.

'I . . .' he began, but got no further with the thought.

I picked my mug up off the side and left the kitchen. As I made my way up the stairs to my bedroom, I could see Stephen through the gap in the bannister, reinstating the photos I'd removed from the display.

Chapter 77

The following morning, Jenny and Stephen were already in the kitchen when I arrived downstairs. As I entered the room, Stephen looked up and our eyes met, just for a moment, before he looked away again. I wasn't sure what he was more worried about, me mentioning to Jenny his confession about the email that he feared had sent Rebecca – quite literally – over the edge, or his violent outburst. Either way he needn't have worried. I planned to have words with him about his aggression at some point – it's not good for a family, to let these kinds of tensions go unchallenged – but I knew today wasn't the day. Today was the day to say goodbye to Luke. And hello to the rest of our lives.

At the hospital, the on-duty nurse explained to us what would happen.

'People often imagine that it's just a simple case of one switch, but it's a little more complex than that. So we ask relatives to give the doctors space to disconnect the life-sustaining equipment. We'll move him to a private room, then we can call you in to be with him at the end.'

'How long is it . . . after you . . . ?' Stephen asked. Jenny sat completely motionless, staring at the wall.

'It can vary from a few minutes to a lot longer than that. It's hard to say.'

There wasn't a single word exchanged between us in the time between the nurse leaving that room and them calling us through to sit at Luke's bedside.

It was strange, to see him free from the machine and tubes, after getting so used to seeing him attached to them. It was eerily quiet too, without the sound of the ventilator, without the beeping and the whirring.

As we entered the room, Jenny turned to look at Stephen and he took her hand. We stood on either side of the bed – me on one, them on the other – and Jenny put her hand on Luke's shoulder. Steady silent tears were falling down her cheeks, faster than I'd ever seen before. Stephen, whom I had seen cry numerous times, seemed too shell-shocked even for that. We stood like that for a time, none of us speaking.

Then Jenny looked up at Stephen and said, 'I think he's breathing.'

Stephen looked at her, and then to Luke. 'I don't think . . . Is he . . . ?'

'He is! He is, Stephen,' Jenny said, her voice louder now. 'Look. Look at his chest!'

Stephen placed his hand gently on Luke's chest. Then he held his ear close to Luke's mouth. 'Yes, I think you're . . . I think he is . . . ? Is that . . . what they said? What does that mea—?'

'Go and get someone,' Jenny said. 'This is a mistake. He wants to live! Go and get someone, Stephen!'

Stephen took one more look at Luke then bolted out of the door. Jenny leant in closer to the bed and started talking to Luke in a low, urgent voice. 'Just hold on, baby,' she said. 'Stay with us, darling boy, someone's coming.'

Just hold on, she kept saying. Just hold on.

And with her suddenly so hopeful, with Stephen rushing off to wherever he'd gone, I felt everything I'd learnt about the situation – everything I'd read and everything Anne Moriarty had said to us – slipping away. There were always mistakes, weren't there? You'd hear about them, against-the-odds, one-in-a-million, inexplicable miraculous recoveries.

As I stood there, watching Jenny leaning over Luke, whispering to him, telling him to keep fighting, I began to play out a scene in my mind. The doctors would come. They would talk to each other quietly, trying to mask their surprise from us, but clearly flabbergasted by this turn of events. They would make checks and measurements, perhaps issue an injection of some sort, then Luke's eyes would begin to flicker open. Jenny and Stephen would be talking to him all the time and he would blink in confusion, wondering where he was, where he'd been, what was happening. And all the while Jenny saying things like, 'We knew you'd come back to us,' and 'We knew we'd never give up,' and other things which were blatantly untrue.

Once Luke had come round and had a glass of water, and had been filled in on what had happened to him and what had occurred over the last few weeks, he would look at me and say, 'What's that woman doing in here?'

And that would be it. I would be moved out, and Luke would be moved in – I was only ever a consolation prize after all – and I would be alone again. Maybe, once in a while, at Christmas time, the Burleys would turn to each other and say, 'Remember that strange girl who hung around us for a while? What was her name? Charlene? Odd, all that business, wasn't it.'

I had a choice to make, in that moment. I could turn and run out of that hospital, and out of that town and that family and that life, or I could stay. I could fight and claim what was mine before they had the chance to pull it away from me.

I stepped out of the door and looked up and down the corridor. 'Still no sign of them,' I said to Jenny. Then, 'Oh! I think that was Anne Moriarty, down at the end of corridor?'

'Get her!' Jenny said. 'Get her.'

When I didn't move, Jenny came to join me in the doorway. 'This is ridiculous!' she said, looking up and down the corridor. She turned back to me. 'Stay with Luke, watch him!' Then she jogged off down the corridor, in the direction I had sent her.

I closed the door to the room and I went back over to Luke's bed. He was definitely breathing, there was no doubt about that. I took his hand in mine and as I did so I felt, I was sure a twitch. A squeeze. But then as soon as it had happened, I thought perhaps I'd imagined it. I squeezed his hand but there was no response. But I was sure I'd felt something. He'd moved. I was *sure*.

But then I thought, it didn't matter, really, either way. For weeks we had been waiting and seeing how things went and not knowing, and having to accept whichever course of events fate had thrown our way. I was sick of it. It's impossible to plan any kind of life with so much uncertainty hanging over it, and now here I was again, not knowing. Not knowing what was going to happen when Jenny and Stephen returned with a doctor in tow. Not knowing what it was all going to mean for me. Where I would go, who I would be. And I realised, at that moment, that it was quite within my power to put into motion a course of events where I *did* know what the outcome would be. Where everything would be final and conclusive, and from where we could all move on, once and for all.

I took the pillow from the visitor's chair, lifted it above Luke and after just a moment of hesitation, I held it firmly over his face.

I think perhaps I'd expected him to struggle, as if I imagined this sudden direct interference would cause some survival instinct to kick in and he would push me away, but of course it didn't. He was no more able to fight that pillow than he was the decision to turn off his machines.

He was helpless. He was in my hands. He always had been, right from the start.

Chapter 78

I'd had the pillow in place for just a few seconds when I heard voices and footsteps outside. For the briefest of moments, I considered staying as I was, waiting to see if they passed, but I knew it was too risky and, reluctantly, I pulled the pillow away and replaced it on the chair next to the bed – just as the door to the room crashed open.

It was Jenny and Stephen together; they must have bumped into each other on their quest for medical assistance. Jenny was talking in full flow: 'Because it happens, doesn't it? Scans never tell the whole truth.'

The nurse accompanying them was clearly trying to listen to what Jenny was saying, but at the same time keep the sudden surge of optimism in check. 'Sometimes patients do manage to breathe on their own for a short time but sadly that doesn't usually alter their ultimate prognosis.'

'But surely,' Jenny insisted – they were inside the room now, but none of them acknowledged me – 'Surely if they thought he couldn't breathe on his own, but he can . . . well, that means there may be other things he can do on his own too? And that could mean . . .'

Jenny's voice trailed off. She watched the nurse intently as he went to Luke's bed, and made some checks, taking his pulse, watching him closely.

'He is, isn't he?' she said after a few moments had passed. 'He's breathing? On his own!'

The nurse nodded slowly. 'He is,' he said. 'He is indeed.'

Jenny let out a little gasp of delight and pressed her hand to her mouth.

'But,' the nurse went on in a cautionary tone, 'that isn't, in itself, as significant as you might hope. I'm sorry, I don't want to be negative, really I don't. I just don't want you to get your hopes up too high. Luke breathing without assistance doesn't necessarily mean that other signs of recovery will follow, I'm afraid.'

Jenny nodded but it was clear that she wasn't taking in the nurse's words. She returned to Luke's bedside and was stroking his cheek saying, 'Come on baby, come *on*,' over and over again.

'I'll ask the consultant to come and speak to you,' the nurse said quietly, and slipped out of the room.

Jenny nodded, not taking her eyes off Luke's face, at his chest, quite slowly, but quite definitely, rising and falling.

Chapter 79

I know they think I didn't know what they were all saying about me, after the fire. They thought that because I stopped talking, I stopped listening too. Stopped hearing. But I didn't. Obviously I didn't.

And I wasn't too keen on it, I have to say, their interpretation of it all. That I drugged Aunt Frieda with sleeping pills, set fire to the house, then left her to burn alive, because – why? – because I was jealous that she didn't love me as much as the others? Because I was angry that she was going to kick me out, when I thought I'd found somewhere I could stay? Somewhere I was wanted?

I was jealous, and I was angry, but there was one big thing they all overlooked when they were busy gossiping in the street, reporting me to psychiatric professionals – that I would never have deliberately hurt Aunt Frieda because I loved her. I still love her. I just wanted to show her how much she needed me.

She had so many, in that house. The little ones, the big ones, her own ones, and the ones who just called in even though they didn't need to because they had their own homes, their own parents. I'd started to feel lost in the crowd. I just wanted her to single me out, just once. I just wanted her to *see* me.

That was all the plan was. To create the fire, but then to rescue them all, to show them all – to show Frieda – what I was capable of. And I did – I did do that. People barely paid any attention to that bit, but it was me who rounded them all up, who held damp towels to their faces to protect their lungs from the hot smoke. Who took them by their hands and guided them out.

I was so careful about it all. I knew it wasn't on to be reckless with people's lives, so I'd researched how to do it – where to set the fire, the direction it would spread, which route we would take to escape. It was all meticulously planned. I thought no harm could come of it.

All I'd wanted was for the pills to keep Frieda asleep just a little longer than she would otherwise. I just wanted a little extra time so I could be the hero for once – before she jumped in to take control.

I don't know why she wouldn't stir. I suppose they were stronger than I'd realised. Perhaps I used too much, when I'd ground them up and added them to the glass of water on her bedside table. Either way, it was a simple mistake.

I know it killed her, but it really was just a mistake.

Chapter 80

When we returned home to the White House that evening, that day when we should have finally said goodbye to Luke, when Stephen and Jenny should have *finally* been freed from their purgatory, I felt flat. It had been such a relief when we'd felt that an end was in sight, and that we would soon be able to move on, as a family. To mourn the past, but to not let it drag us down any longer. But now here we were again, stuck in the middle of it all with no idea what would happen next, our lives still on hold.

The consultant had confirmed what the nurse had warned us: the independent breathing didn't tell us anything very much, but they reattached Luke to the ventilator anyway, put things back to the way they had been, just to give us more time to 'come to terms with things'.

I suppose what she had been saying is that we would, more than likely, be back in the same position, in the same room, with the same painful goodbye on our hands in a few weeks anyway, but she was giving Jenny time to get over her brief flash of hope before we had to do it all again.

Jenny, though, showed no sign of getting over it. In fact,

her optimism seemed to grow daily. There were more articles downloaded, more tales of against-all-odd recoveries recounted excitedly over breakfast. She was at the hospital more than ever, and she was now on constant high alert for any signs that supported her firmly held belief that Luke was going to pull himself out of this.

'I was holding his hand and I gave the top of his finger a little pinch – not too hard but he'd definitely feel it, you know? – and do you know what he did? His forehead twitched! Just a little bit – only someone who knows his face as well as I do would have seen it probably – but it was there. A flinch! Like he was saying, "Oi, Mum, cut it out!"'

Outwardly Stephen seemed to be trying to hold Jenny back from getting too carried away with what she saw – or thought she saw – Luke do, but I could tell his heart wasn't in his caution. He too wanted to believe more than anything that the doctors had been wrong to give Luke such a dismal prognosis.

It fell to me, then, to try, as gently as possible, to provide a voice of reason, to echo the message of the doctors and to attempt to save them from more crushing disappointment. Taking this role proved difficult though because it was clearly one Jenny didn't appreciate.

At first she seemed not to hear what I was saying at all, simply not replying when I suggested other explanations for what she'd interpreted as a clear sign of progress, but then she began to seem irritated by it.

'There!' she cried during one visit. 'I squeezed his hand and he squeezed back! Didn't you see his fingers move?'

I hadn't meant to, but I'd sighed. I started to get weary of these stories. 'I think that was just you though. *You're* moving his hand by touching it the whole time.'

'I didn't,' she said quietly, turning away from me. 'I know what I felt. I'm not a total idiot, you know.'

I started to realise it was safer if I just avoided coming to the hospital, as far as possible, so I told them I'd had to go back to work and took myself off for whole days at a time, passing the hours in the library or, more often, a pub. I told them I visited Luke when they weren't around, that I'd just missed them, that I'd been there earlier that day.

So on the evening when Stephen and Jenny crashed through the front door, kicking off shoes and talking over each other in excitement to get the news out, I hadn't seen Luke myself for nearly ten days, and was in no position to provide my usual pragmatic explanation for whatever sign of recovery they thought they'd seen.

And actually, that didn't really matter when it came to it, because even I had to admit there was no way Jenny could have been mistaken about this one:

'He's opened his eyes, Charlotte!' Jenny sobbed, grasping me by the top of my arms. 'Our boy has woken up!'

Chapter 81

I'd sat down heavily on the stairs, such was the shock of the news. Naturally Jenny and Stephen read this reaction as delight – positive surprise – but what I actually felt was panic.

I had been so sure that Jenny's hope was misplaced that I hadn't seriously considered for one moment that Luke could actually be on the road to recovery. But now, there he was, lying there with his eyes open, seeing things around him. Which meant that very soon indeed, he would see me.

Luckily it was late in the day by this point, which meant that Jenny wasn't able to immediately dash back to the hospital as she no doubt would have liked, but instead was forced to wait the night before we could all return in the morning. From the urgent, excited whispers coming from their bedroom, I knew that Jenny and Stephen would spend this time picking apart what had happened, analysing what it would mean and how things might develop from here.

I too used the time to plan what would happen next, and by the morning, I felt more relaxed – confident that I could handle the situation.

I knew from my own research, and from what I had heard

from the various medical professionals over the last few weeks, that it was highly unlikely that Luke would wake up in any normal meaning of the word – in the way he might from a long afternoon nap, for example. Opening his eyes didn't mean he was about to sit up and begin chatting away, ready to catch up on what he had missed. I knew that his open eyes might not actually be seeing anything at all, that he might have no way of taking in images and processing them into anything meaningful. In which case, I reasoned, I would be fine – and at no greater risk of discovery than I had ever been.

I did, however, have to contemplate the possibility that this development could be the first in a number of bounds forward in his recovery, and that at some point on the journey, he might regain the ability to communicate in some way, however basic. Still, if that stage ever did come, and if he – somehow – found a way to let people know that I wasn't his girlfriend, that I never had been, that he didn't want me near him, I had a very simple plan of action: I would stay in role, exactly as I had been, altering not one bit of the backstory I had provided to Stephen and Jenny.

Any concerns that Luke was able to communicate from his bed could be explained away as amnesia, exactly the type of confusion you'd expect from someone who'd suffered a serious head injury and been out cold for weeks on end. Maybe, I thought with a little smile, in time I might even be able to convince Luke himself that we were a couple.

As soon as we arrived on the ward though, as soon as Jenny rushed over to his bedside, I realised my plan wouldn't be needed any time soon. I felt quite sure that Luke wouldn't be throwing an accusation my way, or doing anything else, for a good while yet. His eyes were open, there was no denying that, but it was clear he was far from alert.

He stared blankly at the ceiling, showing no sign that he

even realised we were there, much less who we were. If anything, I thought this new development made him seem more lost to us than he had before. When he'd been unconscious it had seemed like he was asleep, just like any of us might be, and that he would at some point wake up in the normal way. Now, though, he seemed truly like an injured man. A ravaged man. A shell, with all of his working parts – his essence – gone.

So eerie did I find the sight of him, that I couldn't bring myself to go to him at all, to even pretend to interact with him. And certainly not to kiss his face as Jenny was doing.

Instead I hung back and watched the three of them nervously, for the first time feeling like perhaps these weren't my people after all.

Chapter 82

I suppose it was my reaction that day in the hospital that marked the beginning of the unravelling of our little unit of three.

Jenny and Stephen would continue to discuss Luke's progress with me, but the tone became more formal and succinct. I felt that they were saving their real conversations – the speculation, the optimism – for each other, sharing with me only the bare facts.

I was still surprised though, when, two weeks on from the day Luke had opened his eyes, Jenny announced he was to be transferred to a residential care and rehabilitation facility. It was the first I'd heard of the plan, but Jenny's tone made it clear the wheels were already in motion, and she wasn't seeking my input or approval.

'Which one?' I asked, trying to conceal my resentment at having been disregarded like this. 'Where?'

'It's called The Meadowrise Unit. Just outside Huddersfield.'

'Up north? But that's miles away! How are we supposed to visit him all the way up there? Isn't there anywhere closer they can send him?'

Jenny frowned very slightly. 'It's forty-five minutes from home, so not on the doorstep but not bad, all things considered. And it's one of the best places in the country apparently, for Luke's situation.'

It took me a few moments to piece together what she was saying. 'So we'll all move up there? To be near him?'

She paused. That frown again. 'Well, it's not moving, is it? That's where we live. That's our home.'

I didn't know how to reply to this. I knew what she was saying was true, but so much had happened in the last few weeks, we'd established such a routine, that I thought we'd considered the White House was home, to all of us.

Despite my irritation at being left out of the decision-making process, and my disappointment at the idea of having to up sticks again when I'd just started to make Brighton my home, I managed to console myself with the knowledge that a new place meant a new start, a new blank slate and new opportunities. I had enjoyed Brighton but not everything had worked out as I'd imagined, so perhaps it was time to be thinking about moving on anyway.

By dinner time, I'd come to terms with the sudden change of plan and was even starting to feel quite excited about the move.

'I was just wondering,' I said, helping myself to salad from the bowl in the middle of the table, 'if it would be OK if I stayed with you for a few weeks? Just until I can get myself sorted, find a flat or a room or something?'

I had only really asked the question because I felt confident what the response would be. I was sure that they would look at each other in surprise, then perhaps Stephen would let out a little chuckle and put his hand on mine and say, 'Of course! Of course, you'll stay with us, for as long as you like. For good, if you want,' and then shake his head in bemusement at the idea that I'd felt I even had to ask. I'd been feeling so left out of things since Luke had opened his eyes that really, I'd only asked the question to engineer a little bonding moment between us. To draw out some reassurance.

Stephen's reaction was not at all what I expected though. He paused and looked at Jenny and she gave a little nod as if to confirm he should go ahead with whatever he was about to say.

'Listen, love, we just don't think it's a good idea you stay with us. For you to uproot yourself, because of this. You've got your whole life ahead of you. Luke's recovery could take a long time. A long, long time . . . and we're just not sure you're cut out for that. If you've really thought it through, I mean.'

I opened my mouth to protest but he cut me off.

'I don't want you to take that the wrong way, love,' he said hurriedly, 'but we know you hadn't been together very long and . . . well, when you agree to go for a few drinks and dinners with a fella you're not necessarily wanting to be signing yourself up for years of caring and . . .'

He trailed off.

'I don't . . .' I began, but then I stopped myself.

I had been ready to fight my corner, to insist I *was* up to the task, that I was more than happy to change my whole life for Luke, prepared to give up everything for them, when I stopped to consider: was I though, really?

Although I still had to be wary about the possibility that Luke may one day regain the ability to communicate, to object to my presence, in general Luke himself didn't really factor in my feelings on the situation. He never had. It had only ever been about Jenny and Stephen. About how they made me feel useful and needed and wanted. But now, here we were. And they could dress it up as concern for my welfare

367

and my future all they wanted, but it was quite clear what they were saying:

I wasn't wanted. Not any more.

I had served my purpose. I had only ever been second best, a distraction. Now they had Luke back – or at least, they felt he was on his way back – I was surplus to requirements.

And right there at the table, over the dinner of fried eggs and bread and salad that Jenny had thrown together because she would far rather be at the hospital than wasting time preparing meals for me, I realised I didn't want them either. I had been there for them, I had made sacrifices for them, but still, they were rejecting me. They were selfish. Self absorbed and obsessed with their precious son.

Who really, from what I could tell, was nothing very special at all.

Chapter 83

I left without saying goodbye in the end.

It had meant getting up before sunrise and spending the next few days sleeping with my head resting on my hold-all in the doorway of a disused car park but it made me feel powerful, to know they would be wondering where I'd gone and what had happened. I hoped in a way that they'd look for me, that they'd try to contact me, so I could have the satisfaction of ignoring them, or rejecting them right back. But they didn't.

There was a period of adjustment then, because I couldn't just go back to my old pre-Luke life. I had no job, no flat and I was coming to terms with the fact that Emily, Meredith and Alison were just more names on the long list of people who had, just for a moment, made me feel human, but now were simply part of my past. So I did get my new start, but it was London, rather than Yorkshire, that provided it. I'd enjoyed living in a city and was ready to take it to the next level. The anonymity of it all appealed to me.

I've found a job answering the phone for a little cab company in Dalston. I work nights, which I've never done before and

I like it. I feel like I see things other people don't get to see. That I inhabit a completely different world from everyone else. Although, I suppose, in a way, I've always felt a bit like that.

I call myself Polly here. Nobody could object to a Polly, could they? And it was sensible, I decided, to distance myself from Charlotte Wright. To shed that skin. I didn't want anyone to come looking for her, to get dragged back into that life again. Far better to have a clean break, I've always thought.

I'd let DS Leech ask her questions eventually. It seemed easier to let her have her way and be done be it than to have her hounding me for the rest of my life, so I went to see her myself, shortly before I left Brighton. I laid it on thick of course, apologising for not coming sooner but talking about how emotional and stressful and confusing the last few weeks had been. Then I rolled out my story about the open relationship, explained that it was well within the agreed boundaries of our arrangement for him to spend an evening in a bar with another woman. She'd seemed dubious about this, particularly as I hadn't mentioned it earlier, but the fact was it was beyond the police's duty – and their interest – to pass judgement on the private agreements reached between consenting adults. They did put to me the course of events proposed by Rebecca – that I had attacked Luke myself, in a jealous rage brought on by the discovery of his time with Kelly – but as they had to admit, they had no evidence for such an accusation. The ramblings of a bitter, vindictive oddball were hardly conclusive – especially considering she'd topped herself shortly after.

It was Kelly's ex, Flint, who was tried for grievous bodily harm with intent in the end. He was acquitted though, as there simply wasn't enough evidence to convince a jury. That was disappointing, I'm sure, for Jenny and Stephen, because really, the police knew they'd found their man, so all the momentum went out of the investigation at that point.

It will just be one of those crimes that go unpunished. I suppose that's just the way it goes sometimes.'

Chapter 84

Jenny unfriended me on Facebook, I noticed soon after I left them. I suppose that was her way of registering her displeasure at my rude departure. However, due to her lax privacy settings, I can still view her updates, if I'm ever curious about how things are working out for them.

The last time I looked, Luke's progress in the care home seemed slow, but you wouldn't guess that from the upbeat tone of Jenny's posts. In her most recent dispatch, she'd been gushing about the 'incredible moment' when Luke had managed to blink once to signal 'yes'. How she could tell the difference between a 'yes' blink and a normal blink I didn't know, but I knew it didn't really matter.

In a way, all Jenny's dreams had come true. Her whole life from now on could be focused on Luke – caring for him, sitting at his bedside, reporting his every move to an audience of loyal supporters. I wondered if, secretly, she was happier now than she had been before, when Luke had been living his own life, down in Brighton. When she had been having to make do with a ten-minute phone call once a week, to watching his life from afar.

I still see Luke's face sometimes, in my dreams. Interestingly it's not his face as I knew it best – eyes closed, wired up to those machines. It's how it looked in the picture he used on the dating app. That picture of him next to his bike, with the hills behind. That was the picture that would make my stomach turn over with excitement every time I saw a message from him appear in my inbox. Because at first those messages had been exciting. When you hit it off with someone, when the banter – the flirting! – flows easily, it all feels so full of brilliant possibility.

We had planned to meet. We decided to quite early on, and I will never know to this day what put him off, why he cooled suddenly. He asked to postpone our first date, citing work or other vague obligations he needed to deal with, but then the promised text to reschedule never came. I messaged him, in case there'd been some mix-up, a text lost somewhere in the ether, but when there was still no contact, I'd grown sad, and then, I suppose, a little desperate.

The connection had been so strong, I was sure of it. And that doesn't come along every day, does it? Someone you can just bounce off, someone who gets you? I felt we had a real shot at becoming something. I felt I had a real shot at finding someone who wanted me, to take me in, to make me their family. And so, feeling I had nothing much to lose, I wrote him a message telling him so, and begging him not to let this opportunity slide.

He did contact me then, but it wasn't at all what I wanted to hear. I don't know what had happened in the intervening weeks but he'd changed. Gone were his flirty jokes, his teasing, his attentive questioning about my likes and dislikes, and instead he was cold. Brief, formal and, actually, a bit cruel. I wasn't to contact him again, he said. If I did, he would report me to the app administrators.

I was shocked, and I was hurt. I sent a few angry messages in response, but as far as I know, he never carried out his threat to get me banned from the site. Instead, he just removed himself entirely, leaving me no way of contacting him.

It was four weeks after that last message that I saw him with Kelly. It stung, naturally, to find him there with her, but I took comfort from the fact that he was clearly having a miserable time. 'You see,' I felt like saying to him, 'it's just not true what they say about there being plenty of fish in the sea. Sometimes you catch a really good fish, and if you throw it back, you'll find yourself stuck with a rotten old fish in cheap perfume instead.'

It wasn't planned though. There's no way I could have planned it even if I'd wanted to. It was just coincidence that I saw him in that alley, taking a short cut to wherever he was going. On to meet another girl, probably.

I called out to him and he turned around and waited for me to catch up, obviously not knowing who I was, not able to see me properly in the shadows.

'All right, Luke?' I'd said, when I was in front of him. I gave him a moment to look at me, connect me with the photo that would have popped up on his app each time we'd messaged. But he didn't seem able to.

I chatted away for a bit, dropping in references to things we'd discussed in our messages, saying it was nice to finally meet him in person, just as we'd planned, but still: nothing.

When I eventually revealed my identity, he was neither pleased as I hoped he would be, nor embarrassed, as, all things considered, he should have been. Instead he was immediately cold and rude.

'You're not as fit as your photo,' he said.

I let that slide – he had always been one for the banter after all – and worked hard to continue the conversation. I struggled to break through though, to translate the easy chat we'd shared in our messages to this real life, face to face conversation.

It was at that point that I remembered what one of the girls at school had taught me: when it comes to boys, you have to let your hands do the talking.

I put my hand on his belt buckle and – rather to my surprise – managed to undo it, in one swift movement. This got a reaction out of him, but it wasn't exactly what I'd been looking for it. He pushed my hand away – he swatted at it, like I was a seagull after his chips – and took a step away from me. Then he started laughing. And really, this was where it all started to go wrong for him, because I am no stranger to rejection, but I just cannot tolerate ridicule.

Fine, if you don't want me, but don't make out that the idea of me is so preposterous that it actually causes you to collapse in a fit of mirth. I lost my temper. That's the truth of it. So I lifted my hand – which just so happened to still be clasping that silly glove puppet with its chunky little club that Kelly had stolen from the bar – and I swiped at the side of his head.

I understand from what the doctors in the hospital told us afterwards that it was something to do with the particular part of his head that I made contact with that did it. I must have found a weak spot, because he went straight down like a skittle at the bowling alley, his phone smashing against the kerb as he fell.

I stared at him for a while, and truly, my initial feeling was irritation. We had been mid-conversation and I had more to get off my chest – I wanted him to acknowledge how unkind and how unnecessary he had been, to concede that he had made a mistake by thinking he could find someone better than me.

When I saw the blood, I began to feel nervous. It did seem an awful lot to be coming out of a head like that. I realised he must have smacked it on the concrete as he fell, which I suppose was less than ideal.

I picked up the broken phone and slipped it into my bag. At the time I'd just been thinking of the money I might be able to get for it if I got the screen fixed, but I later realised how lucky it was that I'd done that, and was able to toss it off the end of the pier on my way home that night. It would have been annoying to have had to deal with awkward questions about why I wasn't listed among his contacts if the police had found it on his person.

I turned and ran away but then I stopped at the end of the alley and looked back at his legs sticking out. As long as no one had seen me run from him – and I didn't think they had – then there was no problem with me being caught seen going *to* him. It's what anyone would do, surely, if they saw someone lying motionless in an alley.

I told the story so many times – how I hadn't even realised who the figure was at first, how I'd thought it was just a rough sleeper taking shelter in a back alley, and it wasn't until I got close that I realised it was Luke – that the version I'd created pushed aside the real memories. Those other images – the shock on Luke's face as he registered the blow, his whole body lurching forward like a felled tree – would only come to me if I concentrated very carefully.

I had to recite my own account so many times – to Jenny and Stephen, to the doctors, to the police – that I think I started to believe it was quite possible that it was true. My version of events existed in the minds of so many people by the time I was done that it seemed to me there was a good argument to consider it more real than anything that might have happened when there was no one there to witness it.

I'd been surprised, really, that I'd been able to manage the police quite so efficiently. It had begun as a simple matter of evasion – the leaving of a wrong phone number with the hospital that first night, a few hastily made exits from the ward – but by the time I sat down to have a proper conversation with DS Leech I just told her the story as I wanted them to see it, and she didn't seem to have any real grounds for disbelieving me. She had her doubts and I suppose I knew it was only ever really a matter of time until those doubts led her somewhere awkward – to Kelly, as it turned out – but there were a good few weeks when I definitely had the upper hand.

Anyway, regardless of the technicalities of how Luke came to be lying there in a pool of his own blood, I am pleased with how I managed to respond. I didn't waste any time calling the emergency services, and I was calm and cool-headed enough to do some truly textbook standard CPR. I loved hearing that afterwards – how I had saved his life.

I know I don't always get everything right, I know sometimes I get carried away, I jump to the wrong conclusions, but one thing I can say without a doubt is that I'm always there for people.